[NSFW]

David Scott Hay

WHISKEY TIT
VT & NYC

Published in the United States and Canada by Whisk(e)y Tit: www.whiskeytit.com. If you wish to use or reproduce all or part of this book for any means, please let the author and publisher know. You're pretty much required to, legally.

ISBN 978-1-952600-26-5

INTRODUCTION
to [NSFW]

WELCOME TO THE BLUR.

An opening to a possible present-day.

<p>

There was once a viral video.

It has since been flagged and removed.

Let me describe it.

Outdoors. Daytime. A festival concert between sets. Hundreds of people in a holding pattern. Every single eyeball fixed on their phones. No one talks; no one laughs; no one is aware of anything IRL, not even the fact that they're being recorded.

A caption appears.

What have we done to ourselves?

David Scott Hay torpedoes straight into that question mark.

> —Existential:
> exploring human existence
> on the subjective notions of
> thinking, feeling, doing.

As a futurist, Hay has vision. As a populist, a story to tell. As a satirist, venom. And as a novelist, words— really the only thing that separates us from Winston Smith's rats.

#FREEDOM_IS_SLAVERY

But Hay brings more to the party than just a future world. He brings us something experimental where the experiment clearly works, encased in a style that would make Chuck Palahniuk proud.

Take a group of social media moderators, besieged by trauma. Stick 'em in an office. Promise health benefits and a mystery bonus in 90 days. And let the rot begin. This is where the story starts. Soon after, a love story is introduced, then a breakdown, a breakthrough, and a sea of tough choices.

As Philip K. Dick implied in his own works, this novel is not science fiction, but a treatise on what will become of us if we continue this way, fed by self-actualization, technology, de-evolution, laziness, and solid historical precedent. Huxley, Atwood, Burgess, Butler, Orwell—they all did it, too: showed us the LATER while reflecting on the NOW. Cautionary tales, for sure, but also pulpy reads stuffed with humanity.

Much like social media moderation itself, artificial intelligence can only do so much. In the end, the act of moral judgment is an exclusively human field. These great works open our eyes to cultural dead ends, to our perversions and our aversions (as in averted, as in we don't want to look. Resist! Look those demons squarely in their demon-red sockets).

So this is speculative fiction?

No. Not really.

Is it a romance?

In a way, it is. There are two people in this story who connect and, yes, at the end, we care about their fate as deeply as they care about each other's.

But really, it is more of a horror story—one to make the demons proud—yet lacking the usual guideposts.

> Americans don't like to be reminded
> that bold moves are still possible.

It helps if the reader catches the references. This story is built from the fragments of all we have known and experienced. Hay drops bits about typewriter ribbons alongside high-tech buzzwords—inches apart on the page. September 11 and November 2020 exist on the same flat plain. You can't enter this story from the outside; you must enter from the inside. Know *this* thing. Remember *that* happening. Make the connections.

And it can be hard to tell where Hay stands on ANY of this—as everything from the low-stakes sex to assessment of *Citizen Kane* is thrown like grenades with the pins pulled out. For Hay, tacit approval or complete damnation is a fine line.

> Kids' movies, gardening, and #BDSM.

Hay's first splash was *The Fountain*, a novel of astounding depth and complexity that, at the same time, is one helluva page-turner. Now he is back with a second novel of EVEN MORE depth and EVEN MORE complexity—one that STILL! SOMEHOW! manages to entertain.

In the early pages, you may suppose *[NSFW]* is just a fortune cookie, aided by some goddamn art degree, or something tossed off by a writer who drank from the notorious fountain of *The Fountain*...

...then the boss jumps from the office rooftop and you're like, wait—this is going to GO SOMEWHERE??? I guess it is! Strap in.

You may consider Hay's choices, like:

Do I want the characters to be named with their handles?

@Sa>ag3. @Jun1p3r. @Babyd011.

Then you nod. Fuck yes I do.

Once you discover a style lifts a theme, you COMMIT! And again on the next page. And the next page. All in the service of a singular result. That's what great writers do; they bring you into their world, not make you comfortable in someone else's.

And you can say the same for social media—our Information Age, on the heels of the Industrial (and equally sooty). Social Media is Committed. Upper case C. Unstoppable. Grows with purpose and effect. Whether you want it to or not.

Maybe past generations believed the same thing about newspapers. For example, look to that one popular meme: a 1920s photograph of men stuffed on a commuter train, skulls planted in rumpled ink—vintage echo of my concert-crowd viral smash.

In the Gutenberg days, there were gaps longer than the 70-second buffer @Sa>ag3 counts down when deciding whether or not to switch off a livestream (one of the novel's many suspenseful set pieces). Time to sift... Time to censor... Take a moment to wrap our heads around it... No. Not today. Now all that addictive junk just pours into us—context and mental health be damned.

So what's the book trying to say?

What we experience through screens is nothing short of psychosis.

> Pharmaceutical topsoil.
> Eagles of death metal.
> The Summerland.

As David Scott Hay says through his characters:

This is NOW.

<p>

Darren Callahan is an award-winning writer, director, and composer who has written drama, fiction, and non-fiction for many major outlets. He is mostly focused on the horror genre. You can find him with a search engine.

This one is for Shel.
Who you mad at today?

The following is based on a true story.

Trigger Warning: sex, drug use, witchcraft, profanity, gun violence, collapse, suicide, harm to a minor, terrorism, civil unrest, hate crime, social media, religion, capitalism.

de·vice

/dəˈvīs/

1.

A thing made or adapted for a particular purpose, especially a piece of mechanical or electronic equipment.

2.

A plan, scheme, or trick with a particular aim.

—Oxford Languages

NODE I

"I am alone and miserable. Only someone as ugly as I am could love me."

—Mary Wollstonecraft Shelley
Frankenstein; or, The Modern Prometheus

[ORIENTATION]

Copium.

We had sex in a lactorium the first day of training. People knew. We were not discreet or quiet. But HR did nothing; there was no one waiting to breast-feed.

It was also not the worst the other trainees at Vex would hear or see that day.

We did not exchange sexual histories. We were not safe. Not in the way you think. We locked eyes on a break, others in the kitchen picking through the high-end organic snacks. Maybe she saw me tremble and reached out a hand and we pulled each other away from the idle chitchat as the other trainees checked their devices, thumbing through their own addictions.

Wordlessly, she pulled me into the lactorium, a small cubicle-sized room designed for breast-feeding. I had not noticed it. The door and handle blended in seamlessly with the wall opposite the break room, lest it offend anti-breast feeders. We rent our clothes, torn shirts and blouses as jagged and destroyed as the bombing victims we had just seen on a giant screen.

Our embrace tightening as close as tandem parachutists.

We climaxed together, unaware the other had orgasmed. We only knew that we shuddered in each other's arms.

Catching my breath, I looked down and saw her hanging name tag.

@Jun1p3r

<p>

We were late joining our fellow trainees, stealing branded hoodies from the coat closet to cover our raw flesh. With all eyes locked on the immense screen, we were issued a verbal warning no harsher than a *tsk tsk*.

@Jun1p3r had not yet joined a coven.

That was later.

Before she learned blood magik.

<p>

We met at Vexillum Co. We were social media moderators. Video Division.

Recruits in the war on savagery.

<p>

Day 1.

[N S F W]

1

To work for the *f*ace, the NDAs are ironclad. Of course, they are. Even to spouses. Employees of the *f*ace make a quarter million a year. Not including perks. We make 10 percent of that.

Legally, we don't work for the *f*ace. We're subcontractors here at Vexillum. However, in addition to health benefits, they have dangled a special bonus. *If* we make it through our 90-day probationary period. No one knows what the bonus is, but rumors are cash and perhaps stock options.

Though we all secretly hope this job will be a bridge to the *f*ace. A living wage that enables true savings. Raises beyond the rate of inflation. A matching 401(k). A healthcare program without a crippling deductible. Profit sharing.

All to catch the unicorn of our generation: retirement.

But first we must make it 90 days.

<p>

A pearl is formed from an irritant. What thing of beauty is formed from resentment?

I don't know.

But certain oysters are harvested to be eaten. Swallowed whole. Others fed a grain of sand. So their treasure may be taken.

<p>

NDAs don't apply if you're sleeping with a coworker, you say. We can talk all we want.

I'm sure we'll be lectured on that, I say. Not about the talking—the sleeping.

Instead, we are told we can get a discount on company-approved therapists. There's a punch card and everything. Nine breakdowns and you get your Prozac for free, we joke.

<p>

Up on the large UHD display our trainer refers to as **Mother/Screen**, one of her challenge videos plays. A faulty suicide-bomber belt next to a BMW. Spot all the pieces, the caffeinated and professionally perky trainer says. It's Find an Object until we can account and ID this entire Waldo terrorist. Blood is okay. Flesh is not. Unless pixelated. What do you see? the trainer says, using a laser pointer. As if she is a sniper on high alert for undead movement.

She calls on me with a practiced glance of my name tag: @**Sa>ag3**… What do you see? Here? Here? Here? And here?

My stomach churns and my mouth fills with bile. Even as I answer coolly and enthusiastically. Arm. Brains. Side mirror. Innards. Quarter panel. Sandal. Bumper. A toe.

Correct!

Good job, @Sa>ag3! Good job team!

<p>

A man in Japan, terrified of airborne toxins, sealed his apartment. Plastic drop sheets. Duct tape. Translucent curtains held together with a kidnapper's tool.

He died weeks later. All the oxygen having been consumed.

He forgot he was a part of an ecosystem, you say. Should have gotten himself houseplants.

Nothing functions alone, I say.

<p>

In the lactorium, you suck me as though trying to get all the poison out. You swallow it for me.

In the lactorium, I take you from behind with such ferocity you begin to confess the crimes of others, starting with your father.

Daddy oh Daddy, you say.

I'm sorry I'm sorry, I say.

In the lactorium, we both have to get it out.

<p>

The day ends. We pick up our devices from the Faraday lockers. I ask: would you like to watch a movie with me?

You blush, like teenagers used to do.

Because this is a love story.

[N S F W]
2

Ninety-three minutes later, I'm in a horn-honking match with a white cargo van parked in the fire lane outside the theatre. I never see the driver. Two hours later, there's an explosion on screen. Body parts are kept off camera to ensure a PG-13 rating.

But the sound design is effective. THX surround sound. Named after a film where sex is prohibited and mind-altering drugs are mandatory. Mandatory so that civilians can perform emotionally demanding tasks. The main character rebels. The bass note of the sound system test reverberates through my body.

You squeeze my hand. It's only make-believe, you say. Another explosion happens on screen and we flee through the exit door. An alarm sounds.

We stand there in the sharp cold air trying to catch a breath. A security guard with his hand on the butt of his gun asks, What's wrong?

I can't remember how the film ends, I say. What happened to the rebel?

Are you on drugs? he says. The white cargo van is gone.

I take a deep breath and lie.

<p>

You straddle me in the car. I drive while you grind against me. Denim against denim, the friction rubbing the flesh raw. When I park, our mouths meet violently. A tooth is chipped, tongues box for superior position. Strength is tested, pushing, pulling, sucking. Blood dribbles. The winter night turns our breath to ice on the inside of the car. We don't know how long we're lost. You leave me with a peck on the cheek. You smell like ammonium nitrate.

<p>

The speedometer needle can touch mid-100s. I've put it there before, the needle vibrating quicker than my heart. It's the LSD death run. I do it twice a year. Once in the spring and once in the fall. Lake Shore Drive is a winding road along the lake in Chicago. It stretches for almost sixteen miles. Has curves and a great view of the lake and beaches on one side and harbors and high-rises on the other.

Every few days during the summer months a motorcyclist between 2 a.m. and 4 a.m. will smear himself across three lanes and wrap his spine around a tree. Or bounce his head like a skipping stone three, four, eight times down the white line. The helmet keeping the casket open, and the brains inside a nice jellied mush. Average motorcycle speed on LSD at that time is 99 mph. The speed limit is 40.

I'm doing a winter run. I'm white knuckled doing 15.

There are guidelines for removing a video. The guidelines change almost daily. Given to us in a brief, ten minutes beforehand. Our perky trainer reading the printout, forcing us to commit it to memory. She ends the brief with: Let's be careful out there.

Security camera footage. A college student is shot in the head on the sidewalk by another student. Both are wearing hoodies and blue jeans and ball caps. It's like a twin shooting a twin. I think I FLAGGED it for lack of pixelation. There was no color. Just a flash and the meat puppet dropped. His strings severed with a bullet. Like an Old-West sharpshooter trick. Yee-haw, I say to no one.

At home, in the mirror, I realize I am wearing the same casual uniform. I could be victim or shooter.

I want to burn my clothes, I say. All of them. Instead, we go to a thrift store.

@**Skiny_Leny** says, Nice jumpsuits, as he adjusts his silk blouse. His shampoo-model hair cascades over his shoulders.

We keep them in a locker at the office, our jumpsuits. A second skin to keep the mental associations from permanently staining our good concert T-shirts.

@Skiny_Leny sells drugs on the side at work. A black-market pharmacy in his pencil caddy. Women's clothes are expensive.

The Buddhists talk of desire being the cause of all suffering.

Everybody wants some. I want some too.

The jumpsuits impede our sex, despite the crotch zippers. But not our gropes. Our snaking hands. They are not designed for a quickie, you say, as you hump my leg in the break room.

The stoic manager comes in to refill her coffee and says, Good work this morning. I've only met her once before, at the final interview. She didn't make eye contact then either. I see her pour something into her coffee, but not what. Your face turns red, you thank me, and I bite your neck leaving teeth marks.

We zip up the jumpsuits. I imagine we are astronauts about to be sent hurtling through space.

The training video shows the *f*ace. Eyes jerking as he reads his script from a teleprompter or cue cards. Probably a device an intern is holding up.

You are the first line of defense, he says. The thin digital line. A valued job in making the world a better place. Those that show loyalty will be rewarded.

I can't tell if he winks or smiles or if it's a convergence of microtwitches.

We clap when the video fades to black. That's what we're conditioned to do. I glance over at you even as the sky-blue text fades from the screen.

LET THE WORLD IN

87 days and counting

[N S F W]
3

Sleep does not come. We watch an old Fred Astaire and Ginger Rogers movie.

He's fantastic, I say.

She's fantastic while doing it backwards and in heels, you say. That's how a successful partnership functions: one works harder while the other gets top billing.

<p>

A trainee—no one bothers to look at his name tag—says if guns kill, then spoons must make a person fat.

If you take away the spoon, people will still eat. An intern talking. He's older and has opinions. His name tag reads **@H₁pp3**. If you take away guns, no one dies from gunshots.

And if you're a 2nd Amendment self-defense proponent, then why aren't grenades legal? Wouldn't we all be safer if we could all carry a grenade? It's the same thing.

Because everyone wants to believe you have to be skilled to use a gun, @Skiny_Leny says. This was before he was reassigned as my workstation-mate. @Skiny_Leny and @H₁pp3 both sport long hair. @H₁pp3's, a loose gray rope; @Skiny_Leny's, a tight auburn braid.

<p>

Despite the congressionally mandated Ludovico 70-second delay, a Flat Earther livestreams himself driving off a cliff to prove his deepest beliefs. He proves one thing: gravity.

I flag the video with a yawn, but do not hit the panic button.

According to his recent posts, gravity is the second-most dubious concept schools have forced on us. As no one has ever seen it. He did buckle his belt, but the air bag did not deploy fully. Leaving a skin-and-tissue impression of his shocked face on his shatterproof windshield.

He's currently running third in the annual Darwin Awards. His ribbon will look like the kind they hand out at grade-school science fairs. I had three of them just like it as a kid. I can still hear my science teacher as she handed them out. Good job!

I get called into the office, a shockingly drab affair, by the perky trainer, who I now realize is the interim manager. The previous manager took the last of her GoDrone shipments and did not return. Maybe the mystery of the bonus was revealed to her.

The newly promoted manager says I should have not only flagged the video, but I should have pixelated out the manufacturer's symbol on the car, as we could be named in a lawsuit. Still perky. Optimistic.

I did flag the video, I say. And pixelation is not my purview.

She asks what that's supposed to mean, "Purview."

<p>

In the lactorium, we take off the jumpsuits. I take you on the diaper-changing table. Someone pounds on the door. Tells us to quit being so selfish. You notice I'm bleeding. I'm raw from the denim rub. I don't stop.

Office first aid kits have antibiotic ointment.

<p>

Once upon a time there was a sports hero so enamored with being an American hero he gave up millions of dollars to travel across the world to be shot in the forehead by a coworker.

He has a statue now, so I guess he got what he wanted.

<p>

My mom says when you become a parent, you stop looking for the falsehood in things. You start looking for the bargain in things. The luxury of a worldview diminishes because it's time to cook supper.

My mom has survived a divorce, death of a child, double mastectomy, terrorist bombing on US soil—the non-sexy one—and an F5 tornado. She takes shit from no one and spends her time scrapbooking photos, posting photos, and gleefully drinking white wine. This in retirement.

I want to be your mom, you say.

But I know Dad has lost Mom to her devices, not her vices.

<p>

An old-fashioned beheading video. I recognize it from years ago. It is not a quick process. This is not a forty-pound blade slicing instantaneously through a neck. There is effort. Elbow grease. Sawing. Dry screams. Wet screams. Then gurgles.

A few of the masked terrorists wear championship T-shirts of sports teams that lost the championship. Shirts for both teams being printed ahead of time. Instead of being destroyed, they are shipped to Third-World countries where the Patriots have lost more Super Bowls than they have won. A world where they have a perfect record with the most wins in NFL history.

The Patriot in the video has just lost his head.

<p>

I read certain jellyfish can regenerate. A whole one from even just a tentacle. One species chopped into several pieces will seek itself out and reform and heal. I wish we were all jellyfish, instead of jelly.

Like the suicide jumper ruptured on the sidewalk. My hands tremble at my workstation keyboard. My stomach churns. I run it backwards in slo-mo and watch him regenerate and fly up, up, and away.

<p>

My dad's advice when he gave me his father's pocketknife: that blade won't break or bend. Until it hits bone.

<p>

You won't tell me about the video you saw before lunch. Dismissing the question with a wave of your hand. You take my hand and lead me to the stairwell. You peel your jumpsuit to your ankles. You are nude underneath. The cool air puckers and hardens your nipples. You spread your legs and put your hands against the concrete wall. I've been bad, you say. I spank you. A red ghost print materializes. I smack you again. You bite your lip, denying me satisfaction.

Third one hurts, I say. And smack your cheek a third time. You unsuccessfully bite back a yelp and shudder. I gently kiss your buttock, the red triple-image of my hand, then pull up your suit. Thank you, you say, and slide a hand to my crotch. I stop it. I'm still healing. But no longer trembling.

Dinner on me? you say.

Before we stopped eating out, I'd introduce you as my therapist. My aunt. My boss. My sister. My stepmother. My legal guardian. My cousin. My niece. I forget which one this time.

If the meal and service were either excellent or subpar, we'd leave behind a pair of your underwear. Or mine. Maybe we'd steal a French kiss, an act they could see out of the corners of their eyes. Performance art, our escapism.

One might think there were hand jobs before desert. Maybe I'd finger you during the appetizers. But you can be a germaphobe, these joints having bribed the health inspectors. Other things you've read.

We liked the reaction shots. When we got them. It took quite a show to get people to look up; the glow of their devices at night turning a hip joint into a wax museum of FOMO.

Regardless, we carried our incestuous fantasy home.

Foreplay in the age of unlimited porn.

Time + tragedy = comedy.

Our employee performances are graded, but no one pays attention to it. The reviews and rationales of Vex's management a blur of audio salad. I don't go out of my way to learn anyone's screen names; it's a revolving door. I should have been fired this week; my accuracy inconsistent. But I show up every day. This management team is busy coping with coming up short of their "accuracy" target.

One month, we came just a percentage point short. This is @Skiny_Leny telling me this. I think he's wearing a kilt. He gives us the rundown. He's been here awhile.

No manager lasts that much longer than 90 days. There is an army of us spread out over several offices. Subcontractors. They believe the smaller offices will promote camaraderie. A support system that keeps the snake eating its tail in an endless loop—my words not his.

His words: They call our small groups "pods."

The previous manager, the one that hired you, left to become a paranormal investigator, @Skiny_Leny says. Our office has never made its goal. I suspect the current boss won't last either. Mid-level coffee shop management skills do not transfer. That bonus they talk about is a myth.

Welcome aboard, @Skiny_Leny says, and hands me three tabs of Xanax. These will help.

I want to believe.

<p>

A young kid on the train, on a flip phone, saying he has to meet his parole officer later. It's early in the morning; we're all standing up, swaying with the gentle curves through the city. He has a small tattoo on the webbing of his thumb and forefinger.

How do people do this *every* day? he says.

You chicken wing me in the ribs. We're not the only ones on probation, you say.

COMING SOON

I remember thinking: how hard can it be?

There was one friend, a woman at an old job. We bonded over our obsession with videos of 9/11 jumpers. We didn't see the people on the floors. We didn't see the people in the plane. But we saw the jumpers. When we could no longer see them, we heard their end in an asphalt jungle.

Most of these videos were scrubbed from the net as though the powers that be decided we could only talk about or watch death in the abstract—of the destruction of square footage of office space.

I remember feeling alive inside, this grotesque fascination. The nightmares about planes were not enough to stop me. We saw how the planes ended, not the jumpers.

As far as I know, there is no footage of their end. Maybe a pixelated flip-phone photo of red on concrete

Just the beginning and the ten-second journey. No one will swoop in to save them. They are fated to death. Ten seconds. No one can do anything, only watch.

One evening, with red wine, my friend and I paused the tenth-anniversary edition of a French musical and searched online for the videos. Watched in silence. Then back to songs. I didn't know what to make of the juxtaposition. Other than that, ours was a unique world. At least in our building, if not our block. We lived in a big city.

Maybe this is why I thought the Vex job would be a piece of twisted cake. So, I filled out the questionnaire online. I lied on the cross-reference questions; recognizing their requirement to fit a pattern, connect the dots.

I remember thinking: how hard can it be?

<p>

I am called into the office for flagging a video of a man slicing and cooking a baby dolphin. The most intelligent creature on the planet. It's fake, the dolphin. 3D-printed silicone. A special effect.

Don't be fooled, my once-perky trainer now promoted to manager says. You're smarter than that. Her lips seem out of sync with her mouth and I wonder whose words I'm hearing. Her eyes are sunken into her skull, rimmed in dark flesh as if rot has taken hold. Her trash can is overflowing with used tissues.

ـshe mentions the bonus. She repeats herself. I had briefly forgotten about the bonus. I can't tell if she's reminding herself or me.

<p>

Employment forms. Sexual Orientation. Gender ID. Preferred Pronoun. Marital Status.

All boxes to check.

◊   Single.

◊   Married.

◊   Divorced

I respect my own privacy and fill in the blanks instead.

◊   Single <u>malt</u>

◊   Married <u>work</u>

◊   Divorced <u>reality</u>

You, you just check them all. Because you contain multitudes.

The newly promoted manager comes out of her office, waving the forms like an incensed schoolteacher. Who did this?? This will go on your Permanent Record. Do you hear me?

You and I are assigned to the same pod. Our jokes outlasting her career.

<p>

A large object passes by the window. I think it's a snow cornice from the edge of the building. I only notice it because I'm staring at you. The tiny crow's feet. The perpetual frown when you're concentrating.

The next morning the cracked and splattered sidewalk is roped off. The shoveled snow, raspberry colored and copper flavored. We are informed that we'll be getting a new manager.

<p>

What color is your parachute?

[N S F W]
4

79 days to benefits and bonus.

<p>

Most of us have adapted the jumpsuit for the office. Some thrifted. Some delivered by GoDrone. Specialized patches, indicating service time, the nicknames we've given our pods. Favorite banned book. Creating our own culture. Except @Skiny_Leny, as they do nothing for his figure.

<p>

A Faraday cage or Faraday shield is an enclosure used to block electromagnetic fields. A Faraday shield may be formed by a continuous covering of conductive material or, in the case of a Faraday cage, by a mesh of such materials. Faraday cages are named after scientist Michael Faraday, who invented them in 1836. This according to the net.

In a Faraday cage, no device can transmit or receive. In a Faraday cage, devices are inert.

<p>

@Skiny_Leny is excited. A friend has told him about a 9/11 comedy web series that's going to be posted soon. Laughter is the best medicine. He tells me this as he becomes my workstation-mate; my previous one, an acne case, has gone MIA. I now sit a roundhouse away from my drug dealer. @H₁pp3 and @Skiny_Leny discuss the merits of subversive comedy. Bruce. Carlin. Hicks. Raine.

<p>

I chew the Xanax. Twirl the sludge to under my tongue. Bitter but faster acting. You pass. Organic only, you say. You have an idea, but don't share it yet. In another state you can valet park at a cannabis store and buy items sealed in corporate packaging. Here, we go to @Skiny_Leny. He has a green thumb and is a mycologist.

His special strain helps with the nausea when I get a run of UHD terrorist videos shot with a mini-Steadicam.

<p>

That old commercial: a sledgehammer flies at a dominating black-and-white screen. Shattering the big face of conformed thinking. Out of the box we go and into another:

the *f*ace

now on a small screen we carry with us. Now the *f*ace on your wrist.

<p>

An early adopter has voluntarily implanted his car fob chip into his wrist. This chip does not help him see. This chip does not help him hear. It does not regulate his heart. It saves him two seconds, three times a day. He can now refresh his device thirty-two more times a day.

Three weeks later, they find his body. His hand and his hundred-thousand-dollar car AWOL.

I don't know if they caught the culprit. It didn't make it into the top of my feed.

<p>

Feed. It's a noun. What farmers give the cows to fatten them for the slaughter. Feed.

<p>

@Skiny_Leny slips me a counterfeit coupon for a free dental visit. You grind your teeth, my new dentist says, spotting my chipped tooth from our first date. Do you want a mouth guard?

Let me sleep on it, I say.

The next week, I go in for a cracked tooth. How's work? he says. I look over at his tray of instruments. I don't mention the video with the puppy. Or the little girl.

He sees my anxiety. Asks if I'd like the nitrous oxide.

<p>

I like your new smile, you say.

Make 'em laugh, make 'em laugh, make 'em laugh.

I watch a video of humans. Faceless. A thick coat of concrete curing over their faces.

Across an ocean, that terrorist cell is holding a postmortem. What went right? Was it effective? How can we be more efficient? Can we get concrete cheaper? Was this the best angle? Perhaps next time we'll shoot it during magic hour. Perhaps we will do it at night with a harsh flash. A jihadist focus group.

What do the comments say?

To stare in a person's eyes for thirty seconds at a stretch will stimulate love. Ten minutes and you will hallucinate.

Beyond that no one knows, because no one has time.

Make time?

On our train ride home, we stare at each other for ten minutes.

What did you see? you say. This back at the apartment.

I saw an angel sleeping in a garden of lush grass, I say. Rain trickled off the leaves. The smell of damp earth filled my head. And I saw I was in love.

You don't ask if you are the angel. So I don't have to lie.

Look at me, you say, as your hand slips around my throat. Your fingers tighten as you straddle me. Pushing my cock against my stomach with your wetness. Our eyes lock.

Keep staring, you say.

<p>

We used to play assassin in high school. Used to sneak in assault weapons hidden within our oversized camo pants. Batteries in the stock. Water in the magazine. Fully automatic water guns. Everyone laughed. Even the teachers.

We were good kids. Harmless fun.

This before #Columbine.

<p>

America is a hard religion.

[N S F W]
5

@Skiny_Leny wears his hair piled high on top of his head. As though he has just exited from a shower where he did not wash his hair. He wears a shirt with a cartoon bear holding a joint standing outside a Planned Parenthood. The bear sports a college football jersey. The caption below: STATES' RIGHTS.

I want his hair, you say. And his T-shirt.

<p>

The videos with the Americans are the worst. They hit closer to home. I recognize fashion trends. Designer labels.

A foreign-aid worker. A missionary. A journalist.

Compelled to make a mark on this world.

Recorded in HD.

In the beginning, I couldn't tell the difference between New Mexico and Argentina. Now I can. But now I can't tell the difference between terrorists gathered around their black flag and a state-champion high-school football team photo.

<p>

#Microdosing must be done in moderation. Daily use quickly decreases its potency.

<p>

Another blanketing snowfall. By the next morning, cars have been replaced with dining room tables. Chairs. Shoveled parking spots reserved. By the folks who dug out their spot. *Dibs*, they call it in Chicago. Within twenty-four hours we watch a man get stabbed to death because he didn't recognize a broom in a bucket as a strong enough claim. Savages.

<p>

#Mycology is the study of mushrooms.

<p>

Before the incident with the steak knife, before the Garden, we go out to eat. Prepared to leave a pair of your panties behind.

We introduce ourselves to our waitress. A cheerful, sly thing. You dislike her right away. I am @Sa>ag3, this is @Jun1p3r, I say. Slave and master.

She's heard it all before and takes our drink order, reciting back: Slave = Old Fashioned. Master=Manhattan with an extra cherry. She wears a gold name tag, but it's slightly askew and reflective. I don't catch her name.

She's boring, you say.

Because she's not dragged down by the weight of the world? I say.

You snort—your variation on a laugh. It echoes across the dining room. No one looks up. We people-watch, but grow bored of the faces hypnotized by the glow of their devices.

Let's at least order dessert, I say. I think they have crème brûlée.

We don't have panties to leave, our basement laundry having been raided. We suspect the downstairs neighbor.

A free round of drinks shows up. Our waitress plops down beside us, uninvited, her shift over. She pulls her dark tie through her white shirt collar. Introduces herself as **@Babyd011**.

<p>

I used to post pictures of my dinners. As if it was an original thought. I look back now and don't recognize the entrées still unpaid on my credit card. Where they were or whom I was with.

<p>

@Babyd011 asks why you have a tattoo sleeve of classic screen monsters.

They're a childhood memory, you say. I used to watch them religiously. I don't identify with them now, though. The things I do, I don't have tattoos of.

Because they're fresh in your mind, @Babyd011 says.

You give our waitress a doublethink.

Suddenly, I realize I have never asked you about your tattoo sleeve.

Yes, I want to remember things that gave me joy when I was a child, you say. When I could still be shocked and surprised. Why shouldn't I commemorate that stage of me?

The Bride, mouth inked in a frozen scream, is the only female in your sleeve. The others, vestiges of men forlorn with their own curse.

As the Bride stares at me, @Babyd011 fingers the cherries from your drink and pops them into her mouth. Her cheeks pucker for a moment. She smiles and the stems emerge from between her lips. They drop onto the table, knotted together neatly.

You pick up the stems and hold them close to your face. That's a double coin knot, you say.

I'm into shibari, she says.

<p>

Crème brûlée arrives with a single spoon. I feed you and @Babyd011 slow bites. Patrons look up from their devices.

We take her home.

[N S F W]
6

I catch myself staring at @Babyd011 at her workstation. Thinking of the time we took her home. The mental images already getting blurry. The nervousness you didn't show manifested in me. The awkwardness. The divvying up of responsibilities. The balance. I remember four hands on my body. Soft, warm exploring. I imagined myself a sheik. And you two my concubines. I imagined myself a sex trafficker and you two new recruits. I imaged myself a porn producer with Hollywood credits. A screen test. An audition. Nothing worked.

Something had to work, you say. You did get vigorous.

Yes. When @Babyd011 brought out her jojoba oil and beeswax-softened hemp rope, I imagined that you were binding my body with smoke and honey as you prepared a human sacrifice to a pagan god. I was being cleaned. Then cleansed.

What kind of god? you say.

That, I say, I couldn't conjure. But I could imagine the blackness of nothingness. And when I woke it was if I had cheated death.

You mull this over, staring at her from your workstation. I wish I had her boobs.

I'm sure we can find a scalpel in the office first aid kit, I say.

You swat my arm. Don't tease.

@Skiny_Leny pipes up and starts talking about the history of cannibalism. But I quickly lose the thread. His hair is spectacular.

I wish I had his hair, you tell me again at home, as we check on the mushroom bin in the closet.

<p>

Afterwards as she put on her clothes @Babyd011 says, I dislike my job. You know anyone hiring? We transfer device numbers as she glances around the apartment for a lost sock. Houseplants would spruce this place up, she says. Optimistic, cheerful. She gives us each a goodbye kiss of smoke and honey.

<p>

I'm glad I ordered dessert. If crème brûlée is on the menu, I order it. I say this as I look around my apartment. Spartan. Vaguely furnished with post-divorce donations. Futon. Small TV. A VCR and a box of tapes. You haven't asked what's on them, and I haven't volunteered.

Did you like watching? you say. @Babyd011 between us?

Once we got the candle lighting right, I say. Should I have filmed it? Taped it? Shot it? Recorded it? (What do they call it these days?)

Let it be ephemeral, you say. Let it become myth.

<p>

A man on the train plays with an army-surplus compass. I can only think of the end of *Brave New World*. The protagonist's feet pointing this direction. That direction. Unsure of the direction to the afterlife.

I can do anything for 90 days.

<p>

We are an unusual generation along the cultural timeline, you say. We lived pre-internet and post-internet. We lived pre-9/11 and post-9/11. Pre-pandemic and post-pandemic. Pre-Hack and post-Hack. Pre-cryptocurrency and post fiat currency.

The new generation looking to shake things up only knows terror and devices and isolation and connectivity.

The generation that has lived in both can't decide which is worse.

The dying generation fought #Hitler and genocide.

And then they thought Elvis was the devil, @Skiny_Leny says.

<p>

My neighbor's kid has never heard of the Beatles.

<p>

The ƒace is blank for just a moment, his fixed stare frozen up on Mother/Screen. As if lost in thought. Palm trees wave in the background. Suddenly, he smiles and tells us we are the first responders in making the world a better place. That he himself has done the training. Awesome resources will be at our disposal should we have questions.

Welcome to the family. His smile flickers and the ƒace goes blank even as the screen fades to black. Action-Cut.

Our "guru," a supervising trainer on loan from another Vex office, hands out updated NDAs. Along with an organic treat made by a subsidiary of the ƒace founded by his former Ivy League roommate. His other roommate sits in the Oval Office.

The guru reminds us we aren't directly employed by the ƒace, and that video is more of a pep talk. Supplemental NDAs indicate this. A stack of Employee Code of Conduct booklets sit untouched, like set dressing.

We've seen this video half a dozen times already. Something is up.

Across the office, a desk-bike's squeaky heartbeat quickens.

<p>

A figure enters. Black outfit. Black shades. Black pompadour. Black skin. He dismisses the guru with a nod. Waits for her to leave. He collects our NDAs, as well as the stack of the Employee Codes of Conduct.

He steps up to a podium conjured from the ether. Takes off his shades. He's not young, but his age is anyone's guess. Hello, I'm Ray Gunn. You can call me Mr. Ray.

I snicker at his name.

@Skiny_Leny gasps. Looks for a coworker to share his excitement. It's a real name, @Skiny_Leny says. His father was the Soviet sci-fi writer Raymond Gunn.

The entity that hired me has moved on, according to Mr. Ray. He writes a number on a whiteboard also conjured from the ether. This is our accuracy number. Our big goal.

Ninety days, Mr. Ray says. Hit this aggregate number for ninety days and at the end we'll get you not only benefits, but a big bonus. TBD, but I guarantee it will be worth it.

No other office has hit this number, @Skiny_Leny whispers. This unobtainable goal.

Not yet, Mr. @Skiny_Leny, Mr. Ray says. "Mr." is @Skiny_Leny's preferred prefix. We'll be the first. I do not fail. He taps the whiteboard with his sunglasses. This number. Now the clock has already started for this ninety-day window. We're behind. I will not reset it.

Because I'm looking at you and I see hunger. I see the ability to make up lost ground. I won't allow you to lose.

He flips through a pristine copy of the Employee Codes of Conduct, meticulously put together by our formerly perky and now deceased trainer/manager person. Waits a beat; tears up the copy. We are delighted, like kids in front of a circus strongman.

Just win, baby. Just win.

Stacked boxes of Krispy Kreme doughnuts are brought in the next day. When I go to take three, I see half a box worth has been cut in half for the calorie conscious.

Mr. Ray brings each of us into his office for a quick one-on-one. I'm assuming he's watched security tapes. Seen things. I'm assuming he's going to clean house. His rah-rah speech just that, words.

At least we can get unemployment, you say. Licking glaze off my lips.

I hate the job of finding a job, I say. As I'm summoned to the office.

[N S F W]
7

@Sa>ag3, Mr. Ray says. The previous regime was ineffective. They looked at process and not results. You know what kind of guy I am?

A bottom-line guy?

A big-picture guy, he says. Let me know if you or anyone needs anything to make this office sing. I had them put extra wet wipes in the lactorium. Condoms in the bathrooms.

Mr. Ray is also a hands-off guy. Just win, indeed.

<p>

A week later at our check-in, he's pleased with progress. I don't think @Jun1p3r and I had started our microdosing hobby yet.

As I leave the check-in, he says, If I could do Bokanovsky's Process on a few of you here, we'd be unbeatable.

I want to ask for clarification, but the blown-up, framed book cover on his wall distracts me. It vibrates with the retro stylings of a pulp sci-fi novel. *The Aquarist of Ganymede.*

He starts to speak, but I sense he's just enjoying me noticing it.

I like the artwork, I say.

They don't paint covers like that anymore, Mr. Ray says. Cost-cutting AI art, these days. Prompt engineers, he sneers.

I get lost in the color and details. An alien environment painted realistically, like an architect's rendering with soul. An alien blob with tentacles floats near a space station. A lone astronaut stares out an observation bubble. Menacing ships approach low, just off the horizon.

It was published in 1954, Mr. Ray says. Written on that typewriter, right there on that desk.

It is a sleek machine. What I imagine a modern typewriter would look like if they were built today and presented at an annual developers' conference along with other devices.

My father built his own reel-to-reel machine, Mr. Ray says. He would play tapes of experimental jazz musician Sun Ra, from here in Chicago, and Karlheinz Stockhausen—the Beatles put him on the cover of *Sgt. Pepper*—sometimes simultaneously. I think he was inspired by the mash-up of jazz and space electronica. That music was considered crude and ugly then.

But to him, it opened up mental doors. Me, when it wasn't giving me nightmares, it transported me out of there. And I, I dreamed of a better future.

My father was Afro-Russian, Mr. Ray says. My grandfather arrived there after the revolution and was employed as an expert in cotton cultivation. We moved back to the Gold Coast, but after decolonization my father was offered a scholarship in Moscow. Many Africans were. How my father got ahold of that music there, I have no idea. Probably the Khrushchev Thaw. Policies loosened up a bit then, as you probably know.

I nod, just based on the candor in his voice.

I was very young, Mr. Ray says. But I still remember the people cheering at the success of Sputnik. We put the first dog, man, and woman in space. Did you know we landed on the moon first? Luna 9 in 1966. It was unmanned, of course. So, it couldn't plant a Soviet flag. He says this ruefully.

I nod, trying not to lose the thread.

My father saw none of it. Starving in the Gulag because of that book, Mr. Ray says. Policies didn't loosen up enough to get him out. Gunn was his pseudonym. I made it my legal name.

I nod to the painted cover. What's it about? I say.

Now, he says.

<p>

We walk out of the lactation booth. Zipping up the jumpsuits. My mouth and beard reek with your juices and doughnuts.

@Skiny_Leny passes by us, heading to Mr. Ray's office, an autograph book in his hand. His hair tied back tastefully with a broad ribbon.

<p>

You buy me a straight razor shave. This might be the only way to get my scent off your face, you say. I lay back in the chair and let a craftsman do their work. I let my mind wander, fantasies I've already shared with you. I embrace the ritual. The *skritch skritch* of the blade scraping against the skin. ASMR washes over me. My body tingles from scalp to abdomen.

You guide my hand to my face. It's a strange sensation, feeling it naked. The shift in a breeze. The smoothness. You kiss each cheek experimentally. I can still smell me, you say.

The barber asks if I'd like extra aftershave.

<p>

Out for a meal at a high-end/low-rent pop-up, I see a man who could be from the Middle East. There is a knife at his table. A blonde with him. I recognize him from a half-dozen videos. The same for the blonde, her Buddhist beliefs transporting her to a new body here in the city at the steak house. How the devil follows is God's mystery.

I grab my own steak knife. Target the soft spot just to the side of the nape of his neck. A hard hand grips my wrist. You're safe. You're here. I'm here, you say. We're off the clock. You rub my thighs reassuringly. It's not the man from the video. He's an artist, you say. It's not the same guy. It's not him. It becomes a mantra. A buzz in my ear. My tinnitus activates.

But my eyes are not listening.

He opens an art portfolio and they start to spitball project ideas. Is that how they're attacking us now, through subversive art? Genius. No one can argue its inherent subjective nature. I swing by the table on the way to the restroom and glance at the portfolio. I've seen his art before. Hanging in my ex-wife's house and mine. They've already invaded the watchtower.

I splash water on my face, trying to calm down. The air is impossibly stuffy in the bathroom. Thick and viscous and salty. You follow me and pull me into a stall. My tears hit the toilet. Other body fluids soon join them in breathless gasps, the air thickening even more. As we leave the stall, buttons intact, the toilet senses our completion and flushes. It is as if we were never there.

As I pay the bill, I realize I am still holding the steak knife. There is a thin line of blood on it. A violation I do not recall. You sense this and stroke my hair and reassure me it is okay. Later that night, as I draw us a bath, I see the thin cut on your thigh. You clean the wound and patch it up. You don't mind.

I used to be a cutter, you say. This is child's play.

My @Jun1p3r.

Tell me about your first love, you say.

But I'm not ready for intimacy.

‹p›

At the end of @Babyd011's first day at Vex, she says goodbye to each and every one of us. She's memorized everyone's screen name. Evidently, I also work with **@OrKa**, the source of the squeaky desk-bike, and others whose names elude me.

How long has she had it? Have I been that oblivious?

Good night, @Jun1p3r! Good night, @Sa>ag3! Both of us get a playful wink. It was a good day, she says.

I am jealous of the pep in her step. Good night, @Babyd011.

With a wave and a blow of kisses, she says:
Tomorrow will be even better!

[N S F W]
8

The instant I walked out of a room, she pulled out her phone. Thumb, thumb, heart, heart.

The next click.

The next hit.

This the ex-wife, not @Jun1p3r.

I walked out to give her privacy when she filmed herself talking about her newly dead cat. The tears. The *Hey guys… She was a good cat.* See, I'm real. A cry for help. For sympathy. Just wanting to know she's not alone in the world. She read a Rumi quote I'd once posted to fridge. She posted the fourth take, unhappy with the slant of light. She spent the night in bed, her back to me, my hand on her hip as she refreshed. Counting the likes, counting the hearts. Seeing who had seen her message. The emoji comments, a scroll of hieroglyphic sympathy cards. No one called.

When I walked out for good, I saw her pull out her device.

Broken heart emojis were sent across the globe like a virus. I texted her the number of my lawyer. We'd met online. It was fitting.

We'd tried counseling once. Because ███████████████████

After the first session she was on her device, checking work email. Instead of the agreed-upon postmortem coffee. I couldn't contain my anger.

"It's work," she said. Such a good cog.

No, it's our marriage.

I kicked her out of the house.

I don't know if she was unhappy. She never said as much. But things of mine she didn't like disappeared. Trips to Target resulted in a bottom line of half our rent for objects, candles, and wine I could not see materialize. The empty fast-food wrappers stuffed under the seats, in the bottoms of the trash cans.

In the end, she mustered the courage to cast herself as the victim. Righteous indignation. I let her have her narrative. I never spoke to anyone on her side of the family again. I'd had an affair. This was the story. It spread in our work community. I was doing heinous things. A sex scandal. Even the few on her side that I liked sided with her, no final words; silence their goodbye. It was as if the entire family went down in a plane over the Pacific and were never heard from again. Years later, I am grateful for the clean break.

One of the few in my life.

[N S F W]
9

The new generation of the best and brightest from Ivy League schools are not curing cancer. They're trying to get you to like things. To sell not a thing, but sell *you* to strangers.

<p>

(Stop me if you've heard this before.)

It's a self-perpetuating machine. You are the factory workers. Providing content. Tiny pearls (the hit) from an irritant (FOMO). Billions of dollars of content created for free. It's ingenious.

(Stop me if you've read this before.)

One product you buy to turn yourself, your information, and your content into said product. Social media, the marketplace. Advertisers combing the data for consumers. Paying for the privilege.

(Stop me if you know this.)

You are the factory workers producing product for free in the factory.

You are the product.

(Stop me.)

And I am quality control.

(Stop.)

<p>

The greediest are inserting themselves between A and B. Becoming middlemen. Now A to B is A to $(A_1+A_2+A_3+A_4+A_5)$ to B. For just a small percentage.

The newest college dropouts are working to remove that. Remove the intermediaries. This is called decentralization. Identification. Transactions. Currency. The promise of the blockchain.

The new guard already facing a revolution from their tech brethren.

<p>

This is where a true New World Order will emerge, @Skiny_Leny says. True globalization.

Just like in the Book of Revelations, a newbie says, clutching her necklace sporting a tiny corpse. She says it like that: Revelations. Plural. Error.

Mr. Ray terminates her the next day. She files a wrongful-termination lawsuit against Vex for religious discrimination. The suit is dismissed when video evidence from her OnlyFans account shows two videos shot in the lactorium.

I've already forgotten her name.

<p>

#Breadandcircus

‹p›

Emotional addiction. And your dealer a quarter inch away from your thumb. I like. I am liked.

Look, a cartoon heart. I love. I am loved.

‹p›

Four people die today, taking a group selfie. They fall off a dam. I don't know where because I am laughing too hard.

A man died proposing underwater; an indie viral production sure to impress his sweetheart. He'd made a few such videos. Amateurish. But not without a charming grin.

Click like and subscribe.

‹p›

#Ubiquitous

‹p›

Your first car is no longer a rite of passage. A first phone, a first device has replaced it. This before the term "phone" became antiquated.

‹p›

Students trade secrets at school. How to circumvent parental blocks. Showing videos. Videos I have flagged, videos I have removed, videos they wish to reenact on prom night.

Nudes their currency. Children trading child porn.

Pull down with your thumb to refresh. This is called intermittent reinforcement. Coined by the scientist that let rats pull a lever for food. Sustenance.

The effect that built Vegas.

Filling our feeds with threads we have been algorithmically determined to confront. To engage emotionally. Outrage trumps a like. But then your outrage gets liked. The serpent that ate its tail. *Ouroboros.*

#Bots

Have you ever had a relationship where the other person never used your name? Where you can't recall any specific time where they used your name? Placeholders: man, bro, honey, sweetie, love.

As if you've been friends or lovers for months, years, and they've forgotten your name and are too embarrassed to ask? Or as if your identity has been subsumed by their perception of you. Which of you is dancing backwards and in heels?

A generation from now, kids will line up for tech implants when they turn sixteen like my generation did for their driver's license. The car represented freedom to us. Social freedom. Which is what a device provides. They can now be comfortable being social sitting on their bed. Everyone has a definition of freedom. But we don't all reference the same dictionary. The next generation won't know what a dictionary is. But they will rewrite the book.

That is later; I am now.

<p>

#A_FLAT_CIRCLE

<p>

The parolee is back on the train, standing. We never see him sit. He's on his flip phone again. I'm not getting any bites. I'm fucked. And all the jobs are bullshit. He closes the phone with a snap. Looks around the train car. Everyone is head-down, faces glowing with their devices. You can see the despair in his eyes. Existential. He was a prisoner cut off, inside. And now he's an outsider and still a prisoner.

No one looks at him but us. You make eye contact and smile. Go over to him.

My hands start to shake. Just fifteen feet away, I have an overwhelming sense that you will not make it back. That he will slice your wrists even as you reach out to him. Or that section of the train car will blow up. I see several backpacks capable of mass destruction.

You hand him a Vex business card.

He asks what you do. I hear snatches of your answers that beget more questions until he slumps against the train door and slides to the floor. Dropping your card. He bangs his head against the door. Stifles a cry in his throat. This is what waited for him outside the prison walls.

Tomorrow will be better, I hear you say.

Everything goes dark as the train goes underground. Now we're refugees in a boxcar, huddled over electronic candles. It's the only light, the devices.

I close my eyes. Take ragged breaths. Think of your happy place, you say.

Nothing comes. Just darkness. I say this. Which is a lie. I summon a moment in time. My abdomen throbs. As it does every time, the memory comes back faded. Details missing. Except the terror. Maybe this is why I haven't shared it with you. To tell it would be to diminish it, leaving only the cold.

Your hand slides between my thighs. It's impossibly hot. I feel the heat through my pants. Let the heat radiate, you say. Think of the center of the sun, you say.

I let my soul go supernova.

Nothing can attack the chill.

The chill that never goes away.

[N S F W]
10

Standing on the bank, watching the river of my country run by me. It's much faster than the current of my youth. I fear I would drown if I stepped in there. Slick rocks, unseen bottom. But it's fast. It'll give you more time. More time for what?

<p>

I realize others have gotten off the river. Many way upstream. Mocked. For their old ways. Their old thoughts. The occasional message in a bottle arrives downstream and is smashed, mocked, and rallied against. Others start to build canoes, head back upstream to eradicate the bottle throwers. Paddling with their thumbs, up the river.

I don't want them after me. I think of one of my favorite movies, about a loyal soldier on a mission. He is sent to destroy a new way of thinking. "Stay in the boat."

<p>

The news of the minute: A message to a sweetheart is pulled from a beach. Glass, cork, paper. Eternal love.

Ten minutes later, I watch a Molotov cocktail explode at the feet of a female teenager carrying a bag of groceries. Her jilbab and hijab catch the flames. She throws off her hijab, exposing her face. A Mullah runs to her and smothers the flames of her dress, then beats her for removing her headwear.

Later I recognize her scream in a video. Sounds like "uncle." There are three men. In headwear that conceals their identities. They wear nothing else but the scars of a true believer.

\<p\>

Making room for the mushroom bin, I clean out the closet. We go through my old bedroom gear. All gag wedding gifts. The padded handcuffs. The plastic word WHORE hot glued onto a snap collar. The whip customized with the safe word of your choosing.

We chose a safe word. But it has too many syllables and ruins the mood. It was kinda fun, eliciting laughs two glasses of wine ago. But now I'm too embarrassed to say the word. Enduring the pain is more bearable than the shame.

"."

We, you and I, settle on a different safe word. "Uncle." The tried-and-true schoolyard word. It forms on my lips with ease. You ask if I've ever been molested.

No, but it used to stop the bullies. Until it didn't.

David Scott Hay

You put the whip down. Rock me to sleep. Your breasts pillows under my head.

<p>

#NewCherryMacaMocha.

[N S F W]
11

Last time an insidious plot affected millions, it too, was efficient, done to make a better world and push the boundaries. Behind-the-scenes advancements in the bleeding edge of science. This is known as the #Holocaust. Sources say.

This time, we're pushing buttons and feeding digital cows to get our yellow badges. We're being separated into groups. Demographics. They don't want blood but they want to bleed us. We're not being marched into ovens. No, we're rushing into them with glee. Experimentation and extermination. Costing us time. The one thing we cannot ever get back.

But, you argue, they're not killing us.

Aren't they, I say.

People have argued forcefully that neither the Holocaust or Social Network ever took place.

[N S F W]
12

A live feed of an elementary school playground at recess comes across my display. There is a series of pops. A string of firecrackers flash and jump. Then adults screaming and another single, deeper pop. A dozen kids scream. I'm confused and can't make sense of what is happening in this gun-free safe space.

Everything slows. Even the squeaks of @OrKa's desk-bike.

I hit my panic button. The live feed is thrown up on Mother/Screen. Every one pauses the action on their workstation displays and swivels ninety degrees to face the monolith-sized display.

We have the Ludovico 70-second delay to kill the feed across all devices linked to the *f*ace's platform, before it truly goes live. It's an open corporate secret, this *bug*. Because now is never the time and place to discuss gun violence. A closed-door negotiation encouraged by the threat of congressional subpoenas. The *f*ace hates congressional subpoenas.

In the next update you agree to, that bug will be a feature.

Mr. Ray comes jogging out; a key fob on a lanyard around his neck whips back and forth. He tosses off his sunglasses like a catcher tossing off his mask. We all stare at Mother/Screen. He takes it all in with a glance.

A parent is killed. Along with a School Resource Officer. Our live video also shows a teacher bleeding out, writhing in agony. Another law enforcement officer bends over as if to render aid, but instead throws down a small firearm next to an outdated science textbook. Evidence planted. It isn't noticed until independent digital forensics of the footage is conducted.

Mr. Ray presses the single button on the key fob and kills the live feed. That was a close one, he says, solemnly.

@OrKa revs back up and the squeaky desk-bike resumes its normal beat.

The feed continues to play on Mother/Screen. Our private viewing.

<p>

#Terms_of_Service

<p>

Chicago is a union town. When the time comes to renegotiate their contracts with the great city of Chicago, both the Chicago Teachers Union and Fraternal Order of Police Lodge No. 7 will use this incident at the bargaining table. All because a good guy with a gun at a parent-teacher conference couldn't settle creationism vs. intelligent design.

The city does settle with the families. NDAs are signed.

‹p›

Another couple enters the internet-fame lottery. He holds a book incapable of stopping a .45 round. She reluctantly pulls the trigger. But this is what he wants and she loves him. Books only work if you read them.

The video was reported today on the anniversary of his death.

Another cartoon heart.

‹p›

The *f*ace behind the glass takes note.

‹p›

We might want to consider antidepressants, you say.

@Skiny_Leny will be in this afternoon, I say. He has a hair appointment this morning.

No, you say. Get a legit prescription. I found an HSA card on the sidewalk.

Find a penny, pick it up.

‹p›

COMING SOON

‹p›

An announcement of a new-style device that runs without a battery buries every news story in today's feed. The device will be produced by our parent company. Critics are dubious. Stockholders are not. The *f*ace denies it expressionlessly.

<p>

I can't stop shaking.

You say: When is your prescription arriving?

Whenever they deliver it. I should get a text.

<p>

At some point, I purchased a lava lamp. Matching your favorite panties.

Straddling me, nipples popping in soft light. Your T-shirt: daddy's li'l valentine. I take it in, eyes wide open. Trying to remember details. We're half-drunk celebrating the week's end of pent-up hostility, the lactorium having been closed for refurbishment. Mr. Ray knows what we need.

Glowing lava backlights your head, halos and horns forming and dissolving with every deliberate gyration. It's glorious.

My device pings. I glance at it.

NO. You slap me hard.

My leg shoots out and rocks the shelf. The lava lamp teeters and falls and breaks.

I try to sit up.

Stay with me, you say, as if I'm bleeding out in the bush.

The lava oozes out onto the floor like a blob. So much green.

Stay with me. As you shudder and shake.

The lava touches my foot. Warm. And wet.

The text is from the pharmacy. There's a delay in my prescription.

<p>

We sway on our morning train commute to downtown. A fellow commuter watches a video without earbuds, assuming we are all wearing them and thus giving him the all clear to broadcast his filth. We both sneer and lean towards him. The spontaneous bad cop/bad cop routine triumphs and he shoulders his way to the other end of the train car rather than turn his device off.

We need noise-canceling headphones, you say.

They don't make them powerful enough, I say.

When we exit the train, I track the transgressor and bump him deliberately, knocking his device from his hand. He bows up, chest puffing. *What?* I say aggressively. You pull me away. We can't be late.

<p>

I don't know much about handguns. Except what I've seen on TV and in movies. And since there's usually an ex-military technical adviser, it means I've been taught by experts.

<p>

@Skiny_Leny rummages in his purse for a pill to take the edge off. I don't know why you get so worked up, @Sa>ag3. You're looking for a great moral compass, as if you can philosophize the world into something rational and solvable.

We're just a bunch of primates hooting and hollering, he says. We eat. We fuck. If one stands on a rock and does an antic, we ignore them, we hoot more, or we throw rocks. If one thinks your rock is shiny, they will grab it. We protect the young and we shun the old.

How does this shock people still? he says. We're all just animals on a frying pan that is slowly heating up. Our saving grace for the moment is we fuck more than we kill. This is @Skiny_Leny vlogging our conversation.

I can't tell if he's pulling my arm or not. He usually does this solo when we are flogging. What does he generally vlog about? I ask @Babyd011.

Hair care, @Babyd011 says. We could all use pro tips from those locks. So sincere, her voice, that @Skiny_Leny blushes.

Have a great weekend, everyone! @Babyd011 says, as she struts out of work. Monday will be even better!

<p>

Office. Train. Home. Train. Office. Train. Home. Our loop.

<p>

On the commute, you share that you are going away on a three-day women's retreat. Out in the woods. You'll come straight in to work on Tuesday. You share that you are feeling disconnected from the earth and it's the Winter Solstice.

<p>

I used to walk to the lakefront. The beach. Imagine the vastness of the body of water, the infinity before me. The winds are stronger off Lake Michigan than the Pacific Ocean. But lately I look to the horizon, watching for telltale dots of black, the incoming ships, the invasion. As if the end of the world will be launched from the shores of Michigan.

<p>

#Oceansoftime

<p>

The daily videos thread night terrors through our REM sleep. We awake, our bodies flushed, pupils dilated. Clinging to one another, our hearts pounding out of sync. The inconsolable. After a brief conversation, we make a murder-suicide pact. For after your weekend getaway.

[N S F W]
13

Monday. Two newbies in matching olive jumpsuits have already raided @Skiny_Leny's stash. @Skiny_Leny's sees my anxiety manifesting. The restless leg. The trembling hand. The beard scratching. @Skiny_Leny is working on his supply chain and promises to get back to me with a handshake Rx ASAP.

I close my eyes and try to find a happy place. All I see is her face. Why is it fading already?

<p>

@Jun1p3r still absent. I don't know where. I'm in the break room. Staring at the bubbles in the water cooler through closed eyelids.

I'd do that too, if I had the time. Meditate, that is. The woman speaking to me has been with us since day one. She's older than me. The temp agency sent her. We jokingly refer to her as mom. It pleases her.

Gray streaks her fashionable haircut. Framing a still-girlish face with gentle waves. She's gained weight since starting here. She tells me this. I suspect it's her blended, sugary coffee drinks. I just can't focus without them, she says.

I don't need to open my eyes to tell she is on her device. You and I never take ours out of the lockers. But she needs a hit, her thumb refreshing as she checks her hearts, comments, likes, RTs, shares, and DMs. Trying to stay hip. Relevant. Fed.

She asks me how I do it. How do I cope? Please, help me, @Sa>ag3.

I can't recall her screen name or see her tag. But I recognize her voice from Big Pharma commercials. Insurance commercials. Plant-based burger commercials. It is gentle on my eardrums.

I tell her I chalk it up to the hyperfocus a new job can create.

That video... Her voice drifts.

I don't know which one she's referencing. Could be anything.

She sits on my lap, kisses my neck. There's a room here, she says. Right? She kisses me again, stops when her tears streak her mascara, old enough that embarrassment can still be a deterrent. I was born in the wrong age, she says. She curls up further, going fetal.

I hold her, rocking her, stroking her hair, cooing a lullaby in her ear. She falls asleep in my lap. She smells like dryer sheets.

After that she stops wearing makeup to work and her new name tag says: **@MØM**.

<p>

Home. Train. Office. Train. Office. Train. Home. Our loop. Solo this time. An eternity.

<p>

@Babyd011 peeks over my shoulder at the printed piece of paper—20 lb. Recycled.

> The **Maxwell–Faraday equation** (listed as one of Maxwell's equations) describes the fact that a spatially varying (and also possibly time-varying, depending on how a magnetic field varies in time) electric field always accompanies a time-varying magnetic field, while Faraday's law states that there is EMF (electromotive force, defined as electromagnetic work done on a unit charge when it has traveled one round of a conductive loop) on the conductive loop when the magnetic flux through the surface enclosed by the loop varies in time.
>
> **Faraday's Law of Induction** (briefly, Faraday's law) is a basic law of electromagnetism predicting how a magnetic field will interact with an electric circuit to produce an electromotive force (EMF) — a phenomenon called electromagnetic induction. It is the fundamental operating principle of transformers, inductors, and many types

> of electrical motors, generators and solenoids.

She looks at me, perplexed.

I take a deep breath, hoping to catch smoke and honey. It's how you block a signal to your device, I say. Nothing gets in. Nothing gets out. Like our lockers.

Go science, she cheers.

<p>

@Babyd011 gives a pep talk to the squad of new hires. They are having withdrawals, their devices in the Faraday lockers. I'm trying to meditate, but I can only stare at the giant *f*ace on Mother/Screen. Expressionless and muted.

<p>

I step outside the loop. A local hardware store. Keeping our dollars in the neighborhood. Metal mesh. Wires. Solder kit. Duct tape. Translucent plastic sheets.

I build a Faraday cage for the apartment. For all devices. This for the weekends when we don't leave our devices in the lockers at work. I want to thumb you a message, while you are away. But I know it'll be a signal stuck in space, your device inert in the office locker.

The plastic sheets are to help with the drafty windows.

<p>

@MØM is having a hard day. A gas explosion at a preschool caught on security camera footage. She can't differentiate between binkies and dismembered booties. Force majeure, the gas company claims. Strong winds and disease-weakened trees.

You still haven't come back.

Will you?

@Babyd011 steps out of the lactorium, hooks a thumb toward it. You better go in. @MØM needs you.

The recent refurbishment of the lactorium includes designer touches: plush cushions, the voice-activated white or pink noise of your choice (you and I prefer the sound of a river; @MØM usually prefers to coo over an amniotic heartbeat), LED mood lighting, and heavy gauge D-rings on either side. Mr. Ray takes his suggestion box seriously.

@MØM's streaks of gray look silver in the low light. Her eyes are rimmed with red. Oh my baby, she says as I duck into the lactorium. She lifts her cardigan, and pulls out a heavy breast. She pulls me close and I find a comfortable spot, leaning against her lap and chest. She rocks me, cooing her voice in a lower register, the vibrations primal thrumming pleasantly in my head. She's lactating. I drink her. It's what she needs, and my mom did not breast-feed.

I think of Kubrick's Star Child.

<p>

COMING SOON

@MØM clears her throat, breaking my feeding reverie. She takes a selfie. My face hidden. Adding another image to her digital nursery. HR is pleased to hear from Mr. Ray that the newly designed lactorium is finally being used for its intended purpose.

At last, I see you return. But now it's your turn to comfort @MØM in the booth. I give you a thumbs-up. It's enough to know you're back. My body relaxes. For the remainder of the day, I easily pace @OrKa's production using the tempo of her desk-bike as a metronome.

We spread out in a corner booth for six. The waiter gives us side-eye. Attempts to track down the hostess.

I ask you if that makes us twins? Sharing a mother's milk?

Oh, that's a good one, you say. Let's tell the next waiter that. Then: I wish my boobs could do that.

They can, I say.

No, you say. They can't. Your shoulders drop. I hold you like a baby in my lap. Am I enough? you say. A rare moment of insecurity.

Yes, I say. I love you even more, though I don't say it. The words stick in my craw.

You sprinkle a pinch of salt on my tongue.

"The salt is death—it is bitter and yet it is sweet.

"Taste death and know its finality.

"Fall to the ground and feel the coldness of the earth."

You do the same to yourself. The entrees go cold as I rock you to sleep. This is what it takes to get attention in a chain restaurant.

<p>

#Salem_Witch_Hunts. They were different, you say. Or they were perceived as different. Wicca is a different belief system. One more in touch with the natural.

This was your three-day retreat. Initiation into a coven. Witches in the woods. One works for a doctor.

You explain this as you grind the foraged mushrooms. Boil the water. You look at the drab plastic sheeting loosely lining the apartment. @Babyd011 is right, you say. We need plants.

<p>

It's okay, you say, stroking my hair. It must be the drugs. Let's bake a pie instead, you say.

Why?

I like pie. You like pie.

Sometimes it's that simple.

<p>

#Impotence is a side effect, the doctor says. We could try a prescription to help with that.

Why don't they just include the second drug in with the original prescription? I say.

She blinks at me. Shrugs.

What do you do for a living? she says, as she shuffles through sample blister packs handed out by the blonde in high heels with a rolling black bag back in reception. Her face a thick mask of cosmetics and deceit.

I hear the blonde laugh from here. White teeth, fantasy hair, every word out of her mouth practiced, workshopped, even her non sequiturs—weather, sports, your makeup, the cut of your clothes—every flaw filed away, every positive bright spot highlighted by a woman *so jealous of your eyebrows*. There is nothing left to chance.

She peeks her head in my examination room. Get out, I bark.

She blinks, not having workshopped this response.

Or, I say, Your name will be the first listed on my lawsuit. I turn to the doctor, And yours second for letting her access a private medical session.

The blonde who does not compute falters and I throw blister packs for STDs at her. Side effects may include depression, nausea, vomiting, and a scratched cornea.

<p>

In the corner of the apartment sits a small wooden crate. On top of that: a candle carved with symbols. A small dagger. A dildo. A chalice. A bell. A bowl. A bundle of sage. A translucent rock. An antler. A stick.

<p>

The cops are called. But the blonde is gone. I tell them an unauthorized drug dealer came into my private medical session. She was eavesdropping, I say. The woman at the front desk with the good eyebrows and ancient eyes who knows the long game says, Yes, she walked back there unauthorized.

I mouth *thank you*. I see a bit of sage by her elbow.

The cop asks for her description. A woman you would stare at in a restaurant while with your wife on an anniversary dinner. The face you would conjure up to get through your boyfriend's perfunctory blow job. The face you'd hope to rescue in an HBT situation; a meet-cute.

That hot, the cop says.

I crook a thumb at the doctor. Ask her, I say. They're sleeping together.

Do you have any *[inaudible]* samples, the cop asks the doctor.

Everyone is gone now. I bow slightly to the receptionist, but she's meditating. She's put her hair up. I notice the blood-red streak in her hair. She's not on her device. I sniff the carnation arrangement on her desk.

Her eyes open slowly as she comes back to this world. I ask her gently if she would purge my records, shred them. She nods. Tomorrow is a full moon, she says.

This is of significance to witches.

I don't ask to have my prescription refilled or add a second one. I do take a carnation.

Do no harm.

Harm none.

#Protect_and_serve

<p>

Stay in the loop.

<p>

My neighbor knocks on the door. The one across the hall. I'm moving, she says, with an armful of houseplants. I can't take another winter here. I have to leave them behind. She looks around at the plastic sheeting lining the walls. The plastic shielding the floors. Big plans for the night, she asks?

Murder-suicide, I say. Her eyes wilt a bit.

Don't worry, I say. The plants will be fine.

She exhales her gratitude and wishes me luck.

Thank you, I say.

You step out of the bathroom. Naked. A candle in each hand. The carnation behind your ear.

I present to you with armfuls of greenery. You conjured plants, I say. *Wiccan.*

[N S F W]
14

Full moon. We now track the phases of the moon using a bowl and fourteen stones.

<p>

Floating. Weightless in the liquid. Are you alive? Do you dream?

Is it enough space or do you feel caged?

<p>

I do not see how many followers you have, or vice versa. But I ask. One, you say. I have one follower. You kiss me.

<p>

My finger over the blue square of pixels.

Are you sure, I ask.

Yes.

Are you sure, it asks in Helvetica.

Yes.

My beautiful @Sa>ag3.

I press my finger on the glass. My fingerprint remains after the DELETE box disappears.

Your social media accounts vanished.

#Your_Murder

<p>

Or do you feel safe while the predators on the other side consume each other? Or is it just a blur of colors out of reach?

<p>

My finger over the blue square of pixels.

Are you sure, you ask.

Yes.

Are you sure, it asks in Helvetica.

Yes.

My beautiful @Jun1p3r.

I press my finger on the glass. My fingerprint remains after the DELETE box disappears.

My social media accounts vanished.

#My_Suicide

<p>

I feel your heartbeat pulse on my lip.

<p>

Do you wonder what lies beyond the glass?

NODE II

"The world to me was a secret, which I desired to discover; to her it was a vacancy, which she sought to people with imaginations of her own."

—Mary Wollstonecraft Shelley
Frankenstein; or, The Modern Prometheus

[N S F W]

1

Wicca, you say, is more about a practice than a belief in magic. It's a belief in ritual. Like Catholicism.

Didn't they burn you at the stake?

That was the Puritans. They said we (you said *we*) were evil. They said we did things. Those that escaped persecution did exactly what they were accused of. They went into the woods. We became bogeymen. Built gingerbread houses and ate little children.

You tweak my ears and smack your lips.

I am a great-great-granddaughter of the women they could not burn.

I laugh. We all know who the bogeymen are now. I start to speak, when you push me down and straddle my face and gently grind. I hear the vibration of your voice low and rhythmic. A chant. The plants listen.

<p>

#September11.

That day I felt alive. Shaken from a life where every morning getting out of bed was a feat of will. Where routine became reflexive and if you asked me what I did last Tuesday or Wednesday (it's Thursday), I'm just as likely to draw a blank or tell you a menial task I did several weeks ago. Welcome to the blur.

But on 9/11 there was the possibility that shit was going down forever. And it was going to change everything. The big shake-up. These thoughts as I sat in front of my screen joining with fourteen million. New York. Pennsylvania. Washington, DC. I waited for Chicago. Denver. Las Vegas. Los Angeles. Boston.

I sat in a waiting room, to give blood. A true patriot. A pint of my life that I knew would never make it to NYC. But I didn't worry about an alien attack. The zombie uprising. My inbox. The monthly parking spot lottery at work. The endless mailbox of credit card offers. The absent wife. All the bullshit fell away.

The end of artificial stakes.

I had nightmares about jetliners crashing on Michigan Avenue. Lake Shore Drive. Western Avenue.

These national nightmares became the justification of the hawks.

The jumper videos surfaced later. Every one of them running away from death, flying for seconds, still clutching purses and briefcases. Then the videos disappeared. That was the line of what we could consume as voyeurs.

The first digital line.

<p>

They now call folks with no social media accounts "savages."

@Skiny_Leny scoffs at my great act of defiance. @MØM calls me brave. Mr. Ray says nothing.

<p>

With cash, we buy a pressure cooker. Jars. Syringes. Tongs. Duct tape. Plastic tarps. We wear black T-shirts, sweats, sunglasses and hats. We look as conspicuous and cliché as possible. We use our best sitcom voices at the checkout. Isn't Mom going to be surprised, you say.

I elbow you in the ribs. Not if you keep blabbing.

That's why you're the favorite, you say. Firstborns always are.

I'm a middle child, the clerk says.

You give her an *awww*. And just like that we're forgotten and not flagged.

<p>

If you were a warlock what would your familiar be, you say.

Oh, I don't know the secret powers of the animals. It's such an antiquated occult thought.

We have them nowadays, you say. Emotional support dogs. Cats. Rats.

I have you for that, I say.

Or do I have you for that, you say.

<p>

Our first batch of mushroom tea didn't work. It warmed us, but the heat broke down the magic. Literally. We started brewing the tisane the night before and sprinkling the magic on our chilled morning cup.

You're also not supposed to drink caffeine with #psilocybin.

<p>

The *f*ace is unperturbed with any consequences or twists. Just more data to be mined. More results for his experiments. Causation. Exception. What were the variables? Could it be replicated? How to duplicate digitally? We were just data points in the grand algorithm.

I wondered if the *f*ace rode a meteor to our earth. The Lewis or Clark of another species.

Like Mork from Ork, you say.

I don't get the reference, but nod anyway.

<p>

#MOREHUMANTHANHUMAN

<p>

PTSD. I've been in no war. Never assaulted. Never molested. My prescribed therapist replies, You are, in a sense, on the front lines. The thin digital line. He parrots the corporate speak of the *f*ace. He doesn't ask about prior trauma. I don't tell him about the scar. I don't tell him about Paris. I don't tell him the prescription is a forgery. @Skiny_Leny has a diverse psychiatric network.

The therapist takes copious notes. His exit strategy is to write a book funded by the tragedy of a special client. His practice, a constant stream of auditions.

#Alpha_Male_Beta_Male

The antidepressants work great. They act like a bad-stereo equalizer. Cutting off the highs—I can't hear the screams clearly. Cutting off the lows—I can't hear the bodies thump.

I brush off the videos of women shrieking as acid disintegrates their faces.

My job has never been easier.

Side effects may include impotence.

The brown pill bottle says you shouldn't take a dose with alcohol, you say.

That's only if you're going to take a bath, I say.

The next day you bring a box of high-end bath bombs. We order in.

You prefer rituals to electronics. You prefer reality to fantasy. You prefer well-crafted wine to Two-Buck Chuck. But in a pinch, you'll do anything for your daddy.

You tell me what else you prefer. Your voice, precise and plosive, with the tiniest hint of a lisp. I ask you to keep talking. The ringing in my ears subsides. It was dormant for a while. Then earbuds brought it back. When I sleep, I need white or pink noise, both residing on the frequency that masks my tinnitus. Your gentle snoring also works.

For now, please keep talking. The dopamine flushes my head.

<p>

@Babyd011 is right. Everything is amazing from here on out.

[N S F W]
2

We're in a pawnshop. I've never been in one.

When my grandfather passed away, these were the contents of his bedroom safe:

- $25K in cash.
- A handgun.
- A passport.
- A bag of silver and gold coins.
- A deck of nudie playing cards.
- A roll of 8 mm film.

No one mentioned the 8 mm film roll. When it disappeared, no one seemed to notice.

<p>

You dig through my closet and find a VHS collection I inherited from my grandmother. Our devices locked away in a Faraday cage, the cable and cord cut, we leaned on my grandparents' last adoption of cutting-edge technology.

<p>

My grandparents never saw *Star Wars*, my childhood favorite. I believed in the Force.

They were content to watch the black-and-white movies of their youth. Noir. Marx Brothers. Chaplin. Monster movies. Technicolor musicals. They were amazed they could watch them in their living room now.

I inherited their VHS collection; their VCR was my first thoughtful gift to them.

Among the tapes I found #conspiracy videos.

Connecting the dots to aliens. Hollow Earth. Bizarre frequencies. Implants. There are a few tucked even further back in the collection, cocooned in plastic cases the size of airport paperbacks. Unlabeled. Spooled halfway. Stopped mid-watch. Or stopped mid-recording.

<p>

#BE_KIND_REWIND

<p>

@Skiny_Leny's hometown team won a division game. He chants their stadium chant. It originates from a nation we slaughtered and corralled from their lands.

That's cultural appropriation, you say. Not as an accusation, but as if you are teaching a class and citing an example for a student that still doesn't get it.

It's also what the Romans did to the Greeks, @Skiny_Leny says. This what the Christians did to the Druids. It's how culture evolves. Wicca appropriated from the Middle Ages, other pagan religions, @Jun1p3r. It's how a religion evolves. The Christians appropriated the Yule season, the Winter Solstice.

You're flummoxed.

I snicker. Classic @Skiny.

You're about to respond when @MØM motions us over to her video task. It's a warm-bodied creature being pureed. She makes it a Flavor-of-the-Month contest:

Raspberry fudge? @MØM prompts.

Strawberry caramel? @Babyd011.

Strawberry chocolate? You.

Cherry Maca Mocha? Me.

@MØM squints and decrees: Cherry Maca Mocha!

I win. Cherry Maca Mocha.

Say it as a mantra. Cherry Maca Mocha, Cherry Maca Mocha, Cherry Maca Mocha. So Zen, by the time I get to @Skiny_Leny's workstation to tell him about my win, I don't care I missed his 2-for-1 special on tabs of Lorazepam.

<p>

#Hubris

<p>

An island-state makes the feed. The *f*ace's money has landed and the *f*ace wants to become an island landowner. Land with a better view. Land with better security. Land because he can. The burial land is, understandably, sacred to the natives. Native citizens of the US. But the mainland citizens could not care less. They don't surf and it's not Arlington National Cemetery. The *f*ace brings limitless money and lays miles and miles of fiber optics.

<p>

We should get a familiar, an animal all our own. You say this. Or I say it, or we say it at the same time. We snuggle up. Tonight's viewing is *Singin' in the Rain*. We sing along loudly enough my neighbor bangs on his ceiling. Or floor. Sound carries weird.

<p>

During one of Gene Kelly's direct address lulls, you ask me what was the flagged video of the day. Home invasion. Rape, murder. A young woman. When Gene Kelly sings in the rain all I can see is a young Malcolm McDowell's face. I tense and start to shake. You fast-forward to make me laugh. This turns the little old ultraviolence into a Benny Hill Yakety Sax sequence, and the shaking subsides a bit.

I am not a #droog.

Before bed, I pour our milk down the kitchen sink.

<p>

Anything can be dismissed with scale or time. *Citizen Kane* was a vanity project. *Star Wars* was a children's movie. We're all vain children, a priest once said.

My head feels light in the living room. A sense of *déjà vu*. A vision:

We make love in the glow of our creature in its aquarium. Silent. Eyes closed. Focusing on the sounds. The smell. The feel. Slowly. As if in space. In the depths of the ocean among the giant monsters. Bathing in its alien light.

#Dopamine. Where the word "dope" as in drugs comes from. Also, the "it's cool" proclamation: *it's dope*. A generation removed from the word's origin. Lost etymology its own form of insidiousness and misinformation.

"Maroon" from a children's cartoon. I used to think it was a funny way to say "moron." Instead, Maroon is a culture of isolated savages—tribespeople. Dark skin. Stupid to our American way. Children running on the playground casually parroting a racist slur: "What a maroon!"

Is that where "marooned" comes from? To be isolated? On an island?

We scream words we don't understand.

I pull back in my mind. The end of the earth. Another civilization will rise up. Dig up our fossils. Make connections regarding our culture. Parallels to theirs.

<p>

The first talkie movie with synchronized dialogue and music was groundbreaking. Its signature musical number performed in blackface. In 1996, it was selected for preservation in the National Film Registry. It was based on existing IP. A short story called the "Day of Atonement."

<p>

@MØM cries for the future children. @Skiny_Leny hopes to be present at the end. What a privilege, he says. He's going to freeze and save a Cherry Maca Mocha for the occasion.

Hurtling through space, a golden record with a recording of humanity's greatest achievements speeds away from the earth. Our best face forward. When intelligent life finds it, for them, our history stopped in 1973.

Alien anthropologists and archeologists will have to connect their own dots, drawing a line from 1973 to now, or then. Digging through our remains. Did they just miss us or had we been dead and cold on this rock for a millennium?

What would I put on my own record?

How do you record a vision?

I wonder what grainy story would unspool on my grandfather's 8 mm film.

<p>

We watch old '80s movies. Sex romps. Casual sexual assault. Racist jokes. The quest to deflower and be deflowered. The same actors showing up or making cameos in the slasher movies. Their nude quests ending on the chef's knife of a faceless man.

Remember sneaking into these movies as a kid? you say. Risking a mark on your Permanent Record for a three-second shot of breasts. Perfect breasts before the blade strikes.

Why don't they make these movies anymore? you say. Where did they go?

Your device. For free, I say. A thousand-dollar device with an all-you-can-eat buffet of childhood taboos.

Oh right, you say. The reason we have a job.

We clink whiskey glasses. With the *CLINK*, the power in the building goes out.

We spend the evening watching out the window, into our neighbor's bedroom. She's changing out of her office wear before happy hour. A lacy number. Both nipples are pierced.

This is before we hang the plastic curtains. Before our Garden. Before we obtain a familiar.

<p>

I've seen this movie before. I've read this book before. The hero fails. He has to, because he is dealing with society. There is no bomb to defuse. There is no computer virus to upload. There is no central robot controlling the hive. You are one person.

The machine always wins.

So, you have to decide. What statement will I make? And then what is my exit strategy? I only have to live with myself. There is no option for lasting success. Just a gesture, so I can sleep and say I tried. Then I can sleep.

<p>

#Microdosing is trial and error.

<p>

Now, I'm eleven. In line for school lunch. They are serving deer sausage—the kids called them deer turds—which I liked. The line is abuzz with chatter of a space movie. An alien hatching from a human eggshell. Springing forth from a man's sternum as he twitched and spewed blood.

They showed it?!?!

Yes.

Wasn't off-screen??

Nope.

They showed it??

Even as I was eating deer turds. I can't believe they showed it. Hey Jeff, have you seen this movie?

Yeah, my brother snuck me in.

Did they show it?

Oh yeah, they showed it. Bright lights too.

I can't believe they showed it, I thought. Wow. What a cool world awaits me.

I blink. The intertwined vision and déjà vu unravel. Back in the living space. Me staring at the living space. Plastic tarp walls. A handful of plants. The perpetual dripping gray inside. Even across the room you look molded in black and white. Choking on the haze of burned sage. I can't breathe.

We need more plants, I say.

David Scott Hay

[N S F W]
3

#Bubble

[N S F W]
4

Do you ever have disconnected thoughts? This from my therapist with a pop song's worth of time remaining in our session.

The landing outside our apartment looks like an airlock. I hang a series of hooks and stack plastic tubs. Coats, jackets, scarves, hats, and winter boots. Just inside the door are hampers for our commute clothes and next to that a shelf with pj's ready.

Our jumpsuits stay in our lockers at Vex.

Once the garden is built, we forgo the pj's.

COMING SOON

We go to Gethsemane and order sixty-five square yards of sod. Bit cold for sod, the man with the stooped back says. It won't survive outdoors. It'll have to be special order. He's puzzled but takes our cash.

Next stop, a container store. Thinking outside the box.

<p>

At the nursery.

A cadaver plant. Intriguing flower. Smells like rotting flesh. I buy it. Care for it. Every day I smell its fragrance, unsure that I am remembering it correctly. But I do. It smells like you would imagine a steer carcass baking in the Texas sun. Research indicates it may not flower again for years.

<p>

Kids spend more time on their phones than they do interacting with humans. No more sitting around the campfire, and if they do they're on their phones.

Used to be the fire, then the radio, then the TV, @Skiny_Leny says. This is how a culture evolves. The old replaced with the new. You can scoff or adapt.

<p>

#Solipsism

<p>

@MØM brings in cup holders stacked three high with beverages. We help her unload. Everyone has their own. You look at it, holding it up to a sunlamp used to ward off seasonal depression with its warm light.

What is this? You poke a hole in the lid. Take a sip.

Cherry Maca Mocha, @MØM says. Barista Tim at the Grindhouse made it just for me, special order. We all sip it. Wow.

In the kitchen, you and I add a light dusting of ginseng and psilocybin powder.

<p>

I research bulletproof vests. A cost analysis says spend your money elsewhere. I buy another straight razor shave. The ASMR does not come. I do not close my eyes, following the barber as he does his job. I think I am unsettling him.

He asks about my job. As I leave, he apologizes for the razor burn. I never see him again.

<p>

I spend my break staring at @OrKa. She is huge. With bulges of flesh everywhere. Inhuman shapes. I can't fathom where her skeleton is centered. The stress on every bone, joint, and ligament. I am transfixed.

She mounts her desk-bike, puts in earbuds, and rides into the slaughter. The bike squeaks with energy.

She never waivers in her moderator decision. FLAG. PASS. FLAG. Adjudication without equivocation. Mr. Ray confides she is batting a thousand. She is a machine.

Has she been here that long? I can't recall her ever speaking. Or Mr. Ray ever using a sports metaphor.

@Babyd011 skips by. I'm a beard girl, she says, but that's a nice shave, @Sa>ag3.

‹p›

A video flagged by a user.

The COMING SOON text on black. There's a tiny copyright or trademark or signature or logo attached. Too small to read and the resolution pixelates when I zoom in. I shrug and removed the flag and send the canned response back the user.

DOES NOT VIOLATE TERMS OF SERVICE.

‹p›

HR approves petty cash for our Video Division request. It's official: Cherry Maca Mocha Monday.

‹p›

At the garden center. The smell of earth. Damp. Musky. Then floral. I lean into the lilies. I buy a bag of rich soil. At home I dump it into a shallow virgin tub, bury my feet in it while you run to the convenience store for █████████████

I feel the soil squeeze between my toes. Cool damp. Goosebumps up my legs. Ducky-gumps, you say. A relic of your childhood.

Ten or twenty minutes or hours pass. Now I'm shaking and wondering what is taking you so long. I will my feet to take root, to steady my body. I can't help but let scenes of tragedy play in my head. A robbery. A mugging. Kidnapping. Hit-and-run. Your body thrown in a dumpster. I sink up to my ankles. My breathing evens. I want to call you. My phone is over there.

It's okay, I tell myself. It's okay.

It rings. Not your custom ringtone. It's not you.

It's okay. It's okay.

I break into a sweat. Who is calling? What am I missing? Sweat stings my eyes. I wipe them, forgetting the dirt on my hands.

It's okay. It's okay.

You walk in, stepping out of your pants. I dropped my mittens back at the park, you say.

[N S F W]
5

Vex.

Video of the Day. I thought it would be the one where the man has his eyelids sliced off for spying on his daughter's underage friends. But it's a kid with a coffee drink crossing the intersection, his head down over his device convinced the walk signal will protect him from a driver with his head down over his device.

His shoes fly past the bus stop and into an open sunroof. The device lands faceup, screen intact. @H₁pp3 overlays next-gen graphics: the arc and distance of the shoes. The speed of the truck. The height of the body (beating the Olympic high jumper record). It ends on a close-up of the device.

SUPER: *Pedestrian tested, driver approved.*

It's not @H₁pp3's best work. Troubles at home have kept him subdued lately.

We send @MØM out for a refill. It's Cherry Macha Mocha Monday.

<p>

#Humanist

The mistake is thinking we're raising cold-blooded American sons. They are not. They are filled with hearts burning with belief and passion. It's corporate violence that is cold-blooded. This is @H₁pp3's talking. The gold star for Video of the Day lifting his spirits.

He's wearing his hair down in a quaquaversal of neglect. @Skiny_Leny and @Babyd011 whisper about an intervention.

I rub my eyes. In the corner of the office. I'm seeing two of the same person in a cube. High and tight haircuts. Rocking dark, expensive Nomex jumpsuits. I'm seeing double.

Too much mushroom tea, I think.

@Skiny_Leny swivels in his custom ergonomic chair. Oh, he says. Those are the Twins. He's wearing thigh highs. His legs are devastating. @Babyd011 has shared her isometric exercises with him.

They started just after you did, @Skiny_Leny says.

I half watch the Twins throughout the day. They are courteous but curt. To everyone. Occasionally, one of them will engage in a terse back-and-forth with @Skiny_Leny, but the conversation always ends with a respectful nod.

One of the Twins has installed a breast-feeding bib dispensary in the lactorium. No need for a work order. The middleman cutting out the middle man.

@MØM walks by, handing out Cherry Maca Mochas, her eye also on the Twins. They are both delightful, she says. If it's war footage, they are on it. Such stamina, she says. Such patriots,

<p>

History has shown that if the marginalized and oppressed take power they do not become benevolent leaders. Pick your revolution carefully.

<p>

@Babyd011 walks out of the lactorium. @MØM sure is generous, she says to me. Then: NEXT! That perky voice. She hesitates mid-word as if a sneeze is coming on. I pat her firmly on the back. She burps. Thanks. @MØM's going be sore, she says, mischievously.

Our @Babyd011.

I go into the booth. @MØM is gingerly putting away one heavy breast and pulling out another. @MØM says: She's such a good girl. I indicate I want the other breast. The one still hot from @Babyd011's suckling. The bib dispensary jams. @MØM's smile wanes; she lays a sore breast against my sandpaper cheek. The things we do for our kids.

<p>

The form asks my age range. Even though they have my social security number, which, I remember, is our primary proof of official existence. I skip it.

It's an odd question, we agree, engaging the nullifying white noise. This on our ten-minute break, sitting in the lactorium. We idly shred wet wipes as we cool from physical exertion. A lackluster attempt, the antidepressants suppressing any sexual release. But I admire your optimism. And ability to easily orgasm while humping my leg. It's a gift. I make a note to restock the wet wipes as we turn off the white noise.

People identify now by the model number of their device. But are identified by their device number. Area codes now origin codes.

405.

LET THE WORLD IN

The *f*ace says, as he pays us to keep the world out.

This is how you alter reality.

Alter perception.

Because perception is reality.

I used to think this was academic. A thought experiment.

COMING SOON

People lean away when you mention depression. They lean forward when you talk about inertia. The power of rebranding. Pound sign (#) is now a hashtag. An ellipsis (…) is now a dot dot dot.

18th-century typesetters used to construct every newspaper and pamphlet one letter at a time. Backwards. The uppercase letters were kept in the upper-case drawers. Lowercase letters in the lower-case drawers. The more you know…

#Admin_Rights

@OrKa descended from a silent movie star, Mr. Ray says. That's why she's quiet. And fast. She wears hearing aids when working her video queue and riding her desk-bike. She takes off the hearing aids when not flagging videos. Replacing them with noise-canceling earbuds that play a constant Gottfried Huppertz score.

I wish I had her resolve, you say.

We've all gotten hidden skills, @MØM says.

#COMMUNITY_IDENTITY_STABILITY

The system is rebooting. A new operating system. Off-loading backups. That's the memo. @OrKa and Mr. Ray lean over schematics. Talk in hushed tones. Our planned twenty-minute break has just extended into an hour. Then two. @H₁pp3 leaves to attend to personal matters. The newer employees head for the break room to break out their devices. The Twins duck into the lactorium with @MØM, who looks back with a sigh. Duty first.

<p>

@Babyd011 rolls her chair to our circle.

She could be a model. Striking. In that almost odd way that models are in real life. She photographs like a dream. As if she was built with an artist's brush. She knows this, and wears minimal makeup to the office. Dresses smartly and a touch conservatively. A miniskirt and a turtleneck sweater.

The most content feeling, she says by way of non sequitur. That feeling when you've cleaned the apartment. A deep clean. Dusting the layer of human skin from the winter.

You've bought groceries. The pantry is stocked. Two bottles of decent wine. Even an emergency frozen pizza or burrito, if that's your thing.

The dishes are clean and stored and the Tupperware is organized.

The laundry is done and put away. There's nothing hanging on the chair. Nothing in the hamper.

Fresh sheets. Bed made. The spring comforter makes its seasonal debut.

You are content and everything is perfect, she says. You order Chinese food. And sleep on top of the covers. You want it to be perfect. For just another day or so.

We're quiet. Like we're in a church. Imaging contentment.

Breaking the trance, @Skiny_Leny says, They call it staging, like when they're trying to sell you a house.

No, it's not like that, @Babyd011 says. It's that sense of everything in its right place.

This clicks with @Skiny_Leny. I glance over at you just as you look away, pretending not to listen. But I still see the tear drop into your Cherry Maca Mocha. @Babyd011 squeezes your knee reassuringly. Such an empath.

\<p\>

Later, Mr. Ray will call @Babyd011 into his office for a half hour each day. Just before the Cherry Maca Mochas. She never hesitates to go. Nor does she rush.

@Babyd011's numbers are in the green. She works through her morning break to keep up her normal volume with the Mr. Ray office visits.

\<p\>

The operating system is back online. We know because the squeak of the desk-bike returns.

<p>

Once on my way to recycle my paper Cherry Maca Mocha cup and paper straw—this was when @Babyd011 was in Mr. Ray's office. I cocked an ear to the closed office door. I had no idea what was going on in there.

The sound of Mr. Ray's typewriter stopped infrequently. There was no flash of a camera. No crack of a whip. No *please Daddy*. No *no Daddy*. No *good little girl*.

I heard the typewriter. And a slight pause. I heard *hydrogen*. I heard *Jovian*. I heard *tidal lock*. This was @Babyd011. Her voice was moving as if she was pacing. Positive, thoughtful grunts from Mr. Ray. The typewriter clacked away.

<p>

Eastern cultures prize national identity and stability over individual identity.

Western cultures prize individual identity over national identity and stability.

One kills #freethinkers, the other mocks them.

<p>

There's a group that collects and posts sniper videos. A proper shot will split a head in two. It takes me three weeks to work up the courage to take advantage of my corner market's special on produce. I do not buy any melons.

<p>

His *f*ace again. An automaton. A mad scientist only concerned with the bleeding edge. The founder and CEO. The one subcontracting our judgement.

Popping up in person on Mother/Screen. His trademark gray T-shirts, his lab coat. No white hat or black hat for him. Living in the gray area. He addresses the "concerns" of his lab rats. He talks in a measured and practiced way before returning to his algorithm. I clock three buzzwords. One of which is new this week.

The "concerns" are generated by his in-house PR and used to get ahead of potential negative press. SEO results factor in any potential follow-ups. Puff pieces are released to bury search engine results.

None of his executives have social media accounts. None of their kids have devices. No big tobacco executive smokes cigarettes. This is the drug dealer's code. They *know*.

<p>

#America applauds your courage, the *f*ace says.

[N S F W]
6

All my thoughts are connected, I tell my therapist.

[N S F W]
7

An HR officer in a silk and wool suit from corporate conducts a seminar on the ethical and legal ramifications of having a sexual relationship with a coworker or superior. The seminars at Vexillum vary from fiscal quarter to quarter. This from @Skiny_Leny.

Which one are you, you ask the HR person. Coworker or superior?

She blushes.

We all sign the agreement acknowledging the training. With our screen names.

A week later, as part of her HR training, she has to sit in on video flagging orientation.

A week after that she is updating her resume, but a pod-mate mentions the bonus. Stock options possibly. She saves a draft of her resume in a hidden folder. She already has health benefits.

I'm not sure how long we are into the 90 days. Early, I think. The days blur. A week after that, I am flogging the HR officer with a small cat-o'-nine-tails whip in the dusty conference room. Watching her shudder with every lash.

You sit in front of her, giving her daily affirmations from a book bought at a drugstore. When you read, your enunciation is crisp and wet. Like the bite of an apple.

This while @MØM waits patiently in the lactorium; the Twins hold the HR officer's arms. She prefers this to a rope or leather. Bonds of flesh. HR's silk and wool suit folded neatly on her chair.

You place a cube of sugar on her tongue, reciting: "Earth grows, fire glows, air blows, water flows, spirit knows.

"Taste the sweetness of life and know its resilience.

"Arise and know the warmth created by movement and life."

On "life," I whip her bottom one more time. She cries out softly as welts raise, as if invisible ink is revealed. Afterwards, we are dismissed. @MØM, maternal instinct kicking in, soothes her; tells her she's a good person, applying salve to her blood marks. Helping her dress. Helping her reapply her makeup. Now it's the Twins turn to wait patiently.

It's sweet, this team-building exercise.

For a month or two, we all rotate twice a week. Flogging. Being flogged. Except for you—everyone wants you to read out loud. You accept the task with a sense of reverence.

I can't recall why we stopped. I think one week we had a successful potluck instead and moved on.

<p>

#Deep_State

<p>

One Cherry Macha Mocha Monday, @Babyd011 shows @OrKa a catalogue of fashionable clothes for bigger people.

@OrKa looks at her, her Cherry Macha Mocha untouched.

You've lost weight, right? Treat yourself.

@Babyd011 goes over the pros and cons of mixing seasonal clothing and palettes as @OrKa pedals away.

@OrKa with a hoarse whisper: *danke.*

<p>

Turns out @MØM used to be a burlesque dancer. One morning, she sets up a monitor in the break room and runs her favorite performances on a loop. Grainy footage burned from 16 mm film. The Twins are disappointed she is not in the lactorium, but are soon fascinated with her feathers, fans, and pasties. Showgirl headdresses. Impossibly high heels.

@MØM winks at me and I blush. As she leaves the break room, I notice for the first time her dancer's gait.

Oh @MØM...

We all had previous lives before signing with Vex.

<p>

Our first potluck.

Mr. Ray brings milk, coffee, tea, white bread, jam, and inexplicably a bag of processed sugar. @Skiny_Leny nods appreciatively. You say a Wiccan blessing. @OrKa does not participate. Not since the OS update. She is never off her desk-bike for more than ten seconds. Iron bladder, that one.

We can hear the desk-bike squeaking as we clasp hands in the conference room and include her in the blessing.

<p>

There are no new stories, just new audiences. Mr. Ray says this at my performance review. He dusts the large framed artwork of the alien environment, the cover for *The Aquarist of Ganymede*. He's agitated for an unknown reason. Very few copies of the book survived Stalin and Eisenhower, Mr. Ray says. Eisenhower's policies changed, but by then the pyre had been lit. His brow furrows. His hair is near-perfect.

Maybe you should write the sequel, I say. Hiding my trembling left hand.

He nods thoughtfully. @Skiny_Leny is always finding the falsehood in things, Mr. Ray says. I try to find the truth in things, @Sa>ag3. He polishes the 99% UV Museum Glass.

He became an influencer just as they were being phased out, I say. The frame hangs a bit askew. About a quarter inch. I fight the urge to straighten it.

I'd like to find a better use for his acumen, Mr. Ray says, tilting man and alien back to square. Let me know if something comes to mind. You've got a good mind for problem-solving.

He taps my unopened employee folder and says, Keep up the good work.

<p>

@Skiny_Leny says that book, *The Aquarist of Ganymede*, was banned for a number of years. Ray Gunn (Sr.) did an uncredited rewrite on *The Blob* (1958) starring a twenty-eight year old Steven McQueen as a teenager. At the end of the movie, the blob is dropped from a helicopter in the Arctic where it is rendered inert and the world is safe.

"Yeah, as long as the Arctic stays cold," says McQueen before joining a magnificent pod of seven men.

I'm not sure how a writer in the Soviet Union could pull off Hollywood gigs, logistically, I say.

@Skiny_Leny shrugs. Those communists had their methods.

<p>

Your finger traces the scar on my stomach. You lick it as though about to devour a tequila worm. This the night we test fit, wall-to-wall, dozens of shallow plastic tubs. The furniture will have to go.

I dreamt I was a military drone pilot. And in that dream, I also dreamed of working in an office with other people. We all worked hard for our big bonus. We got in trouble with HR for flirting.

And then my device woke me up. I took it as a sign and signed up at a temp agency. And they brought me to Vex, a child of the *f*ace.

Brought me to @Jun1p3r.

This is how I got here.

This is the lie I tell people.

We watch children's movies. Drama is conflict, they say. But I find the most memorable moments of a story are of connection. Ofttimes the connection is salve enough. These days, the level of drama I want is a polite disagreement with civil problem-solving. The pig. The bear. Finding their misplaced galoshes.

That's our escapism of choice these days: kids' movies, gardening, and #BDSM.

Our special order from Gethsemane arrives. We haul the sod up, you and I. Our hands dirty. We haul the plants up. Our faces dirty. We haul the trees up. Our bodies dirty. Between trips, we push my thirdhand furniture out the window into the alley.

Tossing ballast.

[N S F W]
8

#Jellyfish

[N S F W]
9

The flogging breaks didn't happen all at once.

In the break room, @MØM was flustered when neither of the Twins joined her for a milk break in the lactorium. @MØM's numbers were mediocre, but she knew her greatest contribution to the pod came from her morale boost. Droogs will be droogs.

The Twins were demonstrating interrogation techniques on a curious @H₁pp3, the intern trying to ingratiate himself.

Hard to soft: elbow to stomach. Soft to hard: open hand to the face. This mitigates broken bones. He took the punishment. Asked more questions, @H₁pp3 confusing their bearing for authority.

I wonder if this is the only combat the Twins have seen.

@Babdyd011 wandered in, doing recon for @MØM. She clucked her tongue. Boys, she said, there's more than one way to skin a cat. Her stride and breathing changed as she approached @H₁pp3. She took in the intern with her eyes, determined his weakness. His predilection. She pulled out a pair of thick-framed glasses and put them on. Tied her hair up loosely. She knotted her shirt at her belly, tightening it against her breasts.

She leaned into him, her mouth near his ear. I heard *homework*, I heard *detention*. I heard *naughty boy*. I heard *punishment*. Other vanilla admonishments. She bit his ear and he jumped. His pants jumped as well.

You wandered in, nose buried in a book of poetry, reading out loud. One of the Twins shushed you, but @Babyd011 said, Keep reading, @Jun1p3r.

I followed you and quietly took a seat in the corner and took in the show.

@Babyd011 reached down to @H1pp3's lap and undid his belt buckle. Whispered in his ear. He sat up slowly and turned around and thumbed down his pants, revealing hemp underwear.

She deftly tied his hands behind him with a Yuki half hitch. The rope appearing with the sleight of hand of a magician.

I started to touch myself.

@Babyd011 unspooled his belt through the pant loops. Stood silently doubling up the belt. Finally, @H1pp3 whispered, *please.*

The Twins watched. I watched, rising hard, the atmosphere crackling. You continued, but are now reciting from memory. An ASMR VO.

@Babyd011 began a slow lashing. Each time whispering privately in his ear. Two stanzas later, @H₁pp3 told us his social, his recipe for homemade coconut pie, and that he cheated on his SATs.

As she left, @Babyd011 said, Good meeting team!

That was the first time.

<p>

And then it was on. Our conference room becoming a communal BDSM space. We lost many first-timers/interns, the women lasting much longer than the men who huddled together with their broken masculinity at a hookah lounge and formed their own start-up.

Mr. Ray hears of @H₁pp3's grit and promotes him to full-time temp. Now in on the 90-day bonus hunt.

I rarely join in on the flogging. Content to sit and watch you in the opposite corner reading poetry taken from your hidden library. The flogging an out-of-focus pantomime. A shadow play to your storytelling. My body tingles as the videoconferencing equipment buzzes.

No one asks if it is on.

<p>

Now, @MØM is sullen as the HR officer leaves. Maybe I wanted to be flogged, she says.

I shrug and say, Maybe at the next meeting. Just pipe up.

<p>

Now, Mr. Ray sits outside the conference room door with his portable typewriter on his lap, clacking away steadily, a metronome in time with our whip.

@Babyd011 flits between refilling his coffee, sticking positive affirmations on @OrKa's protein shakes, checking the knots, and complimenting @MØM on her underwear choices with naughty admonishments. *@MØM... goodness.*

I slowly stroke myself, listening to you speak. After I cum, @Babyd011 hands me a wet wipe with an empathic thumbs-up. Then it's her turn. Thigh highs and pigtails. One of the Twins takes the whip.

Our numbers increase 13.5 percent. Other offices shutter. We need more moderators. Mr. Ray is pleased.

<p>

Now, a woman on the elevator pulls out her device. And freezes. As if she's suddenly woken from a dream to find it in her hand. Her thumb circles a number of brightly colored, nonexistent buttons. Hesitating, for a moment, as habituation slides into foggy intention. She hits three in rapid succession. Puts her device away. Each floor she pulls it out and her panic grows. She can't seem to scratch the itch. Why did she pull it out? What was she going to do? What was she going to check?

Nice shoes, I say.

She looks at me. Smiles and says thank you. Then we chat about cold feet. Socks. Public transportation. The winter weather. The box of fresh Krispy Kremes in my hands. It's a pleasant exchange. She laughs. I laugh. It's a genuine interaction. Device in hand.

<p>

I hear my ringtone when my device isn't near. I feel it buzzing against my thigh when it is in the Faraday locker.

<p>

The woman from the elevator is the new girl. I'm flogging her in the break room. She's an early adopter. Livestreams it to her feed. Most people have forgotten the 70-second delay implemented since the Hack. It's live enough.

Her first flagged video was a cat video. Funny. Sweet. Then a blur of fur. A Doberman finally having had enough of its lazy roommate.

She asks a lot of questions, but thanks me for welcoming her warmly.

<p>

My favorite movie directors don't have cell phones or emails or social media accounts. Old school. You say, They have personal assistants instead. And alimony payments.

<p>

@Babyd011 smiles at the new girl. The new girl is wearing pigtails and thigh highs. A cheerleader-style skirt and cashmere sweater. The same outfit @Babyd011 wore last week for Cherry Maca Mocha Monday. I like your style, @Babyd011 says to the new girl.

When the new girl gives a cheery *thanks!* @Babyd011's left eye twitches.

<p>

#HelpWanted

<p>

@Sa>ag3 and @Jun1p3r. That's who are to each other. How we coped. We kept it up. Looking away when we had to print our legal names on a form. Legal. Medical. Insurance. Last Will & Testament. Intimacy in the form of interspatial anonymity. We knew each other but not our real names. We did not carry each other's history. Not in the way you think. Our history began our first day at Vex. Moved only forward.

This is known as the Principle of ██████████

It is a flawed principle.

<p>

COMING SOON

<p>

All these women taking half-nude selfies. Posting them for attention. But in most of them they aren't making eye contact, they're looking at their devices, looking at themselves. You look at me, while I look at me.

It is not a celebration of their bodies, you say. It is the myth of Narcissus and Echo.

This is our conversation as we cover the apartment floor with shallow plastic containers. Wall-to-wall for our sod.

<p>

Mr. Ray grinds the coffee beans himself.

"I don't know if my father died or is alive right now," an Asian says. "But I can see the mosque where we prayed is gone."

China is in the middle of a Muslim holocaust. Systematically, their mosques and synagogues are being destroyed. Placed in camps. Forced not to practice their faith. Sterilized.

Soon the extermination will begin. I've seen the photos. The videos. Smuggled out in blood. Or taken for team building later.

We do nothing, since Islam has no GDP. And things from China are cheap. Keeping wage slaves happy with their meager purchasing power.

There will not be any US intervention. This is not like WWII, an article reads, dismissing the issue. The Chinese aren't threatening our way of life.

And besides, regarding Muslims, 9/11 anyone?

Also, I say, spiritual annihilation does not violate company policy.

You laugh and just like that an issue is raised, acknowledged with gallows humor, a higher power is thanked, and then the issue is discarded.

Our cultural privilege.

Mr. Ray pauses and nods thoughtfully on his way past, coffee cup steaming. He starts to speak, but instead prefers to divert his thoughts through his typewriter keys onto pulp.

‹p›

Mr. Ray terminates the new girl for breaking policy about livestreaming. He suspects she is a spy. She leaves behind an unauthorized biography of the *f*ace.

Used to be that flogging content would be considered dirty and unsavory. Now it will buy a semester of college tuition, @Skiny_Leny says. Now it's on her dating profile. Even as college will be the excuse. Chasing the rush. The next generation of leaders will take power with their nudes accessible at the click of a button. It will be common and no longer taboo, like tattoos in the workplace.

‹p›

@Iun1p3r says you're redecorating, @M∅M says.

Did you get more plants? @Babyd011 says.

@OrKa's desk-bike squeaks. I would oil it. And have thought about oiling it, but otherwise I wouldn't know she existed. The squeaky wheel occasionally is its own purpose.

When's the housewarming party, @Babyd011 asks, as she sterilizes the former new girl's former workstation.

On the train, we chat briefly about the day, our daily check-in. We try to get out the bad stuff before we get home. We share tidbits of the horror we've seen, but nothing stands out. Overall, it was a good day. Very upbeat. Very normal. Today, the quiet lulling of the train is enough.

#Equilibrium

We hang our travel clothes outside the front door and enter the Garden, naked. The humidity curls your hair. Immediately I feel a rush, all the pure oxygen from our plants and newly laid sod. Wall-to-wall grass, thick and supple under our bare feet.

This in winter.

The buried plastic tubs form the foundation of our terrarium. Additional plants, ivies, and potted trees, our new wallpaper and baseboards. From the second floor, we connect back to a forgotten earth. The dry-air nosebleeds of previous winters disappear.

s for our morning mushroom
dnesday. Friday.

shroom bin in the closet. Our first
y to harvest. @Skiny_Leny will be
t of business, but happy with our

when @Babyd011 suggested the plants?
d we be without her?

011 finds the glee in every experience, good
ou say. If good, she might do it again. If bad,
still be grateful for the experience.

riety is the spice of life, I say.

No, you say, it's her meat and potatoes. I'm glad we
ree shared a crème brûlée.

You mentioned you still had all your old bondage gear from when you were married, @Babyd011 says. That @Babdyd011 sure pays attention.

I nod.

Great! @Babyd011 hands you and I a flyer. She has signed us up for a performance art piece in the West Loop. Here's the details. She knows folks.

Everything's amazing from here on out.

[N S F W]
10

They assume I'm your husband. You on display, whispering in your ear to make sure that you breathe. That your wrists still have circulation. Us the knots @Babyd011 taught us. Another Yuki h hitch. Quick release. At home the knots would not quick release, but the event has exceeded the number o the Certificate of Occupancy.

After I double-check the emergency exits thrice, I wipe the drool gathering around at the corners of your mouth around the horse bit. Brushing your hair. Your eyes scanning the room. Locking eyes with the patrons never for less than nine seconds for optimal effect. You wear a name tag that says OBEY.

Your real husband does show. Having bought a ticket. He strips to his tighty-whities, gives himself a wedgie, slicks his hair with spit into limp spikes. He runs around hooting like a baboon. A buffoon. Just an unbilled sideshow to the main attraction. He tells @Babyd011 he's just landed a gig in a big-budget action movie. Things are going to change, he says. She gives him a spirited high five and moves on. Everyone else ignores him while a renowned comic book artist draws your bondage portrait.

At the silent auction, it gets the second-highest bid. The first, a date with @Babyd011; your husband being outbid.

As an encore, I remove the thigh separator first, two padded straps around your thick thighs and the wooden baton joined with metal rings. Working my way up. Then the chest harness. Your wrist. You put them, ladylike, in your lap. Then the horse bit. And then I reach into your mouth and pull out a pair of stained black panties. You stand and throw them into the crowd.

They scramble and fight for them like drunken bridesmaids, as we exit the stage. When they look up from the mêlée, we have vanished into thin air.

The shelf life of a porn star now is two years. The smart ones dole out the acts. First time girl on girl. First time BBC. First time anal. Adding a new and exciting act as their freshness wears off. Because there are no new acts of depravity. No new angles. Just new faces. And that's what keeps them coming back.

A new product.

A new face.

Women have admitted to filming a career's worth while they were younger and hanging on to the files in case of financial emergency. There is no data to determine how many porn stars have been lost to power surges, discarded hard drives, and long wait times at tech bars manned by geniuses.

<p>

The next day at work, we watch amateur magicians in a bizarre attempt to make a bus vanish. The trick goes wrong and all the assistants end up splattered over the audience.

Abracadabra Allahu Akbar.

You lean over my shoulder. That show killed, you say.

My heart swells.

<p>

I'm hard. But there is no path to redemption. The door to Nirvana will not open. I choose not to fake it.

Like you did on prom? you say. It's the meds, I say. It's okay, Lover. We'll cope. There's more than one way to skin a human.

I work my tongue. You come. You hump my leg as I hold you close. You come again.

By the weekend, we stop having sex.

<p>

Let's try intimacy, you suggest.

Like what?

Ask me a question. Anything.

[N S F W]
11

When I struggled with the question of divorce, I spent a New Year's weekend in the city with a pagan friend— not a witch. When I was married, we had lived in her neighborhood for years. Back then, the wife and I ordered Chinese regularly. Had it delivered, though it was less than a block away.

You listen with intent, recognizing the importance of history.

During the last great snowstorm, we ordered our regular. The Chinese deliveryman walked it over rather than drive half a block, lest he lose the temporary parking spot he'd shoveled for his business. I know because I watched him cross the icy intersection from my sunroom.

I felt shame at my laziness and tipped him obscenely. He nodded with gratitude.

The pagan friend and I had done a number of projects together when we were younger, when a life in the arts still seemed worthy. Then suddenly I had to move to the burbs. For my bride's new creative job. And now it felt like I lived on the other side of the moon. Divorced from my friends, from my potential.

During that pivotal New Year's weekend, two things happened:

We got news that a show we had worked on seven years ago was named the number two show of the decade in Chicago. We were second to a Pulitzer Prize winner. *Huh.* How about that? We celebrated. And we celebrated our younger selves, who had sacrificed so much. (Talking about it now, I understand your tattoo sleeve.)

That's amazing, you say, putting the kettle on.

But that's not what I remember most, I say, and continue the story.

We ordered takeout to celebrate. Minutes later, the buzz at the door. I open it. It was the same Chinese deliveryman. I had not seen him in five years. He recognized me. We both stood silently for a moment and then broke into smiles.

So delighted were we that we hugged. The embrace you give a long-lost friend.

It was one of the most unexpected bright moments of that time.

An hour later, as the egg rolls and crab rangoon were expanding my waistline, my friend performed a reiki session with sage and I drove home through a snowy night with leftover Chinese, to my wife. I listened to "Here Comes the Sun" on repeat.

I had wanted to tell her about the Chinese deliveryman. Instead, I told her I wanted a divorce.

She packed a bag and left an hour later.

Happy New Year.

Six months later, when the divorce was final and the depression stabilized, I treated myself to a week in Paris. I met ███████ and I stayed three months (90 days). We spent a blissful romantic summer. Every adventure punctuated with her infectious laugh, the encore to my butchering every attempt at her language. I had no plans to leave.

She told me I'm not like most Americans.

How's that, you ask, handing me a cooling mug of mushroom tea.

Americans don't like to be reminded that bold moves are still possible.

[N S F W]
12

A celebrity opens up about a recent personal tragedy. Click here for the full video of her acute psychological self-analysis.

A quick five-dollar wager circles in our pod.

It's hard, she starts. *It's so unfair. You guys....* She adjusts her camera. Non-waterproof mascara for this particular video. She's lost followers recently. A spat with another twentysomething with better skin. I just can't, she says.

She takes a handful of pills.

Are those Tic Tacs? you say.

I hope not, I say.

As she's pleading, her eyes are flicking down to the scrolling comments and emojis.

‹p›

In a whisper of a German accent @OrKa says, Based on her body weight that woman has twelve minutes before cardiac failure. This the most we've ever heard @OrKa speak. She has our attention. She's wearing metal-edge French tips, @OrKa says. She won't be inducing her own vomit.

@Skiny_Leny yawns. It's contagious and @MØM goes down for another round of Cherry Maca Mochas.

@OrKa sets a timer for twelve minutes and sprints "uphill" nonstop on her desk-bike. The squeaky wheel's tempo now like a Geiger counter in Chernobyl.

Can @MØM beat the timer? @Skiny_Leny muses. Now we're excited.

@MØM returns. Seconds later the timer goes off. There's a spontaneous applause. @MØM blushes. Then there's a moment of synchronized silence. If such a thing can exist.

The first RIP post goes up twenty-seven minutes later.

@MØM beat @OrKa and the celebrity! @Babyd011 stands and gives her an extra-slow clap.

One of the Twins pins a medal on her ample chest. I notice his hair isn't as high and tight as it used to be.

Milk does a body good, @Skiny_Leny says.

<p>

The Information Age: we speak in declarative sentences and respond in questions.

Do we?

[N S F W]
13

I want a baby, you say.

<p>

<p>

<p>

<p>

<p>

Do you?

[N S F W]
14

It will take effort and thirty-six hours. We make a shopping list. Step out of our loop. We bring home a baby.

<p>

Mr. Ray posits that PKD will prove to be prescient. Animal products will become illegal; a last-minute attempt to curtail emissions. We will become herbivores. Owning a real animal will be a luxury.

Aquariums will become status symbols.

<p>

The odds of human conception are astronomical, @MØM says. We're already lottery winners.

Most lottery winners are broke inside eighteen months, I say.

Let's transcend that, she pleads.

@Skiny_Leny scoffs. A billion worlds. We're not special. Just a byproduct of the Chicxulub asteroid. He says this with a shrug as he curls his hair.

<p>

An airlock is a device that permits the passage of people and objects between a pressure vessel and its surroundings while minimizing the change of pressure in the vessel and loss of air from it. The lock consists of a small chamber with two airtight doors in series, which do not open simultaneously. This according to the net.

It also keeps out contaminants.

We can't have anything go viral.

<p>

I've decreased the dosage. Still impotent.

<p>

Thirty-six hours pass in our apartment garden.

It's alive, we scream.

We open the valve at the bottom of the tube leading to the brown water. We fill a shot glass. As an extra step we drain the shot with a coffee filter. Little squiggles twitch and pulse.

We feed our creatures to our baby. To them, a monster.

We watch. The brine shrimp drift into the tentacles. Taken to be eaten and digested in one of the fours stomachs in our

Despite the medication, I'm hard.

<p>

Condensation drips in the background. The occasional diamond of water glowing visibly through the foliage that lines the apartment. Plants. Trees. Vines. The diamonds sliding down sheets of plastic. Containing our O_2. Our own diorama of Eden. Our own private Idaho.

You turn around, straddling my cock; your back to me as you face the jellyfish tank. You ride me, slowly afloat on cosmic seas. I can't tell if your eyes are open or closed.

I watch you. The light of the tank makes your edges glow as if in the presence of a minor god. When you sink down on me, the jellyfish reveals itself, slowly floating, turning before it bumps against the glass. And then you rise and the jellyfish is hidden. I can smell you. Feel you sliding in and over, then out and on me and back in. Wet ocean sounds as you paint me with your sex. The jellyfish a silent voyeur.

I close my eyes and lean back, my skull on the sod. The soft sounds of breathing hum in my ears. Slow and steady. My tinnitus fades. You slide a finger into me slowly. In. Out. Your body matches the waves. Your rhythm. You slide off of my cock. Now I feel your hand. Another hand. Maybe your mouth or a combination, but I cannot track what is doing what; it feels like a dozen mouths, a dozen hands. A puzzle beyond my unlocking.

Then a tiny spark; I can see it, The path is clear.

You carry me along it in a natural time. The outcome no longer in doubt. You don't push me, or hurry my arrival. I ignite. I see stars bursting. I cum. Wave after wave. The waves crash and I buck. Soft then pounding then soft again. You coo in my ear: *That's my good boy.*

I lose my mind and drift away into a coda of sleep. The plink of diamonds, an elemental lullaby.

Tomorrow is a day off. And our bodies will wake when rested.

<p>

Garden. Airlock. Train.

Feeding your creatures to my monster. That's what you say later, slapping my thigh as a rim shot. This over our morning psilocybin tisane, still steaming in our travel mugs.

I laugh. You laugh. I laugh harder; you laugh harder. People on the train stare, looking up from the glow of their devices. Their faces illuminated like trophy mounts of a big game hunter.

Now we're in hysterics. It's a kind of magic.

<p>

Our pod spends too much time debating whether a flagged video is of a woman's breast and areola or an elbow and shadow. A fleshy Escher sketch.

Mr. Ray is called out of his office as a tiebreaker. Grateful it's not another live-feed crisis, he takes a moment to test his pompadour. His hair is flawless like a Greek statue. He taps a few keys, checks the video's metadata. Consults a laminated card like a head coach.

FLAGGED.

It originated in Afghanistan. Either decision is a violation of community standards. The elbow/breast belongs to a female marine. Men with stars on their collars dishonorably discharge her.

We are bummed. @Babyd011 says, Men are afraid of boobs.

@MØM says, sotto, Not around here. @Babyd011 giggles. And then realizes it's Monday and asks who is getting the Cherry Maca Mochas.

Train. Airlock. Garden.

Sex magik, you say. Wiccans do not approve of sex or blood magik or hexing or cursing, you say. But this is for a good cause. Just to be safe you'll mention it to your coven, but you're sure most of them. Because if the goddess can't rub a few out for a female warrior, then what is the point of it all?

You put your legs up on one of the half whiskey barrels. The overhead light bulb has been taken out. A series of sunlamps on a timer. But it is early evening in winter and the sun set hours ago. The only light in the apartment is the aquarium with our baby.

The knife, the dildo. You write the female former marine's name on a piece of paper and burn it. Spread the ashes on your abdomen. You take the dildo and lay back on the sod.

May her healing come threefold, you say. Three orgasms later. You release an energy out into the universe to that woman.

The jellyfish hums.

‹p›

LET THE WORMS IN

‹p›

I awake early with you in my arms. The leaves of the ficus and *Schefflera arboricola* glisten in the jellyfish light.

The silhouette of the foliage weaves another layer of insulation. The jellyfish floats, suspended in its tank. I imagine it a giant floating in an interstellar atmosphere. The whiskey barrels have been relocated for the night to the side of the Garden.

With each sleepy blink, the barrels morph. Wooden slats emerging from the earth, half-buried treasure awaiting pirates. Or burial mounds. Or monuments of offering to the glowing god. The slight gurgle of the filter. The hum of the hatchery. The darkening of your toes where they gripped the sod during your ritual.

Tomorrow, I will wash them. Kiss them. Warm them for our morning sojourn.

The sod earth and grass beneath us have warmed with our body temperature. It is like floating in a warm bath, the heat from your body against my stomach. It cools quickly as I separate, and trace the moles and tiny crater of scar on your upper shoulder and neck. In this light, the tiny shadows mirror the surface of an unknown moon. I have never asked.

Just as you have never asked about the jagged star of scar tissue on my abdomen. My thumb beats with its own tiny pulse, a marker for the small cut you made. Drawing a drop or two of my blood to fuel your nightly incantations. In the morning, the chill will finally have seeped into the Garden. And I will grab the woolen blanket rolled up neatly behind us.

Your breathing is shallow, an accent pushing on the exhale. A dreaming feral dog chasing humans. The excitement of the day slipping into night. If I were to lie on my other side, I would hear my ear ringing.

Tinnitus, the echo of the scar on my belly. But now the white noise hum of our alien and the hatchery push it outside the bubble. And around us all the trees and plants, their leaves whispering softly, echoing the protection invocation you used with your magik. I listen for the creaking of the building. The cracks in the bubble. Hear none.

My mouth is dry. A side effect. I think tomorrow I will start to bury my pills in the sod. I can hear you say, I can't wait to see how impotent happy grass grows.

The smell of your ritual sex fades, now mixed with the grass and warm damp earth. The smoke from the candle drifts over us, lingering with the aftertaste of sweetgrass.

Slumber caresses me.

I dream we are in an alien craft, a generation ship hurling through the cosmos as the jellyfish come to return to their home world. Adam & Eve birthing another myth.

Everything in its right place.

NODE III

"One wandering thought pollutes the day."
—Mary Wollstonecraft Shelley
Frankenstein; or, The Modern Prometheus

[N S F W]
1

One warm evening in my youth, I was alone in the backyard when I spotted a large red ant as it moved along our brick-edged patio. There were no nests or hills I could see, nor was it following any discernable trail. With no pressing matters and an interest in an ant's life as it pertained to my backyard, I lay down close to it, not enough to cast a shadow or spook it.

For an hour, I just watched this red ant. I moved occasionally to keep a good vantage point. I wondered if he was lost. I wondered if he was blazing a trail or if he was the sole survivor of a black-ant surprise attack.

Or if, like me, he simply wanted a bit of solitude. Away from the bullies and crude boys that circled the block on their racing bikes, popping wheelies.

The ant walked up and down blades of summer grass, each a towering obstacle. Mostly it stayed on top of the blades. Multiple blades under multiple feet, moving more quickly on top of the yard's canopy. Other times it traveled down to the earth walking around the blades, disappearing in and out of the shade and sun.

After an hour, it nearly completed a twenty-foot circle coming back to the patio.

I spotted the spider before it did. Crouched in the cracked mortar between two patio bricks. No trapdoor, no webs. Just a shadow. Perhaps tired of navigating the blades of grass, the ant walked into the clearing of dirt in front of the spider. The ant came into the full view of the spider and did not sense it. The spider let it pass. Almost. It pounced and that was it. And then it was just the spider and me.

Did you kill the spider, you ask?

I did.

And then you were alone, she says.

[N S F W]
2

COMING SOON

The warnings continue. Simple. Text on black with a simple minor chord under it. Probably some new app or device, @Skiny_Leny says. My tinnitus activates and I mute it.

Office. Train. Airlock. Garden.

A present. You bring me a cupcake with a lit candle embedded with glitter and sparkles, and an unlabeled VHS tape. I tense realizing we are going to watch a video. I have just spent my day watching people become things.

You hit play as I try to take a deep breath. It's a clean transfer of old-school cabaret acts. Burlesque. Pasties and titty-twirlers. Large colorful feather headdresses and jiggles. Bodies curved and without tone. But with smiles that reach the eyes. Proud. We applaud each dancer. @MØM snuck me the tape, you say.

With the last dancer you get up and perform the same moves next to the screen, in near synchronicity. She, your historical shadow. Or you, her modern puppet. It is a moment of unexpected, pure joy. Your unselfconsciousness. Your smile. You turn, arms raised. And the dance becomes much more. Salome before Herod. My brain floods with serotonin and dopamine.

Happy birthday, Daddy. Make a wish, you say.

I do and blow out the candle.

‹p›

Garden. Airlock. Train. Office.

‹p›

More COMING SOON videos. Something big is coming on the digital horizon. But it doesn't violate policy. At the imported-water cooler, it is brought up. It's trying too hard to go viral, you say. Probably an IPO, @H$_1$pp3 says. Good luck there.

The accompanying sound is an anxiety-producing earworm.

‹p›

A deputy sheriff comes into the office and hands @H$_1$pp3, a veteran of a dozen failed Bay-Area start-ups, a manila envelope. After a moment, he refills his daily Valium at @Skiny_Leny's desk and asks him about hot-oil treatments for his thick silver hair.

A silver fox, @MØM says of @H₁pp3 within earshot. But @H₁pp3 doesn't take the bait. His mind on the manila envelope.

Later @H₁pp3 asks me if I have a white business envelope. I haven't seen one in years. As he asks if @Skiny_Leny has anything stronger in his desk stash, all our computers sound an alarm. Electronic tones warbling between minor notes. (All of our devices sit in the Faraday lockers.)

My heart jumps despite the residual Xanax packed in my molars.

@MØM shouts it's just an Amber Alert.

We all breathe a sigh of relief.

Figures, @H₁pp3 says. Disappointed the apocalypse isn't coming soon enough to save him from impending legal fees, depression, and online dating. He says, Does anyone know how many more days to the bonus?

Office. Train. Airlock. Garden.

The house next to our apartment building is being razed. They're going to put in a condo. The top of a bulldozer is just visible over the fence.

I sit cross-legged on the green, green grass of home. You straddle me, envelop me. We wear gauze masks to further enhance other senses. We rock back and forth slowly; sweat forms and drips as we listen to the ethereal sounds of Stockhausen through shared wired earbuds connected to a device in our homemade Faraday cage.

<p>

At 3 a.m., the witching hour, there is a crashing sound in the bathroom. Covered with bits of grass and dirt, we get up.

Is there an intruder in the Garden?

The shower curtain has fallen. Curious. I turn on the light. Moisture covers the mirror. I feel a cold breeze. There is a large crack running down the side of the wall. I look at the window. It's askew. Bricks have cracked.

Outside, in hastily-thrown-on coats and boots, we trace the brick-pixelated crack up the entire exterior wall. It connects every bathroom window from the ground floor to the top floor. We are in the middle. I look at the bulldozer, over the construction fence.

From the bathroom window we can see where they have excavated out a new basement too close to our building. Our foundation has shifted and cracked.

[N S F W]
3

Vexillum is a subcontractor. The ʄace not wanting to subject its direct employees with their custom shakes, skate park, and free day care, to this stream of uncensored content. But if we're good. If we hit the impossible numbers. Maybe we will be invited to the inner circle.

It is the only way @Jun1p3r and I will not die working.

The ʄace company hoodies regulate your body temperature to your preference and have many hidden travel pockets for all your device's accessories.

Meanwhile, our healthcare is a collection of counterfeit coupons, forged prescriptions, and sympathetic vendors.

<p>

@Skiny_Leny, between suicide-by-sports-car videos, taps away at a business plan. An IPO, the endgame for him. It doesn't have to be profitable, he says. You just have to convince people you're making the world better, that it's disruptive, and they will be missing out.

Build your retirement with #FOMO.

A buckleless belt. A toilet for your cat. A footstool to help you shit.

More than once, @H₁pp3 steals a glance at @Skiny_Leny's scribbles. Protect yourself, @H₁pp3 says. Legally.

<p>

In our Vex email signature blocks are our preferred pronouns, e.g., @Sa>ag3 (he/him/his).

@H₁pp3 (we/our/planet) hangs himself Wednesday, at home. Per company policy, Mr. Ray tells us on Friday.

I ask what node @H₁pp3 was in. Political ads, you say.

Now @Skiny_Leny won't have any hair competition. Twin One or Twin Two says this regarding the news of @H₁pp3.

@Skiny_Leny blushes as he fidgets with his van keys. Dangling from the ring and fob, a pink canister of mace in a designer case.

Twin One or Twin Two needs a haircut. If only @H₁pp3 had been lactating, Twin One or Twin Two says. He might have been useful. Their laughter is forced.

<p>

We don't dissuade them. The lies. The propaganda. The links. Policy violations overruled by clickbait revenue funded by foreign governments, @Skiny_Leny says, double flagging a video while experimenting with false eyelashes. He loves a good conspiracy theory.

<p>

In the lactorium, you and I take turns on @MØM's breast. @H₁pp3 was served divorce papers, @MØM says. That was the manila envelope. His wife wants— wanted his IP. Intellectual property.

I know how he felt. Then and now.

I know this because @H₁pp3 left two notes at my workstation. After reading the first, I realize @H₁pp3's wife will be stuck with his student-loan debt (she co-signed back in a more optimistic time), along with the virus he injected in her computer.

All this tucked in a white business envelope.

The second bonus note says: "In the event of my death, my wife did it."

Then he addresses me, directly. *I leave it up to you, @Sa>ag3, whether you want give the authorities no note, this note and expose my ruse, or the "my wife did it" note."* Win-win-win!

@MØM whispers a comment I don't catch.

Hmmm?

@MØM whispers, @H₁pp3 had an S-shaped cock. And then sighs.

@H₁pp3 never was an incel boy.

<p>

Meanwhile, @Babyd011 has a heart-to-heart with @Skiny_Leny after he struggles with fake eyelashes as big as monarch butterflies. It's so hard, he says.

Oh, @Skiny.

@Babyd011 explains what it's like to be a real woman instead of a tourist.

Imagine Amazons, @Babyd011 says. But not nearly as sexy. Not nearly as clean. Not nearly as couth. Not nearly as witty. Pithy. Tall like NBA players. Almost everyone is as tall as an NBA player. And horny. Staring at you. Leering. Coming on to you. Entitled. Relentlessly. Like a child with a hard-on. A child who can easily lift you into a car. Easily knock you out, easily throw you to the ground. Imagine fighting an NBA player. The height. The reach.

@Skiny_Leny drops his keys.

Effortlessly, she applies a giant fake eyelash on @Skiny_Leny. Imagine any professional athlete. And now one that wants you by force. Imagine a world in which any male could turn on you. You know two judo moves from middle school. She hands him his pink mace. How much safer do you feel now? Imagine that world every day.

@Skiny_Leny stumbles over a quote or a statistic from an obscure philosopher.

Or imagine a person wants to borrow your phone charger, @Babyd011 says. Ten times a day. Friends. Relatives. Strangers. Spouses. She applies the other eyelash. Holds a compact mirror up to him. His eyes are devastating. How exhausting it is to be polite lest you be labeled a bitch.

@Babyd011 clucks her tongue and snaps shut the compact mirror. In my head, I hear an actress playing a prostitute snort America's long-forgotten laugh.

Women are better at this job because they've been in a constant state of threat assessment their whole lives, she says. Now she applies foundation to his face, hiding the blemishes, his five-o'clock shadow.

The men do okay at the job, but mostly because of their experiences with movies. Oh, that's rated PG, that's PG-13. That's a definite R, but only for language. That's a hard R because of the blood and bone. A light touch of blush to his cheekbones. That's NC-17 because of choreographed sex.

A woman sees a flagged video and thinks: *That will fuck me up*.

Men think of it as experiential and transient. A nude-colored lipstick.

Women think of it as, will I survive? And if I do, will I tell? Does this need to be stopped and how much am I willing to sacrifice to stop it or do I just pray for it to be over quickly?

She takes off @Skiny_Leny's sensible flats. Slips her own high heels onto @Skiny_Leny's feet. He blushes like Cinderella. His keys slip from his fingers again. A muted jangle on the carpet.

Men are more concerned with the behind-the-scenes of the traumatic. Who directed? Who did special effects? What was she wearing? Had she been drinking? How could she have prevented being in that situation? She unbuttons the top two buttons of @Skiny_Leny's blouse. Are you willing to go all the way?

@Skiny_Leny starts to speak, a clever rejoinder—

Hush, honey, @Babyd011 says. She takes his hand and they stand. Let's walk the streets, @Skiny_Leny. I'll give you a half-block head start to the train. It's not far and well lit. Only a few darkened alleys. Here's your keys with your mace. You'll keep one hand on your bag. The other will be a choice between your mace and your device. Between self-defense and 9-1-1. She squeezes his thigh and whispers in his ear: Don't forget to bat your lashes.

@Skiny_Leny is suddenly mute.

[N S F W]
4

Professor Snowden falls ill at the Moscow International Airport. Poisoned.

‹p›

I thought he was already dead, you say.

I forgot all about him, @Babyd011 says.

Oh Eddie, @MØM says.

Looking at the feed photo, @Babyd011 exclaims, He's got your beard, @Skiny!

The Twins glance in eerie unison at Mother/Screen for a moment then go back to a marathon viewing of suicide bombers at a Middle Eastern market.

Mr. Ray bows his head for a moment. When he walks away, I see him close his small notebook.

‹p›

I guess the COMING SOON mystery is solved. No one says it, but we're mildly disappointed.

[N S F W]
5

LET THE WORLD IN.
MORE CONNECTED.
MORE CONNECTED TO FAMILY.
MORE CONNECTED TO PRODUCTIVITY.
MORE CONNECTED TO THE WORLD.
LET THE WORLD IN.

More time for news. More time for ads. More time to consume. But never enough time to consume it all. That's the game. Who can consume the most? And then you die.

<p>

LET THE WORMS IN.

<p>

@MØM wants to be positive and encouraging about @Babyd011's new mohawk with blue tips. Why would you cut it like that?

It's her body, you say.

My date from the silent auction, @Babyd011 says. His band is having a hard time getting folks to their show. I love them and want to support them. They're playing the Metro tonight. You should all come. She hands out flyers.

LIVE MUSIC!

The flyer is triggering. The room starts to spin. I focus on a flashing cursor. I focus and draw a deep breath. Tell myself I am safe. I am in Chicago.

Sensing my distress, you bring me a compostable bottle of water from your pack. It is cold and jolts my brain and gut back to Vex.

I start to tell @Babyd011 that I don't do live music because of my tinnitus. But my mouth doesn't work properly.

You intervene on my behalf. We have an order of sod arriving, you say. We can't make it, @Babyd011. With regrets.

She gives us an appreciative head bob.

Regarding @Babyd011's new mohawk, @Skiny_Leny says, It's not cultural appropriation if that culture has been destroyed. It's homage.

Assimilation, you say.

The rise of social media has also seen the rise in cruelty. #Cruelty grows quicker than #Inspiration.

<p>

I post a mistake, distracted by @Babyd011 trying to reconcile the freshly scrubbed schoolgirl and new punk esthetic. It scares me, her power. I tell myself she does not look familiar. Whatever lie it takes to get through the day. I do not remember the last 100 videos I have adjudicated.

<p>

Right before a flogging-break, Mr. Ray summons me to his office. *Thwacks* a piece of paper with a flick of his finger. Sighs. @Sa>ag3. I don't get it. How could you blow this call?

I can't guess which video I missed. I lower my head. My thoughts start to drift.

Far away, I hear his voice say: Any lost ad revenue and corporate might cut our budget. Poof. There goes our Cherry Maca Mocha budget. It affects the whole pod, your performance. Does that make sense?

He clears his throat. *Ahem.*

Did he ask me a question?

He brings me back by tapping his sunglasses on his whiteboard. The numbers. The important numbers. We're off target for the bonus. Your bonus. The pod's bonus. He leans closer. His hair is sculptured perfectly, a tidal wave, frozen and shiny.

I've never missed my numbers. Mr. Ray says this gravely, confidentially, as if sharing this for the first time.

I let my personal life affect my performance, Mr. Ray. I'll get refocused.

He nods sagely. Softens. At least it wasn't a live feed, Mr. Ray says. I don't worry about you with those. Look, I'm sure you can get your numbers up. @OrKa's already running anchor. Find your rhythm, your routine. No need to make the homestretch interesting for the folks at home.

I nod.

He absently taps the space bar on his typewriter. How's @Jun1p3r? he says, cocking his head in her general direction though she is out of sight.

We're on a break, sir.

I'm sorry to hear that. I thought you two—

No, we're on a break from microdosing. Two weeks.

How's it going?

We're coping.

The mushroom hasn't evolved in a million years, he says. Same for the jellyfish. Five hundred million years. Just the same thing. He stares into space for a few seconds. Buffering.

Ah, he says. Well, if there's anything I can do, let me know.

<p>

The FTC says that jellyfish as a memory supplement is a hoax. Another study says it can help fight cancer. It does, we agree. It fights so many things.

<p>

Office. Train. Pet store. We break our loop. We're out of baby food.

<p>

The clerk at the aquarium store tells us that piranhas are outlawed in states where it's too warm. People get tired of cleaning the tanks due to the carnivores, the detritus of half-eaten goldfish clouding their tanks. So, they dump them into lakes. And they propagate.

Them fish don't go into a feeding frenzy when there's just a few of them, she says. Instead, they go for their prey's eyes first. They yank out the eyes with a quick bite. Then watch their prey swim around blindly. Then they bite off tails. Fins. It doesn't kill them. They exhaust themselves just to stay afloat. And then sink to the bottom. Most times the piranha don't even eat them. Just killing for sport. It's kinda beautiful.

Sounds like ████████████████████, you say as we complete a cash transaction for brine shrimp eggs.

<p>

It looks like a translucent mushroom, I say. But your thoughts are elsewhere.

If we let our jellyfish go, you say, we can't put it into the sea. It's filled with microplastics. They're inside us even now. Everywhere. Even the rain is filled with microplastics.

<p>

Garden. Airlock. Train. Office.

<p>

The next morning, @Babyd011 comes in with a black eye and a fat lip.

We all gasp. It's different when violence walks into your office. The need for an explanation. To comfort. To ignore. To bite back the gallows humor.

I moshed!!! she says.

She did, says @MØM, who now has purple tips in her hair. They giggle later when they pass each other. Their night out at the punk show a memorable one.

Cherry Maca Mochas arrive courtesy of the assistant manager from the coffee shop. *To @MØM, compliments of **BARISTA TIM** at the Grindhouse.*

I check my calendar. It's Tuesday. @MØM gives me a wink. Keep grinding. And flashes me the devil's horns. \m/

@H₁pp3's drink sits on the break-room counter unclaimed. Eventually one of the interchangeable interns claims it.

<p>

Climate change. Racism. Corporate personhood. Ten-dollar coffee drinks.

How much more can we adapt, I ask. I look at the jellyfish. No brain. No eyes. Alone in the aquarium. But he's safe. Ask the animals lower on the food chain if they want to leave the zoo for the Serengeti.

<p>

An email from a senator hits my inbox. They wish for me to participate, to be part of the solution. To answer this survey, to have my voice be heard. The last question isn't a question but a donation box. I won't be heard unless I give them money.

<p>

#Bai_lan.

<p>

We picnic in the living room on our lush grass.

Every time I accomplish a goal, I want it to be notable and acknowledged. To be visible. I won the first thirteen games of chess I ever played, I say. I haven't won since, but I still own three different sets. Am I an optimist? Superstitious?

Or just a loser, baby, you say.

At least I'm not a quitter, I say.

That night we fall asleep on the sod, the bedroom long abandoned.

<p>

We don't want foreigners killing our civilians and soldiers. But our tolerance for domestic terrorism inside our borders keeps rising. *First Amendment vs. Second Amendment.*

Yes, you are a quitter, @Skiny_Leny says. You quit winning. He pulls out a mini magnetic chess kit. He's white. Opens with Queen's Gambit. I counter with French Defense. His sculpted eyebrows knit in alarm.

I play @Skiny_Leny to a stalemate. You celebrate like it's my first victory in twenty years. You didn't lose, you say over and over.

We celebrate. You create a yard sign with balloons congratulating me. It weathers the winter, losing only its helium. You have such a sense of occasion. *My @Jun1p3r.*

I see you, you say.

I am seen.

Perhaps for the second time in my life.

#Asch_Conformity_Experiments

You got anal, didn't you, @Sa>ag3? @Skiny_Leny says. That @Jun1p3r knows how to spray the champagne.

I look at you with adoration. You hum a novelty song from the '70s as you watch whales breathe their last off the coast of Japan. Slaughtered in their homes in HD. I think of the killer whales ramming into the sides of their concrete tanks.

\<p\>

Outside our tiny apartment:

Going the distance!
Draw in 27 moves.
@Sa>ag3 vs. @Skiny_Leny

[N S F W]
6

The revelation: I finally understood Johnny's sentiment to June.

They figured it out.

We figured it out.

The only time we said it to each other.

<p>

In the future, as society breaks down even more to grant individual rights, we will all incorporate, @Skiny_Leny says. Become our own city-states corralled by a figurehead who will bestow new technology on those that show it favor. @Skiny_Leny twirls his long thick hair with a finger. Ringlets form effortlessly.

Our government will become just a house of straw men, he says.

How far in the future did you say this was?

@Skiny_Leny shrugs and slurps the last of his Cherry Maca Mocha. **@S_L INC** in thick marker on the side. He stays after-hours to boost his slipping numbers and work on his Big Idea, his retirement idea. At his elbow, a hacked list of venture capitalists and cabalists tracked with unhackable paper and pen.

@Skiny_Leny's apologizes for his aggro comments regarding @Jun1p3r. Bath salts do not agree with me, he says. But I think it was @Babyd011's thought experiment. He's planning on a long soak with Epsom salts after work—he says this as he asks for a sip of your tisane.

\<p\>

My dad didn't help me much when I was growing up. Figure it out, he'd say. And I would. Later in high school and college everyone would call me. Call █████████, they'd say. He'll figure it out.

\<p\>

That's where culture evolves, the convergent path of science fiction and science. Where Big Ideas meet Engineering. This from Mr. Ray as we stand over our respective urinals. I couldn't tell if he was pontificating in the manner of his father or reciting his father.

But I understood his point.

You're an asset to this office, @Sa>ag3. I've got my mind's eye on you.

@Skiny_Leny comes in; his hair is a loose French braid. He hikes his skirt over the urinal to my left. *A Clockwork Orange*, the novel, he says, has two different endings. Depending on where you lived. The UK or the

US. One had a more redemptive, rehabilitative ending. The other one, not so much.

They censored it, Mr. Ray says. Unsure what it would do to the masses. Afraid of a Big Idea.

Much like our prison system, @Skiny_Leny says.

I shrug. Being white, it's not a concern of mine.

They banter about what constitutes a Big Idea.

<p>

So, did your dad help you? you say. By making you more independent?

I finish my Cherry Maca Mocha, thinking.

<p>

COMING SOON

[N S F W]
7

There's a new web series. The one @Skiny_Leny has mentioned: a low-budget 9/11 comedy. Episode One is flagged. We put it on Mother/Screen and gather 'round for a pod watch.

MT. RUSHMORE

Two brothers in brownface lament the fact that they have just been assigned Mt. Rushmore as a target on the eve of 9/11. One brother wonders if they can trade targets with the other cells, as the civilian damage will mostly be symbolic. The other brother cannot be happier to drive a jetliner into Lincoln's brow.

The other tries to bribe his zealot brother with gifts he has been buying with a credit card obtained through offers arriving at their Chicago apartment. The zealot's bald spot is his weakness. His brother knows this and shows him how he can paint it. All the more to impress the seventy-two virgins that await each of them. The zealot tries out the product with the help of his brother and they both are impressed.

Suddenly, there's a knock at the door.

To Be Continued...

Finally, some decent entertainment, @Skiny_Leny says. We all chuckle. A group laugh standing in a semicircle slurping our personalized slurry of carcinogens. @Babyd011 starts quoting lines. One of the Twins smirks, the other is stone-faced.

It's the first time I see them not act like a mirror image of each other.

<p>

In our lifetime, we saw cultures shift six times: Video games. Internet. 9/11. Devices. Pandemic. The Hack. What happens when they shift together? What happens when the human brain can't keep up with the input? @Skiny_Leny says.

"The most merciful thing in the world is the inability of the human mind to correlate all its contents." Mr. Ray says this as he comes back from the rooftop drone pad with a box of fresh typewriter ribbons.

Lovecraft, @Skiny_Leny says, nailing the source of the quote.

Mr. Ray pauses as if regarding @Skiny_Leny in a new light and then continues back to his office. @Skiny_Leny sits a little straighter and crosses his legs. Straightens his kilt. I think it's a kilt and not a skirt. But I can't recognize any clan's colors.

I made up my own tartan, @Skiny_Leny says. If that's why you're staring at my legs.

He notices my stare even with ten videos playing on his display at once. The average baseball graphic on a televised game will give you sixty pieces of information in addition to the pitcher attacking the batter. That's twice the number on a jet fighter's HUD.

I am a clan of one, @Skiny_Leny says, with a wink. His legs are smooth and oiled.

I find it alarmingly titillating. I'm hard.

<p>

I can recite two humorous poems from my childhood with the practiced ease of a classically trained actor. And I do.

@MØM claps. Good intonation, she says.

<p>

I applied for corporatehood today, @Skiny_Leny says. To shelter my stock options if that is our bonus.

Or to shelter his new Big Idea. I've seen him putting away pie-chart presentations and spreadsheets when we return from our flogging break. He's committed.

Or you could bury them in a pickle jar in your backyard, @MØM says. Physical resources. That's what's going to matter. No panic room was built with thoughts and prayers.

I heard a Twin say these words earlier. He discreetly slips into the lactorium.

No church was built with just thoughts and prayers, either. They made you tithe. On a sliding scale. The NRA should tithe every mass shooting. Thoughts and prayers and tithes. These are @M∅M's words.

I ask her if she's going to run for office.

She blushes. I'm just too busy. Unbuttoning her cardigan as she heads to the lactorium.

\<p\>

You'd be better off in a cabin in the woods, @Sa>ag3. I think you're Amish at heart, @Skiny_Leny says. And I don't mean that as an insult.

I don't know if I believe in God, though.

Not sure it matters anymore, he says. Sooner or later, there's going to be another asteroid.

\<p\>

As a kid, I hated connect the dots. My straight lines from point to point turning a perfect rounded picture into a rudimentary constellation.

\<p\>

If you were given the chance to exchange freedom for the illusion of luxury, would you? you say. Or have you already?

No. I haven't, I say. And yes, I would. I always wanted a car with suicide doors. And bondage office wear.

You lick your lips.

Then again, maybe I am a big battery being drained by the machine. Maybe that's why I'm always fatigued.

<p>

My computer pings. My queue is full. I'll have to work through my break. But @Skiny has extra go pills. An early form of this drug fueled the German *blitzkrieg*. One of the Twins has stopped taking his.

[N S F W]
8

A live feed event comes across my screen.

#Insight

Early morning at a school bus stop. You can hear shouting in the background. Shouting that there are kids around. The kids screaming. The fathers, children themselves, shouting, bowing up. Kids are crying and pleading now. A cop cruiser pulls up. A siren tapped and then a POP.

I hit the red panic button on my desk. The alarm sounds in Mr. Ray's office and the feed gets kicked up to Mother/Screen so all can see.

@Skiny_Leny peers over my shoulder. You got another live shooting! He claps my back. Lucky!

Mr. Ray comes out of his office. Wifebeater. Boxers. Sock garters. I run hot when I write, he has said. He consults his laminated card while looking at Mother/Screen.

I can confirm a Ludovico 70-second NIST livestream delay, you say. Smooth. In control.

I think Mr. Ray should stop the stream. He fondles the red key fob hanging around his neck like a talisman. Are you sure you heard gunshots? He's distracted.

Why isn't he stopping it? I think—

Another POP. A muzzle flash. Multiple screams.

A small body falls. A girl, I think.

Mr. Ray pushes the red button and the livestream is killed. Frozen and eliminated well within the 70-second delay before propagation. Devices recording are not affected. Even the *f*ace's reach has limitations.

But it keeps playing on Mother/Screen. A dozen more gunshots.

I watch it until Mr. Ray deactivates Mother/Screen and it resets to the default wallpaper of VEX in gold font with red banners hanging on either side.

Queues ping and everyone goes back to their workstation screens.

@Babyd011 walks by and gives me a wink and a finger gun. And then one of her thumbs up.

I catch your eye and you mouth, Are you ok?

It didn't show anything, I lie, as my abdomen throbs.

<p>

Mr. Ray urinates on my left. My mother had strange end-of-life visions on her deathbed, he says. She begged her sister not to tell Dad she was pregnant with me. She was sixty-five. But that moment had been imprinted deeply. I saw a video of it later. It was surprisingly humorous. Seeing her behaving as a scared teenager, I suspect it was a result of DMT.

DMT? I cock an eyebrow, my own urine stream sputtering. I can't relax.

It's a hallucinogen, he says. They say it occurs naturally in the body at birth and at death. Which could explain the end-of-life stories of those that have had an NDE.

NDE?

A Near-Death Experience, he says.

Oh.

You can also brew it with ayahuasca leaves, Mr. Ray says. Make a tea.

Hey, @Sa>ag3, that'd be right up your alley, @Skiny_Leny says, hiking his skirt at the urinal next to me.

The ambient sound of three streams splashing. It's really unfortunate, Mr. Ray says. Snowden's demise.

Pardon?

Ed Snowden passed away this morning, Mr. Ray says. Sequential organ failure. Poisoned. Probably polonium-210. Maybe Novichok. Poor bastard.

David Scott Hay

I grunt noncommittally. My jaws ache from clenching.

@Skiny_Leny flips his hair over his shoulder with a head toss and a long snort. Says, what did he think was going to happen?

Mr. Ray focuses at a point in space beyond the cheap tile wall and speaks:

"You will hear thunder and remember me,
And think: she wanted storms. The rim
Of the sky will be the color of hard crimson,
And your heart, as it was then, will be on fire.

"That day in Moscow, it will all come true,
when, for the last time, I take my leave,
And hasten to the heights that I have longed for,
Leaving my shadow still to be with you."

@Skiny_Leny shelters his thoughts as tears escape the Venus flytrap of his eyelashes.

‹p›

I see her silhouette fall in my dreams. A dark shadow of pigtails and a turtle hump from her oversize backpack. She collapses as if God cut her strings. My memory blurs and I try to visualize her getting back up. Dusting off her knees. Another small shadow helping her up. Lucid dreaming.

‹p›

The feedback from the band's amplifiers resonates with the scream of hundreds. The ringing in my ear never stops. The story I tell no one. This in Paris.

<p>

Magical thinking vs. magikal thinking.

<p>

Everyone has forgotten the school-bus-stop shooting. But the funeral and the subsequent protests come across Mr. Ray's feed. A new alert sounds on my computer and Mr. Ray flips the feed to me.

Cross fire. Drug gangs or cops. Or a personal beef from years ago. Or mistaken identity. The verdict is still out. I kept thinking it was about homework. Child custody. Chinese cuts. No one saw the live feed once Mr. Ray hit the kill switch, but multiple narratives are edited together with footage from various devices.

No matter your take on socioeconomics, guns, race, parenting, gentrification, there is a video that supports your view. It's a moving Rorschach test: *Look at the evidence.*

A few police officers attend. No one shouts *Blue Lives Matter*. Recognizing the inappropriate forum.

A few gangbangers attend as well. Guns left in glove boxes. Afraid of Mama's wrath. Not in church. This is Chicago. Not Texas.

<p>

The body cam footage of the cross fire is leaked. FAKE. REAL. ALTERED. VERIFIED.

The girl is black. Nine. Unlike in my dreams, she did not get back up.

The shooter is a cop. Black. Former gang member. And off duty. His BAC just below the legal limit. He'd had a tough case that night. Not all the bodies he pulled out of the wreck survived. He'd get a commendation.

Why was he still in uniform? Who fired first? Did the bushes hide the kids from plain sight? Did a parent really have a gun or a cell phone? Did the officer identify himself? Was he violating his custody agreement by visiting his kid at the bus stop? Was the other shooter his ex-wife's Caucasian boyfriend?

The sides to this one are slippery. The narrative pliable.

<p>

Violence has always been a lottery ticket. But now a lucky civilian or two might profit with video of an event. The real lottery.

<p>

When I was younger, I found four-leaf clovers. Usually within a few minutes of looking. My folks laminated one. As I grew older, they became more elusive.

<p>

The small girl's small casket is the center of the livestream from the church. The preacher opens his mouth for the eulogy, but doesn't know what to say. You and I discussed attending. You sensing that I might need closure.

But I couldn't go. One tiny casket in my life was enough.

Also, we had seen the body cam footage earlier that day. Another leak.

We knew why the South Side church mourned and the casket was closed. A mother, a cousin, a sibling all cry for answers. We have them. And NDAs.

#Loop

Molotov cocktails are just messages in a bottle sent priority. But with the cost of gasoline there is less correspondence than you imagine. Here in the States anyway.

The school-bus-stop shooting, one of thirteen that day, sparks a protest of civic-minded civilians that turn onto our boulevard, marching and chanting, as they stream below Vex's office windows. No one in the pod remembers looking out the window prior to today. We're here in case the event goes bloody on a live feed.

Everyone can protest the death of a nine-year-old girl. Adopt it for their cause. Rail against the root of it all.

Less cinematic than a California wildfire and about as compelling as an inauguration aerial. But all the news outlets send professionals. Their bosses ready to plunk down life-changing money for civilian footage. Plus, the 24/7 news cycle's voracious appetite is never satiated.

In the crowd, everyone has his or her or their devices out hoping to capture a moment that can boost their followers, their likes, their cartoon hearts. The savvy ones have media contacts stored in their burner phones.

I'm sure a drama-starved teen is thumbing firecrackers in one pocket, a lighter in his other. I didn't mean for anyone to get hurt, he will say, chained to a metal table as his bravado exits in sobs. The DA will weigh charging him as an adult instead of a juvenile. What happened to foresight?

The smell of microwave popcorn fills the office.

<p>

The protestors march down below our office window.

This is not recreational outrage, @MØM says. Referring to America's new pastime.

Mother/Screen juggles news feeds of multiple camera angles from the street below as footage is stitched together live, like for a sporting event. A few aerial shots from news GoDrones to give the viewer the big picture with establishing shots, to show scale.

But most of our Vex pod watches from the stationary window, a static view unenhanced by graphics and broadcast commentary. We're used to raw footage and do not get bored. @Skiny_Leny and @Babyd011 pass out compostable bowls filled with full-butter-and-sodium popcorn.

<p>

One nation under God. Indivisible.

<p>

A *SQUAWK* cuts through the crowd noise. Chants through a bullhorn. Where do you even get a bullhorn? Mothers of color, cousins of color, siblings of color marching like ants. The men of color institutionalized.

All this on our day off. They've seen just a small percentage of what we've seen. I've been on the feed. I've seen every color of man fall to every color of man. Every animal. The things we've protected them from seeing… If only they knew.

But that's a complicated narrative and the new stream of counter-protesters comes around the corner. White. Masked. Having learned lessons on 1/6. Everyone wants peace, but the outrage needs to be vented. And directed at a target.

Anonymity a MiracleGro for hate.

<p>

America: Commies love it or leave it. Patriots riot.

<p>

Once again, the youth lead the charge. Civil rights. Normandy. Viet Nam. Chicago. Young enough to take risks based on principle, yet wise enough to know that repercussions could derail their future. Taking the long shot that they are putting the country back on track one railroad tie at a time.

I can hear both sides chanting as they face off. I can't hear their words and I don't have to understand their positions. The sun peeks out and the protesters are now half in each other's shadow, half in silhouette. Part of me wants them all to fall over like that little girl.

<p>

Any hard-boiled detective will tell you that people only kill for two reasons: love or money.

How quaint, eh?

<p>

@Skiny_Leny sprays popcorn when he talks. His hair hasn't been washed in days. We should give free cable and A/C to the South Side, he says. That would quell violence.

I don't know what to say to that. My brain pulled into several arguments.

Mr. Ray says that every cop should foster a black child for a year.

@Skiny_Leny asks who's going to shoulder that financial burden, the government?

We can't shoulder the current burden, Mr. Ray says. They argue polices enacted by the Federal Reserve.

They are arguing the fisherman parable. But I can't decide which side represents which.

In other countries, inalienable rights are grounds for execution, Mr. Ray says.

They're just going through the motions, @Skiny_Leny says. They're just following a pattern of grief. It's nothing new. A moving truck would solve most of their problems.

Every car I see in an alley below, I imagine it is revving its engine, waiting for the protest parade to come into view. A legacy on either side of the windshield about to be created.

Mr. Ray has seen his father's stories of the Gulag transferred to a sci-fi setting in *The Aquarist of Ganymede* to such universal acclaim it got him removed from his country's history. His body never thawed.

On occasion the concept of scale eludes my pod-mate. Venture capitalists concur, as evidenced by his desk trash can overflowing with the confetti of his rejected business plans and pitches. A graveyard of Big Ideas.

These are my silent observations.

<p>

#Incite

<p>

Seriously, if a moving truck plowed through that crowd, @Skiny_Leny says. Think of the financial settlement. The GoFundMe windfall.

Suddenly, the Twins are restraining me and pulling me off @Skiny_Leny. I have a handful of his hair and a bit of his scalp in my hand. His eyes widen with shock and surprise as I pound his head into the Cherry Maca Mocha-stained carpet. No one recalls exactly what I screamed.

Eventually, the primates turn on one another.

[N S F W]
9

Subject: @Sa>ag3

Age: 49

Title: SMCM

Test: Short Post-Traumatic Stress Disorder Rating Interview (SPRINT)[1]

Administrator: Raymond Gunn II

In the past week, how much have you been bothered by unwanted memories, nightmares, or reminders of the event?

> 0 = Not at all
> 1 = A little bit
> 2 = Moderately
> 3 = Quite a lot
> 4 = Very much

---

[1] Test results are the sole intellectual property of Mahalo Inc. and are not to be disclosed without proper authorization.

In the past week, how much have you been bothered by pain, aches, or tiredness?

> 0 = Not at all
> 1 = A little bit
> 2 = Moderately
> 3 = Quite a lot
> 4 = Very much

Repeated, disturbing memories, thoughts, or images of a stressful experience from the past?

> 0 = Not at all
> 1 = A little bit
> 2 = Moderately
> 3 = Quite a lot
> 4 = Very much

Feeling very upset when something reminded you of a stressful experience from the past?

> 0 = Not at all
> 1 = A little bit
> 2 = Moderately
> 3 = Quite a lot
> 4 = Very much

Avoid activities or situations because they remind you of a stressful experience from the past?

> 0 = Not at all
> 1 = A little bit
> 2 = Moderately

3 = Quite a lot

4 = Very much

Feeling distant or cut off from other people?

0 = Not at all

1 = A little bit

2 = Moderately

3 = Quite a lot

4 = Very much

Feeling irritable or having angry outbursts?

0 = Not at all

1 = A little bit

2 = Moderately

3 = Quite a lot

4 = Very much

[N S F W]
10

Train: I tremble, doubled over. The darkness spins and I feel a wave of impending doom. It's either a panic attack or a heart attack. The symptoms are the same. Knowing which doesn't relieve the terror. It's drowning, slipping below the surface. Trying to swim to the surface, with concrete blocks of anguish and despair chained to my legs. Death and madness inevitable.

You lay over my body, a human security blanket. We look like unhoused people curled up in a corner of the train car, riding out the winter from end of the line to end of the line.

This is what happens when you attack your drug dealer but need his lorazepam and alprazolam.

<p>

Garden: I can't stop shaking. My lizard brain is on fire, the chemicals in my brain a firewall keeping me from the lucidity of rationality.

Amazingly you get me home, through the park, down the block, up the stairs.

My hands curl and my arms lift of their own volition. It's a seizure. I'm stroking out.

<p>

Bathroom: The tub. You run freezing water, even as the winter wind cuts through the cracked wall and forms ice on the bathroom mirror. You plug the drain and hold me as the shower dribbles like a cheap watering can with its second-floor water pressure.

Your rapid breathing is causing you to lose carbon dioxide, you say. This is why your arms and hands are curling, you say. You put your mouth over mine and breathe out as I pant in, then reverse it. I breathe in your oxygen and then expel it into your lungs. You do the same. We are trading a single breath, back and forth, the CO_2 increasing. You a human brown paper bag.

The water in the tub rises; my muscles contract with the cold. I feel another wave coming on. It would be easy to just let go. Let this be the end. The end of pain. The end of worry. Just the end. The peacefulness of nonexistence. I must have muttered or rambled these thoughts out loud. I'm sorry, I say.

Shhh, you say, and straddle me in the tub. I think we still have our clothes on—a direct violation of the Garden. You put your hands around my throat and push my head under. My tinnitus stops. The shock of cold on my neck, my face. My eyeballs. I see clouds of dirt drift in front of me. I can just see your eyes distorted by the tainted water. The wind whistles in through the crack in the wall, a bolt of lightning in negative. Roses blossom on your cheeks. Ice forms on your eyelashes.

You hold me under and I do not struggle. Your lips move as you say a prayer, a baptism, or wish me luck on my journey. My body does not seem to be producing DMT.

I get a clear look at her face. The other face. The face before I met yours. Remembering and seeing her with perfect clarity. I can smell her perfume. I remember the words I tried to say. And maybe I do, but they are lost again, this time under an inch of water. The words forming bubbles that burst with their own language.

It's a gift, this vision.

Blackness.

‹p›

I gasp and humid air fills my lungs. You're kneeling behind me, the wool blanket around us both. Tendrils of your hair spill from a hasty put-up. I roll out of my cross-legged position. The sunlamps have evaporated the cold. A not-unpleasant breeze drifts from the hallway, the bathroom exhaling its chill.

It feels like a resurrection, a return from hell, a reprieve from Yahweh. I shrug off the blanket. You roll up behind me. The room feels like Spring. The Garden is whole.

‹p›

We stay up watching the jellyfish. It hovers and floats as if waiting for the mother signal. You take my hand. In the glow of the jellyfish, we stare into each other's eyes for ten seconds at a time, falling deeper…

Jellyfish are used in anticancer medicines. Maybe this one will stop the spread, you say.

Neither of us have cancer, I say.

…then for ten minutes at a time…

It's working already, you say.

…until we began to dissolve. We disassociate.

There's no panic, only weightlessness.

[N S F W]
11

Mr. Ray taps the paper with my psych test results. Takes off his glasses. Cleans them and peers at the results again. Sets them aside. Tells me nothing came of the weekend protests. No violence incited. Externally, that is.

Asks if I know where the term "basket case" came from. He explains, in WWI soldiers that had both arms and legs amputated had to be carried in a litter or basket. Such soldiers were warehoused, and fed and hosed down like livestock. A secret slush fund was created to bring in women from France in exchange for US citizenship. Comforters for the basket cases. After six months, when their flesh had healed, the basket cases were shipped off to Germany, in exchange for data achieved from experiments that became the basis of the German Research Foundation. It was on these shoulders Josef Mengele stood.

This deal supplanted a similar deal with the Soviet government. They've never forgotten the US breaking that deal and we've been rivals ever since. Mr. Ray adjusts his sock garters and slips into his slacks. Nobody remembers this because of Operation Paperclip, he says.

And now basket case means one who can't get their shit together or one who can't cope.

<p>

My father Raymond Gunn the First—he takes pride in saying his father's name. I wish I could do the same— he left me this. He taps his industrial-green, sleek Groma Kolilbri typewriter. A West German product. Not much bigger than the first laptops. This machine kills fascists, he says. He scribbles on a Post-it note and slaps it casually on the desk. He excuses himself from his office with a false narrative.

I move around to his desk to admire the typewriter. Next to it is a sheaf of paper, on the Post-it, an address.

A Hawaiian address. The home address of the *f*ace. Twenty thousand square feet of temporary home while his army of lawyers annex land for his dream compound.

Instead of the blank paper, I roll in the results of my test and begin to type on the back of them. The satisfying clack of the keys merges with the physical sensation of physically creating words by mechanical means. There is no delete. No spellcheck. No autocorrect. Just ink stamped into pulp. I feel as if I am doing work for the first time at Vex.

<p>

We are the thin digital line, the *f*ace says.

<p>

I type the *f*ace a letter. I type it slowly, hunting and pecking each key, keeping the number of typos to an acceptable level. A human touch. My ink-stained fingerprints evidence of physical collaboration between man and machine.

Before I do, I spend half an hour deciding how to address him.

<p>

I mail the letter in a white business envelope. You thumb a Forever stamp onto it, with an image of the Liberty Bell.

A second stamp goes on an envelope containing @H₁pp3's suicide notes. All of them. I won't lie by omission. One might call me a snitch, but I won't shoulder his responsibility or revenge. And I will not take any of his secrets to the grave.

<p>

#selfcare

<p>

You bring home a copy of a banned book. We take turns reading its new language and vocabulary with Cockney accents. When we take a break for tea, you put the kettle on and hum "Singin' in the Rain."

Which version is this book? I say, flipping through it. You slap the book out of my hand and say, we'll know when we get to the end.

The fact there will be an end fills me with a foreign feeling.

You read my mind. Optimism?

No, I say. Closure.

[N S F W]
12

#Device

[N S F W]
13

The unions created a middle class. The gig economy is destroying it. The only way to get a substantial pay raise is to change jobs. Especially for women.

The trouble with college is they expose you to new ideas without their context in your current world. Tenured professors teaching and gifting you an understanding of a world that no longer exists. Sharing a path to success that can't be duplicated.

All this to children just smart enough to ingest big ideas, embrace them, and become a danger to themselves and others.

The college dropouts are the ones changing the world. The others are shackled with crippling debt, and a worldview skewed by righteous indignation. This is how the status quo is maintained. Keep the workers poor. Keep the rich kids marrying one another.

@Skiny_Leny on a rant.

@Babyd011 brushes his hair and nods agreeably. His new part hides the small bare patch I pulled out with my hands.

This I see and hear as I settle in with my new workstation-mate, @OrKa. I greet her with a nod. She responds with the slightest twitch of her nose. The squeaky desk-bike does not miss a beat.

@Skiny_Leny's volume drops when our eyes meet through a tangle of monitor cables. Conflict resolution is not part of the training protocol at Vex.

<p>

"Who cares what they are saying on social media, as it's less than 1 percent of the population. If someone gets a million retweets, that's still less than 1 percent of 330 million people in this country. Fifteen years ago, that type of audience would get a TV show canceled. Now we live in a bubble society where nobody caters to the masses anymore, we think these small minorities are the majorities." This from a keyboard warrior on the net.

I suspect @Skiny_Leny is boosting his own comments from a burner account.

It's given a round of online applause. Then another keyboard warrior points out that the "who cares" line doesn't reach the PACs and Super PACs who spent half a billion in the last presidential election. That will triple in the next. This is how 1 percent of the population at the booth can change the course of a nation. Incite, incentivize, normalize, pulverize. That's who cares. Maybe the commenter was a plant. "Don't worry, folks. There's plenty of lifeboats."

This is where the real world connects to the web, @Babyd011 says. Like that movie with the red and blue pill, right?

You say, that's the one where they explore Plato's Allegory of the Cave.

Before that movie, back in 1977, PKD theorized the world as a computer simulator, @Skiny_Leny says. But a kid's space opera smashed the box office and indoctrinated a new generation into Eastern philosophies and chivalry. PKD also posited déjà vu as being a glitch in the system.

You can learn so much from popular entertainment, @Babyd011 says, impressed with this new information. I don't think deep thoughts like that, she says. It's a rabbit hole away from the present.

@Babyd011 never was a cornflake girl.

Mt. Rushmore is a viral hit. @Skiny_Leny and @Babyd011 have memorized bits and are trading lines, waiting for the next episode to drop. Their timing and farcical accents are spot-on.

I feel a flush of jealousy, but @Babyd011 gives me a reassuring wink when @Skiny_Leny's baby-soft face follows @MØM into the lactorium for the first time.

I cross and uncross my legs seductively and @Babyd011 giggles.

Graying directors continue to grouse about cinema these days. They had their revolution. But can't recognize the next one as anything but heresy. They've gotten out of the boat, off the river.

Hitchcock says suspense trumps surprise every time. But he didn't have to compete with the internet. His audience dressed in their finest for an evening out.

‹p›

At my workstation, I pretend the thing in the microwave was dead before the start button is hit. The microwave has an internal light and rotating glass plate. It showed everything.

FLAGGED.

‹p›

@H₁pp3's widow is suspected of his murder. The investigation prompted by a note in @H₁pp3's handwriting fearing his own death and blaming his wife. There is no mention of any of the other notes I'd included. This in the middle of my feed.

I guess @H₁pp3's mom intercepted her dead son's mail and is not a big fan of her daughter-in-law. I wonder if his computer virus was as successful.

‹p›

#WAZZU

‹p›

I slurp my Cherry Maca Mocha. The paper straw collapses under its own weight. The bright side is I've been ditching my meds to surprise you tonight.

The whiff of @Babyd011's perfume. @MØM's silver streaks and full sweater. The plastered ringlets that frame @OrKa's face. Your clunky glasses. Even @Skiny_Leny's beardless cheekbones. Everything quickens my heart.

Was it always this easy?

I skip the lactorium, the flogging, using @OrKa's squeaky wheel as a metronome to stay focused on the videos. Sex trafficking. A snuff film. A political ad. A YouTuber in a high-speed accident on the 101, slowing traffic to the happiest place on Earth.

After the flogging, you ask if I'm okay.

He's hard, @Babyd011 singsongs. And he's going to take it out on you tonight.

You clutch your pearls in mock shock.

So much for the surprise. We just have to make it through the day. Easy peasy lemon squeezy.

<p>

X amount of days and counting. #WAGTMI

[N S F W]
14

A familiar position, you straddling me, facing the tank.

<p>

The day did not end well.

You watched a video. Among hundreds. Thousands. One.

@Babyd011 saw it too. She seemed melancholy and I suggested she take a break from the stuffy office. Crisp, clear winter air clears the head.

She nodded, left, and did not return. I remember she grabbed her scarf, her Cherry Maca Mocha in her hand, the lid keeping it from spilling against her thigh. She kissed @Skiny_Leny's head. She hesitated briefly at Mr. Ray's door. A hand even went up to knock, but instead dropped back to her side and she left without a word.

You didn't return from the video either, spiritually. @MØM was shrugged away. Even I was rebuked with a hand slightly raised. A head tilted slightly away as though eye contact might unleash an outburst.

Oh @Jun1p3r.

A pod-mate commented later it was the closest they'd ever seen us to getting into a fight. @Skiny_Leny put two bars of Xanax on your desk. They remained untouched. Though @MØM took them at the end of the day.

We did our commute. You never made eye contact with me. Once home, you stripped your clothes even as we trudged up the stairs, hoodies and sweats shed like a snake's skin. I made tisane, even as you contemplated your altar, standing in silence for a moment and then retreating to take a scalding shower.

Then you appeared naked in our living room jungle. Toes digging into the earth, you wiggled your feet as if to take root or grind insects into powder. You stood, arms out, basking in the sunlamp and luxuriating in the humid breath of the plants and trees. Water slid down the plastics sheets, a rain collecting to feed the sod. Sweat oozed from your pores. A trickle down your face. Your back. Your breasts. Between your thighs.

I'm mesmerized. Instinctually I lie on the sod nude before you. An offering to the gods.

You take it.

Facing the tank, muscles ripple under your shoulder blades. I can't tell if your eyes are closed. I can't tell if you're here or elsewhere. The jellyfish tank highlights you with a glow so, so beautiful.

There is no escorting me. There is no pushing me or pulling. There is only my body, a vessel for your rage and purification. You grind and pound against me. The tempo that of a heavyweight boxer throwing cross after cross at a punch-drunk opponent. There is no ref to stop the fight. My fingers dig into the sod to steady myself. A poor mooring in this thunderstorm.

<p>

You grunt in a language that is not English. An ancient tongue.

Exhausted and catching my breath, I think of the Wiccan Rule of Three.

[N S F W]
15

@Babyd011 has not returned to the office. @MØM is worried she won't be eligible for her bonus, let alone healthcare. There are only so many promo codes we can pirate. @Skiny_Leny says maybe she went back to her waitress gig. Where the only carcasses are served on Buffalo China.

I'm still waiting for you to return. Your spark.

<p>

I used to get sad when emails I sent went unanswered. Now I consider them messages in a bottle. Maybe they come back, maybe not. Maybe the tide turns.

You remind me of the river. The flow of information. Always moving. Always eroding. Fearful of stagnation.

<p>

I try to cheer you up. You're still your dry, sardonic self. But the smile in your eyes. The this-is-all-a-joke glint is dulled. You're on autopilot while you try to determine the best course forward.

We try to watch kids' movies. The first part of the first act only. Before the inciting incident. Before the parents are killed. Before the wife dies. Before the earthquake. Before everything is knocked out of its right place. This is usually ten minutes in. The first ten are setting the world. Then the "event" happens. Then ten minutes later, the story shifts and takes a new direction. End Act One.

Act Two is abandoned when your imagination takes over. Your body vibrates with anger.

<p>

I had an imaginary pet alligator when I was young. It lived in the backyard behind a row of trees. I was also chased by a bear when I was three in that same backyard. This I swear.

My grandma said maybe it was a black man, as our postman was black. Though, as I was three years old, my parents said it was probably a German shepherd. My mom says I created the alligator to protect me from bears.

Experts surmise that in a hypothetical battle, the bear will win unless the alligator gets a devastating surprise attack. Maybe that's why I made him invisible.

<p>

I mistakenly take my meds when we get home. We should label these things better. I dig in the closet next to the mushroom bin. I find an old gift card from a previous life. Let's go to dinner, I say. Get a crème brûlée. You nod.

Look for @Babyd011 at her old workplace, I say to myself.

Dinner. Two tables for one. From across the restaurant, I watch you float by the other diners. I have the remote control for the vibrating device. The batteries are weak but you'll hopefully climax, biting your lip, forcing your own eyes to stay open before they take your salad plate. Me, I've got all night.

When the hostess seats you, I begin to worry you are out of range. I order the tasting menu.

You take a deep breath as your waitress brings you a glass of water. Your eyes, still open, go elsewhere. I can only imagine what you're imagining, what firewall you're summoning as I thumb the remote.

Your panties buzz and vibrate as if you have an incoming call. You're in range.

Made in China.

Our parents worked for the same company until they dropped. If we don't survive at Vex, we'll switch companies until we drop. Climbing higher and higher without a rope, looking for that parachute.

But what a view, eh?

<p>

She'd answer your questions about love with: Why the Big Bang? Things like that, not to trump you but because you liked a girl that could take a cosmic view when needed and foster an air of mystery. And she liked that you thought she could be that kind of girl. An indie film star. A Wes Anderson storybook character.

<p>

I see your eyes moisten, but it's the wrong glint. The bread basket full of seeded rolls dumps over. One makes its escape from Old Smokey.

Our rushed waiter says crème brûlée is no longer on the menu.

You pound the table in frustration. *Oh, @Babyd011.*

<p>

I hope our words feed and stimulate our plants the way classical music does.

<p>

A patron at the booth next to you, face lit by their phone, says to an audience on her device: I'll have what she's having. Wink. Wink.

You throw your crab fork at her, screaming: What? A panic attack?? The seafood tines crack her screen.

WOW!! The patron screams.

I tell the waiter I'll take care of your tab.

The patron turns off her damaged device, turns to you. OMG! THANK YOU SO MUCH FOR THAT!

Already the device is blowing up with cartoon likes and the emojis interspersed with sprinkles of FAKE! STAGED!

Check, please.

<p>

The early wave of talkie movies was witty with great banter, *The Thin Man* series, etc. Why did these movies crackle in the early dawn of the art? Because there were no screenwriters back then. The first screenwriters were playwrights and radio dramatists. The dialogue had to crackle. Defined character with trackable wants and needs. Their wits and verbal repartee as engaging as any car chase, any gun fight, any sex scene.

Eisenstein says the perfect movie has no dialogue. His theory of montage says that Shot A + Shot B, even if they are shot and filmed at different times or different years and locations, = Effect C. A twig snaps. A deer raises its head, thus Effect C = Danger.

In this example, there is no dialogue either. No language barrier. Terror is terror. Blood is blood. The unimaginable. Filmable.

This as @Skiny_Leny and I try to one-up one another. Get a room, you say, nodding toward the lactorium, as you flag a video of a celebratory machine gun wedding reception. This before I turned on my pod-mate. We ignore you.

When did things become unimaginable? Have we not seen enough irony? Enough coincidence? If anything, movies have taught us to expect the unexpected. Not to laugh at the wit, but to laugh at the punch line; we've been conditioned to laugh there whether it's funny or not. Recycled gags, trotted out time and again.

Remember this: there is no such thing as a new story. Just a new audience.

This is where the skill of editing is underrated among film students, until they need it. Everyone wants to direct.

<p>

Our VCR eats seven brothers and their brides.

We hadn't given up all devices. We didn't know a time before TV.

And, as you have pointed out, we're not a slave to our own concepts.

Plus, our eyes and brain needed the occasional sweetener. To dilute the bombardment of daily images. The earworms of old musicals muting the echo of violent ends.

I hope a sing-along will bring you back.

And now black ribbon overflows the VCR slot like a nest of tapeworms. I say a prayer for the Pontipee brothers. We watch the jellyfish, then, wordlessly, fall asleep on the sod.

<p>

Office. @Skiny_Leny laughs. That musical is based on a short story based on the Roman legend the Rape of the Sabine Women. You should say a prayer for the women.

<p>

Garden. That night on the sod, staring at the jellyfish: Didn't Malcolm McDowell play the Roman emperor in *Caligula*?

<p>

You spend time in silence at your altar. Not meditating or casting a spell, but in contemplation.

I keep the tisane warm and harvest the mushrooms and load the dehydrator.

You are spiraling in front of me. Revving an engine on the edge of a cliff. There's a hint of sun peeking through morning clouds. Let's take a walk, I say, swallowing my own fear.

I can't tell if my words are registering.

Then you say, I'd like to go to church.

<p>

Music swells.

[N S F W]
16

We try three different churches that Sunday. My tinnitus acts up. The choir and congregation try to sing in the falsettos of long dead castrati. Later, after you're gone, I'll go back to a different one.

That day, though, we also went to a black church. They hit the notes and we clapped. Contagious joy and energy. A feast welcomed us. Despite the current state of affairs, there was the spirit of hope. Participating joyfully in the sorrows of their world.

<p>

I stare at your tattoo sleeve as the preacher tells of a story about fishing. I realize the Church is built on classic horror tropes: reanimation, vampirism, and cannibalism.

<p>

Together we prefer the priest who has taken a comedy-writing class. Each sermon and parable drawing a laugh. Each sermon and parable sprinkled with setups and payoffs. Each one containing a turn, a twist, and a surprise ending. Each one an IP ripe for being optioned by a studio, a writer, a production company.

The church mailing list including cousins of Hollywood executives.

Afterwards, at the coffee meet and greet, we overhear him talking about his agent. And complaining about his manager's notes. Raise the stakes, they keep telling him.

What they really mean, you say, butting in, is raise the emotional investment. He blinks at you and glows with enlightenment.

<p>

As we watch others partake of the blood and body of Christ, I marvel at how calm you are in church for a Wiccan.

You tick off the differences between Christianity, Satanism, Wicca, Paganism, and Humanism. The end result is the same. Love and hate are the same. Indifference is the opposite.

You have a guiding principle or you don't.

<p>

The *f*ace appears on Mother/Screen. Light makeup. Or maybe it's a filter. The audio has been muted. It looks like a still photograph with moving lips. A producer off camera must be timing his words between blinks. I lose count around 330.

<p>

Modern interactions. Beautiful behind glass. Despicable behind glass. All sight and sound. No tactile. No smell. No feel. Unobtainable. Shouting at the glass. This rumination again.

\<p\>

There's a reason your devices no longer flip close. Its psychological note to yourself that you are done. Open-face devices are always ready. Your business never done. One brand thinks it cutting edge with their always-on display, a perpetual beacon.

\<p\>

The Twins have a rough time with a video shot from a Hollywood exec's dungeon. Is it consensual? Is it real? Or props? Are there air holes in the Saran Wrap? What is the significance of the bags of cotton candy?

@OrKa takes the video and flags without breaking stride, but wounds the Twins' pride. @MØM takes them by the hands and leads them to the lactorium. I imagine the lullaby she is cooing and the greedy stubbly mouths at her nipples.

They'll never be done before the end of break, you say. We quietly wreck a stall in the unisex bathroom, my hand firmly over your mouth. Mr. Ray and @Skiny_Leny discuss Stanisław Lem's *Solaris* at the urinals across from our stall.

Mr. Ray wants to discuss the German opera adaptation, while @Skiny_Leny tries to justify

Tarkovsky's seven-minute highway sequence as art vs. artistic pretention. Mr. Ray asks if he has actually read the novel. @Skiny_Leny flushes the urinal as you bite my hand to stifle your moans.

I see glimpses of the old you. My heart is bursting.

<p>

Where'd you go, @Babyd011?

<p>

The feed fills with Iranian citizens at a protest. Their government machine-guns them down. Including a sci-fi writer. He used to dine with my family, Mr. Ray says. Since @Babyd011 left, cracks have appeared in Mr. Ray's pompadour. The click-clack of his typewriter, now a handful of random bursts throughout the day.

@Skiny_Leny is right about us being primates with sticks and stones. But a few of us keep an eye on the stars.

It's easier to attack small ideas than to embrace big ones.

It's easier to kill big ideas than it is to nurture them.

Scale.

You can't kill an idea once it goes viral.

Mr. Ray says this as he peers at me over his typewriter. These, he says, tapping his writing machine, were once ubiquitous and are now obsolete. But with oil and craft and care they will last forever. Your new car will not. Your new device will not.

He pauses and stares at his stack of pages.

Do you ever imagine what will be the last act of the last human?

<p>

I contain multitudes.

<p>

Office. The *f*ace is frozen on Mother/Screen. @OrKa reboots the system as we walk out the door. Do you think he's the mad scientist and the network is the monster? I say.

Train. *Creature*, you correct. It's originally called the creature. It's not a monster until later. When it won't be a slave.

Airlock. That night by the glow of the jellyfish you pull out your book. The pages rippled from the humidity in our bubble.

"Everywhere I see bliss, from which I alone am irrevocably excluded," the creature laments to his creator, Victor. Your voice crisp. My skin tingles. "I was benevolent and good—misery made me a fiend. Make me happy, and I shall again be virtuous."

Garden. Did you see me and think, he's harmless? Or, he's out of my league. Or, he's levels below me?

These were normal questions with easy answers. Normally. But the way we met, the where we met, the how we met. My mind was flailing, just looking to connect, to find a tether to keep me from spinning off into orbit.

You have a surprise planned for me this weekend.

Trauma bonding, I believe, is the term they use. I have not looked it up. I don't want to be told our connection is a disorder.

Because this is a love story.

[N S F W]
17

You bring home a commercial-grade piercing kit.

Every savage should have a piercing, you say. We look through a reference book. Lip plates, neck extenders, pierced septums. Tattoos hand-inked with wooden needles and tiny mallets. Art chiseled into flesh.

This inspired by our latest Video of the Day. We watch a video of a woman who is tattooed over ninety-five percent of her body as a living skeleton. Including a peek-a-boo brain, dark circles around her eyes for sockets. A black nose to feign the lack of cartilage, the ultimate skull look. Teeth tattooed above and below her lips to give the illusion of none. A nipple inked over one breast, muscle and sinew on the other.

She's got a nose ring, I point out, dismayed. She's ruining her own illusions. Illustratively she is suggesting she has no nose; anatomically there is not supposed to be anything there to pierce. Kids, I scoff.

Or maybe, you say, she's not a slave to her own concepts.

...., I leaf through the other pictures in the ...ook. The penis piercings. I like this one, I ... little bar bell running under the head of a penis, ...ear the glans, giving it the impression of a bow tie.

You imagine the possibilities. Then a small frown. It says here you have to be erect for the piercing. That makes sense. But my impotence has returned. We tag it with a Post-it note from work, for future reference. I hate disappointing you.

So much for our weekend plans.

[N S F W]
18

Maslow's Hierarchy of Needs.

<p>

Barista Tim asks: Would you like an extra shot? We're buying Cherry Maca Mochas on the weekend. It feels like a betrayal, having one here at the Grindhouse on the weekend without our pod. Rape, murder, you say. It's just a shot away.

<p>

A stack of logs form. I've waterproofed the tent. Lightning to the west. Where the good witch lives. Lightning again, enough to power a Victorian experiment.

I read back through my journals. I wonder which of us was the scientist? Which was the monster? Who built whom?

Or am I thinking of a different movie?

<p>

Hanging at the Grindhouse coffee shop. Like regular people. Since we don't have Wi-Fi at the house and our

Faraday law applies. I can't decipher the drink menu and don't want to ask questions while you crack the code to the restroom, so I order two of the regular.

We create an online dating profile. The picture of me is a candid shot looking out the window of a pub. Beard. flannel. *Financially secure. Creatively successful.* I don't put much else. It feels good to use the device.

We split a scone, waiting for an electronic bite.

Nightmare is a word used often enough that it's lost meaning. It's just a word, that conjures no images. It stands in the place of the indescribable. No, that's not true. I can describe all of the nightmares. But they won't make narrative sense. Just cinematic moments stitched together. A postmortem might reveal the origin of the components.

But I know.

And yet I do not fear falling asleep. I don't understand why.

I ask you about your dreams.

I don't dream, you say. I used to have night terrors when I was a child. My parents thought I was possessed by a demon. They took me to a priest.

What happened?

He splashed water on me. Gave me candy.

And that worked?

Yes, you say.

Was it holy water?

My parents thought so. He asked for an hour alone with me. Took me into his private chamber, closed the door. Lit lavender incense. There is enough evil in the world without inviting it into your home, your bed, your parents' mind, he said. So cut this shit out.

And then we ate baklava and he showed me how to play Chinese checkers. And we talked about his former life as a drama teacher. I took my first acting lessons later that year. He sent me roses when we did *Our Town.*

<p>

What's the worst thing you've ever said to a human?

I once told a woman to go home and drown her kids.

What was the context?

It doesn't matter. I meant it.

<p>

My device blows up with dating app notifications. Messages of vulnerability. Leading with their heart. Smiling with sad eyes. One messages asking me not to judge their tattoos. One wants a man of faith. One says she just wants a faithful man. She has five kids. *Land a plus.*

You decide to get in on the action and create your own profile. Maybe we can double-date, you say.

<p>

The jellyfish has no central nervous system. No eyes. No face. It just exists, floating in space. It doesn't care the size of its tank. It could be in the ocean for all it knows. Bliss.

I ache with jealousy.

It still needs us to feed it. Clean its tank. Make sure it has enough oxygen to breathe.

Are we its caregivers?

It's a symbiotic relationship, you say. We both benefit.

<p>

You use a picture of @Babyd011, post-mohawk, for your dating profile pic. You settle on a pithy screen name for your dating profile, and cast the net.

I mute my device which is buzzing and jumping with notifications of desperation. I delete my profile, feeling guilty for using them as entertainment. I've miscalculated the depths of despair that are not mine.

<p>

We bought a half whiskey barrel and set it upside down for a coffee table. You also bought two Mexican ponchos from the thrift store. Brightly colored blankets, each with a hole for our head. We wore them, forcing our rods and cones to take in the full spectrum.

I broke out the coloring books. A conservative affair with happy shiny families. The cover suggested their skin be a lovely shade of pink. We leave that color at work. Along with reds and browns. The color of viscera.

This before the plastic went up. Before the real nesting.

<p>

Your device now dances. A river of puns and farm innuendos flood your profile.

Plow. Till. Fertilize. Coral [sic]. *Bit. Break. Milk. Udders.*

You're disgusted with the lack of wit. You tell me all this as your eyes linger on the photo of @Babyd011. The drugs from @Skiny_Leny are working. Nothing is vibrating or shaking. Yet, there is a rising panic underneath the pharmaceutical topsoil. Tendrils pushing upward from underneath.

I sense this coming off you in waves. You're on a precipice. Like cops, we all need a partner who sees us. Someone who has our back. Someone with a throwaway piece.

I reach for your hand and squeeze, anchoring you. Two other patrons on a first date *awww* at our tenderness.

<p>

Drifting through liquid space. A starship beyond comprehension. Engineering not achievable. Tendrils like sine wave cosine. Purposeful and elegant. Perfect.

Oxytocin.

Oxycodone.

Love in pill form.

GoDrones buzz the coffee shop. News. Police. Consumer. Neighborhood watch. A few illegal with no markings or color banding. Each gathering and hunting. Even the delivery drones.

I sip my Cherry Maca Mocha as I search-engine the ingredients. It's a cancer beverage with sprinkles and your name misspelled on the cup. Served with a smile and paper straw.

I slide you yours.

Here's to our chemical romance.

You kill your profile; the entertainment value of misery dwindles quickly.

Murder-suicide is becoming our forte, you say. You lean over and kiss me. A soft gentle thing on my lower lip.

You taste of pesticide residual, GMO milk, carrageenan, high-fructose corn syrup, and traces of 4-

methylimidazole. A chemical of which there are zero safe amounts.

\<p\>

Love, sister, is just a kiss away.

[N S F W]
19

They found @Babyd011's body.

Mr. Ray tells us this before the morning break.

<p>

The Five Stages of Post-Hack Grief[1]

1. The shock of the evaporation of a future time line.
2. Resentment of the lack of social media acknowledgment.
3. Indulging in risky behavior.
4. A recalibration of a sense of scale.
5. Creation.

<p>

@Babyd011 won't know how *Mt. Rushmore* ends, a pod-mate comments.

---

[1] Anthony, Hobart. "The Five Stages of Post-Hack Grief." *Liminal: Children of the New Country*, edited by Abigail Shaffer, 38-50. Chicago: University of Chicago Press, 2026. (Reprinted with permission in *The Vexillum Employee Guide, Revised Edition.*)

It doesn't matter. It's fiction. This IRL.

<p>

Authorities interview our pod. Did something happen, anything usual?

No, I say.

What was your impression of her?

Renaissance woman. Fashionable dresser. Optimistic. Rope expert. I don't even know her real name.

What do you do here?

Flag offensive videos. Mostly of cats.

The detective smirks. Tough gig, he says. His scars are visible. His partner, though, puts an arm on his. Leans forward. Whispers: Do you know anything about the new phone the *f*ace is releasing?

They call them devices now, I say. We're just grunts.

I hear it's going to change everything. "Let the world in."

I find myself asking, How did she…? I watch their hands; afraid I have said the wrong thing and they will pull out a police photographer's photo of her body. Maybe video. I don't want to see it. I just need a mental image. A mental image that will eliminate the thousands of mental images my brain is overlaying on my memory of @Babyd011's face.

<p>

9-8-8 is the new three-digit suicide hotline number. Sixty-three percent of callers are cops, vets, and domestic abuse partners. Nine percent are teenagers who have had their devices taken away. The social workers who are answering the phone have had a rigorous weekend training course.

The news of @Babyd011 must have made it up the ranks. On Mother/Screen, the *f*ace tells us how valuable our contributions are. Pioneers. First responders (a focus group approved this term ranking with **Enthusiastic**). This appears to be an effort to boost morale.

I ask the *f*ace about the potential bonus, stock options, employment, reparations, benefits. Not sure if this is a live feed or prerecorded, or an AI deep-learning exercise.

He tells us congratulations and then looks to the side as though he is actually looking at Mr. Ray. Then he smiles. I see his head twitch as though new information is being downloaded into his brain. I think I can just see a wireless IFB nestled in his ear like a *Naked Lunch* bug.

Mr. Ray's eyes flit about unsettled, instead of his long contemplative stares. As if the answer was stuck in a corner of the office overlooked by the janitorial staff. Despite his best efforts, Mr. Ray's pompadour is frozen at low tide.

They're playing the wrong video, you say. We've seen this one.

<p>

We grieve. @Skiny_Leny doesn't cut his hair. But for a week he does not wash it. Keeping it in a sloppy ponytail. @MØM's breasts go dry for a week or so. This makes the Twins sad. @OrKa takes over @Babyd011's feed for a week before they cut @Babyd011's account. @Babyd011's run at Vex ends with posthumous stellar numbers.

<p>

@MØM is disappointed when no one drinks the latest round of Cherry Maca Mochas, but says nothing. She reminds everyone we're only a few weeks out from benefits. From bonuses. We've lost count of the days. Our big countdown. It doesn't cheer anyone up, so @MØM suggests a round of flogging for old times' sake.

I take her up on it. Partially, because she needs the attention and I want to express my anger. @Jun1p3r takes the whip from my hand. *You can take it out on me tonight.*

You give @MØM a cathartic flogging while reading. A book in one hand, the whip in the other. Despite being off your game, @MØM will start lactating the next day. The Twins will be happy.

You are good at reading a room.

[N S F W]
20

After the break, Mr. Ray announces he'll be moving on, his job done here at Vex.

I just want to say how proud I am to have served with each and every one of you, Mr. Ray says. We lost good folks along the way. But I wouldn't have done anything differently. I'll be handing in my badge. Next week will be my last.

With luck the transition to new leadership will be seamless, he says. I'll do my best to facilitate that. He does not mention the numbers or the bonus. Mr. Ray can read a room.

@OrKa slows her pace, but keeps pedaling. She's lost a significant amount of weight, except in her thighs. Her thighs are massive, a speed skater's quads. The jiggle replaced with the rippling piston action of a machine.

You pull out your holy book. We should have a funeral service for @Babyd011, you say.

@Jun1p3r, my @Jun1p3r.

We don't know her real name, a Twin says, the clean cut one. Or her next of kin or family.

We are her family, @MØM says.

You go to @Babyd011's Faraday locker. Return with her cashmere sweater. No one asks how you got in.

@Skiny_Leny hands @OrKa a pill. She picks up her pace and sorts through videos nearly keeping up with our entire team output. I marvel at her strength of will. That desk-bike will give out before she will.

You get @Babyd011's trash can and bring it over to our circle. You say we will cremate her symbolically. And each of us will take a pinch of her ashes so we may also bury her or dispose of her as each of us sees fit. This will allow her to transition to the Summerland.

You consult your book once more. We join hands as we burn her cashmere sweater in the trashcan. You take a deep breath. Unprompted, we all do the same.

Outside, snow falls.

<p>

Down the ashes drift, our jellyfish tank a snow globe. Just a pinch. The jellyfish gathers bits for its four stomachs. It pulses with @Babyd011's spirit.

Another pinch. Scattered across the Garden. The sod pulses with her life.

Another pinch. In the tisane. We pulse with her heart.

She is always with us.

<p>

"Heavy misfortunes have befallen us, but let us only cling closer to what remains, and transfer our love for those whom we have lost to those who yet live. Our circle will be small, but bound close by the ties of affection and mutual misfortune. And when time shall have softened your despair, new and dear objects of care will be born to replace those of whom we have been so cruelly deprived," you recite.

Thank you, @Jun1p3r, Mr. Ray says. Wiping a tear. That was lovely.

[N S F W]
21

I have been tasked by the office to ask Mr. Ray if they are going to keep the office open. I've been standing at the urinal for fifteen minutes hoping our bladders sync. I don't want to ask him in his office. I don't want it to be an official ask. I stand long enough my bladder lets me know evacuation is imminent.

My urine smells like rotten fruit. Is it the mushrooms?

Mr. Ray comes in. Takes the urinal to my left. Tells me I have a sharp mind. Asks what my degree is in.

Journalism, I say.

Substack?

I nod. Until the Hack, I say. I start to ask him about the office's fate.

@Skiny_Leny comes in. Takes a urinal to my right, leaving an empty one as a buffer between us. Unzips his denim miniskirt.

Mr. Ray tells me he has a degree in cliodynamics.

@Skiny_Leny laughs at this. Psychohistory, he says, by way of explanation. Applying mathematical models to cultural evolutions, society, and religion. Civil wars. Predicting the rise and fall of empires. It was Asimov's biggest plot device.

Mr. Ray points out that before anything was science fact, it was science fiction. Kirk's communicator, our cell phones. Private flights to the edge of space. The moon.

Mr. Ray sniffs and wrinkles his nose.

Cliodynamics currently has two hundred theories on why the Roman empire fell, @Skiny_Leny says. That field needs fine-tuning.

Mr. Ray just smiles at @Skiny_Leny, his eyes hidden behind his sunglasses.

@Skiny_Leny sniffs and wrinkles his nose at the rotten fruit odor.

It's the Cherry Maca Mochas, I say. It's in our streams.

<p>

I listen at Mr. Ray's office door. The *clickety clack* of his typewriter firing spastically like a machine gun. Pausing as he reloads his thoughts. Occasionally, he laughs to himself. Occasionally, there's a sniffle.

I poke my head in. He's in old-school boxers and a wifebeater. Dress socks and garters.

Sir, are they going to keep us open?

He keeps typing.

Any word on the new manager?

He keeps typing.

Our numbers are borderline, but he's respectful of our mourning. Maybe he's run the projections already. Maybe he doesn't want to know the financial cost of being alone with his thoughts.

A new episode of *Mt. Rushmore* has been uploaded, I say.

As he continues firing away, Mr. Ray motions for me to take a seat.

[N S F W]
22

Subject: @Sa>ag3
Age: 49
Title: SMCM
Test: R-PAS

Administrator: Raymond Gunn II

A series of inkblot cards. My responses:
Card 1: A fox mask.
Card 2: A blood bond.
Card 3: Witches at a cauldron.
Card 4: A close-up of a fly's face.
Card 5: A bat.
Card 6: A bearskin rug.
Card 7: Two women in a tantric pose.
Card 8: Ovaries.
Card 9: Cross section of a white rose.
Card 10: *Le Quatorze Juillet*.

<p>

The jellyfish requires significant upkeep. In a separate tank we breed brine shrimp. Live prey instead of powder. I check the water religiously.

The web says once the novelty wears off it's a chore, as jellyfish give nothing back.

But we chose to make it a priority. We don't do it consciously; we just do it. Keeping the delicate creature alive. Something has to make it through the 90 days.

<p>

I sit across from Mr. Ray as he goes over the results. His hair is solid and high. With just one hair out of place. I fight the urge to make it conform. To snip it. He must see my eyes behind his sunglasses. His hand smooths his hair and now the bulk of it is separating.

I think of the crack running up the outside wall of my apartment. His fingertips are freshly stained from replacing the ribbon in his typewriter. Looks like this one was a bit more of a struggle, as though he has wrestled a squid.

He takes off his sunglasses and taps the paper in his hand. The skin around his eyes is loose. *@Sa>ag3, @Sa>ag3, @Sa>ag3*, he says.

[N S F W]
23

You spend an hour watering the plants. You overwater a section of the sod and create a mud bath. You take garden shears and prune our forest walls without rhyme or design. I circle you warily. The mud sucks at my feet, as I gather the cutoffs for disposal.

You saw what @Babyd011 saw, the video that made her walk out. That diminished your light. I thought you'd made it through the experience, the video, @Babyd011's absence, but now she is dead.

You tell me to make a fist in your hair. I can't get hard. You call me names. I can't get hard. You dare me. I can't get hard. You beg for mercy. It twitches, but I do not get hard.

The long fuse of grief burns towards its powder keg. You're trying anything to stop it. To keep peace in our Garden.

You're manic. I can't corral or contain you. I can only be present.

I hold you while you scream the lyrics to "Singin' in the Rain."

Then, guttural and manic:

Ten and six.

A dark mantra. Ten and six.

He made them do it.

Ten and six. Ten and six. Ten and six. Ten and six. Ten and six. Ten and six. Ten and six. Ten and six. Ten and six. Ten and six. Ten and six. Ten and six. Ten and six. Ten and six. Ten and six. Ten and six.

He recorded them doing it.

Ten and six. Ten and six. Ten and six. Ten and six. Ten and six. Ten and six. Ten and six. Ten and six.

He posted it.

Ten and six. Ten and six. Ten and six. Ten and six. Ten and six. Ten and six. Ten and six. Ten and six. Ten and six. Ten and six. Ten and six. Ten and six. Ten and six. Ten and six. Ten and six. Ten and six. Ten and six. Ten and six.

She was screaming.

Ten and six. Ten and six. Ten and six. Ten and six. Ten and six. Ten and six. Ten and six. Ten and six. Ten and six. Ten and six. Ten and six.

He made them do it.

Ten and six. Ten and six. Ten and six. Ten and six. Ten and six.

He watched.

Ten and six. Ten and six. Ten and six. Ten and six. Ten and six. Ten and six. Ten and six. Ten and six. Ten and six. Ten and six. Ten and six. Ten and six. Ten and six.

He got off.

Ten and six. Ten and six. Ten and six. Ten and six. Ten and six. Ten and six. Ten and six. Ten and six. They were *ten and six.*

And then: *That video killed @Babyd011.*

You double over, grabbing your stomach. Then hands on your knees. Animal sounds are coming from your throat.

Then you're coming at me with glazed eyes. Thrusting shears. I numb your arm with a quick blow and pull you toward me. Your nails rake my body and dig raw furrows on my back. I spin you and throw you down. You land in the mud and I roll you over and push you down. Your legs and arms flail as I contain them. I feel you wear yourself down, like a boxer in the later rounds. You fight me until you can't lift your hands. I push you deeper into the mud. You're sobbing, then whimpering, and then just shaking.

David Scott Hay

I gather handfuls of mud and finish covering you, ritually outlining your face, then covering your eyes, your mouth. Leaving your nostrils clear. I turn on the sunlamps and angle them on your body, hoping to draw out the toxins. All the things you couldn't absorb.

I hunch over a half whiskey barrel. Notes of oak, sherry, and peat fill my nose. I inhale a toke from a thin joint, careful not to induce more paranoia. I exhale as the mud bakes, and the jellyfish floats with a low hum.

[N S F W]
24

I love you.

Even the part of you that's inside me.

As you tuned your guitar.

On a playground. Perhaps the merry-go-round. Instantly regretting it.

During a winter's night. A blank stare.

Over messenger.

Over email.

Watching *Taxi Driver*. Your lips wet with semen.

Scratching it on my back.

A double-dip cone of mint chocolate chip. My favorite flavor, not tasted in a decade.

Inside the wreckage of a classic Mustang, hands intertwined.

Shouting it over the pre-show of a concert.

These are all the first times I can remember saying it. Hearing it.

Which one was the first time?

I don't remember. But I remember the last. My ear rings still.

<p>

The clay bakes slowly, cleansing.

<p>

Do jellyfish dream?

<p>

You sleep the sleep of the dead. Your chest gently rolling and cracking the baked earth. You wake. I fix you tisane with honey to soothe your shredded throat. You emerge from the dry clay, your skin crumbling off. A pink golem underneath.

<p>

The jellyfish floats centered in the tank.

<p>

I had a dream, you say. You don't elaborate. You smile. You pack your altar. An extra set of clothes into an urban backpack. A pinch of @Babyd011's ashes. I have to leave, you say. The glint is back in your eye. Purpose. Intention.

I hide my trembling left hand behind my back as I nod supportively.

<p>

Better to plan your suicide than to let others plan your murder.

Delete > dox

@Babyd011's frozen body had been discovered in Welles Park. Slumped against a tree, her Cherry Maca Mocha still in her hand. Her cashmere scarf knotted loosely around her neck, inviting the cold and snow to purify her one last time. We realize we walked past her on the way home the night she disappeared, our winter commute acting as blinders.

[N S F W]
25

You're gone now.

I am alone in a bathroom stall.

I have just had a meeting with Mr. Ray.

<p>

You insist I don't ride the train with you to the airport.

I've never begged for anything in my life. Not my life. Not a job. Not a date. Not a second chance. Not an autograph.

I am begging you not to go. I am begging you to let it go. I am begging you to sweep this one more thing under the sod. Let the jellyfish absorb it. Let us trip into another universe, let the light out. I am screaming that it will be okay, we have each other, and that's enough. That I can't lose you. I just can't. I'm not a loner. And that I don't have to explain things to you, and I can't do this alone.

I can't be alone with my thoughts.

But I don't. I don't say any of those things the voice in my head is screaming.

The first black hole known was Cygnus X-1.

Your naked body against my impotent one. I finger paint with your menstrual blood, recreating today's video splatters that did not get flagged. Your body an imitation canvas of concrete. My inspiration the lesser of the day's evils. Before the kid video, this would have been art therapy. Now it is blood magik. Protection for the task ahead. I paint the runes per your verbal instruction. You chant as I paint.

The human body slowly replaces Its cells every seven to ten years. This never made sense to me. I still have childhood scars. A tattoo of a dot when a 00 ink pen jabbed my thumb.

Did those cells not get replaced or did they get replaced with exact replicas?

Would I pass the Voight-Kampff scale test?

Is that why your luck returns seven years after you break a mirror? Your old self no longer exists? The curse has nothing left to dissolve?

A black pearl forms when an irritant gets stuck in a black-banded oyster; an oyster with a black lip. The closer to the edge of the oyster, the more the grain of sand inside will absorb the color of the black band as the pearl forms.

A white oyster that produces silvery pearls may have a slight black coloring just inside its edge. If a pearl forms here, you will get a black pearl, i.e., black pearls from a white-pearl-producing oyster. This happens once in 10,000. Not a miracle, but an anomaly. A natural surprise. And thus coveted.

<p>

I am alone, hunched over my black pearl. Sitting in a bathroom stall at Vex.

Two other toilets run, my own private babbling brook. One of the Twins masturbates in a stall at the other end of the bathroom, humming a military fanfare. My own private soundtrack.

I prefer the solitude of the lactorium, the white noise, which quiets my tinnitus, but @MØM needs the room for her own coping and comfort. She's shaved one side of her head as a tribute to @Babyd011. With her gone to the Summerland, you out of the office, and me here, I wonder who @MØM will find to cradle at her breast under the white noise. The other Twin's hair is not regulation length anymore. Tiny curls form at the base of her neck. And now, to @MØM's chagrin, this Twin has also given up dairy.

I tell you this now, looking back. At the time, it just felt like me and the black pearl and me and the black pearl and me and the black pearl.

#*f*Ōne.

This is the new branding of the *f*ace's new device. The *f* being the company logo. There seems to be a graphic between the *f* and the one. As in, we're all one. We're all connected, the hive mind coming online. Are we supposed to call it a *phone* or an *F-1*?

LET THE WORLD IN

The *f*ace tells us that this new device will need no battery. We are the battery. The slight bioelectrical charge from your body will keep it going. You can fast recharge, but just holding it will recharge it. They factored in the amount of time people hold or wear their devices and suggested just a bit more time with the device will keep it charged with even heavy use.

There's a haptic tingle when you hold the *f*Ōne. I'm sure it causes the brain to release endorphins in the body. I imagine a clothing line that will have very thin pockets allowing the phone to stay in constant contact with the skin, but the *f*ace says it works better in the hand. Wearables, it seems, are fading. The natural position of the arm and wrist not conducive to long-term doomscrolling.

<p>

The device is your key to the modern world. Cryptocurrency. Bill pay. Taxes. Payroll. Healthcare. Purchasing. Biometrics. Sleep patterns. Health. Identity. All run through your device. All monetized information. This is life in the modern age. You are your device.

They talk about it with the fever of the old guard excited about the possibility of the World Wide Web. When the possibility of access to the world's knowledge, culture, and music could be at your fingertips. Back when it seemed a utopia of a future.

Even then, there were the detractors. But now you can't go to a college without being wired, you can't attend class without attendance being pinged from your phone. It's a surveillance state.

And no one cares.

<p>

#XSuperApp

<p>

The device (already I'm resisting the branding) assimilates the information from your previous device through your *f*ace account. Those that want the device will have to reactivate their account to use it (those with deleted accounts are offered a recovery process). It's proprietary. If you do not, you cannot use it.

It is the hottest tech item this decade or century. The comments of resistance are either removed or genuinely drowned out with the flood of bots and the fever of early adopters. Fringe opinions and articles are written about the dangers.

But here is the bottom line: conform or be cast out.

‹p›

Suddenly, I can remember my high-school locker number. My generation's first PIN.

‹p›

You've been gone two days on your mission of vengeance. A self-appointed advocate for the children of ten and six.

The seat next to me on the train is empty. People choose to stand. I must be giving off dark energy. I dare not pull out the ƒŌne. I want to look at it. I dare not pull it out. Tech spies everywhere. Double dare. I dare not pull it out.

What will it fix? Triple dog dare. What will it cure? I try to shake the rumination. The loop in my head. I just want to look at it. Bile stings my throat. I just want to hold it. Now. I want to show everyone. Now.

‹p›

It is a thing of beauty. Black iridescence, like a butterfly wing. Seamless, a barely discernible matte logo on the back. Not that it will even be seen, covered by your hand. Biometrics being read every millisecond.

It is the future and the future is now.

I hand the device back to Mr. Ray.

He says, Keep it. It's yours. Tomorrow, I'll pass them out to the pod. His hair is under a ball cap. His sunken eyes glazed in red spiderwebs. His jowls sag and gray now streaks his temples. Presidents don't age as quickly.

Good job, @Sa>ag3, Mr. Ray says.

He talks to me but he's staring at the device. He says more things. He doesn't indicate whether his statements are good or bad, whether we are crossing the Rubicon or terminating with the device. I don't know if he's capable now. He's looking at me. A wan smile on his face.

Now I have other news, he says...

The black pearlescent finish of the device is mesmerizing. The subtle Damascus pattern of the cosmos swirling as I turn it. *Thus Spake Zarathustra* echoes in my head, drowning out Mr. Ray's soft voice.

This is not a black mirror. Nor is it a black pearl. It is a black hole that absorbs with its own boundary of no escape; held in my hand this event horizon.

David Scott Hay

NODE IV

"I greatly need a friend who would have sense enough not to despise me as romantic, and affection enough for me to endeavor to regulate my mind."

—Mary Wollstonecraft Shelley
Frankenstein; or, The Modern Prometheus

[N S F W]
1

Mr. Ray pours a flute of champagne for everyone. We've hit the numbers. We've won.

That was easy, @Skiny_Leny says. Dryly.

There is no confetti, no horns, no spinning sparklers. Without @Babyd011 and you, the celebration is muted.

Now what do we do?

We're full-time, yes?

What are our choices of healthcare plans?

And that fat bonus, what about it?

That's just paperwork, @Skiny_Leny says. The real question is when do we get a new manager? @Skiny_Leny is nervous about an office culture change.

The bonus is forthcoming, Mr. Ray says. Please be patient.

We give him a silent hoist of glassware. Respect. But he hasn't answered the question on all of our minds. Everyone looks at each other afraid to ask. Afraid to ask when the new manager is coming.

There is no need to ask, Mr. Ray answers. *@Sa>ag3.*

What? I say.

He makes it official in front of the pod. Congratulations.

He fixes a Velcro-backed patch to my jumpsuit, on the sleeve. Congratulations, Interim Office Manager. You'll be in charge when I leave Thursday, Mr. Ray says to me. They're interviewing new managers, but I posited that things might best continue with continuity. Promoting from within, so to speak.

Mr. Ray takes the fob from his neck, the kill switch. Drapes the lanyard over my neck, as if I've podiumed in an inaugural Olympic sport. I hear the national anthem play in my head. I wish you were here.

He says a few nice words. @MØM tears up, so proud. One of the Twins gives me a formal salute, the other double thumps his fist to his chest. I can barely make eye contact with them. Except @Skiny_Leny. If he's jealous it doesn't show, other than a flush creeping up from his décolletage.

Officially interim.

<p>

@MØM comes out of the lactorium with one of the Twins. She buttons up her cardigan. Ruffles his shaggy hair. Despite his steel jaw, he blushes. Dairy is hard to give up.

The other one exits behind them. His hair high and tight. By the book. I can see his erection waning through his flight suit.

The Twins have official government-issued flight suits, stripped of all insignia and rank. Plausible deniability. @MØM says, Both of them have flown combat missions without ever leaving the ground.

@Skiny_Leny nods as if this confirms his suspicions. Drone pilots, he says. Military.

<p>

Mr. Ray still does not know what our bonus will be. I try not to count chickens before they hatch, but I will finally be ahead. Finally recovered from the financial ruin of a just-get-it-over-with divorce. The medical bills in a foreign country.

<p>

Office. Train.

<p>

I can't stop thinking about it. I can't stop looking at it. The iridescence moves like viscous liquid. Oil on glass. I touch it repeatedly and swipe it with my finger just to prove it isn't wet. Not even the natural oils from my finger can smear its living Damascus pattern.

<p>

Airlock. Garden.

<p>

The iridescent blackness sinks slowly to the bottom of the jellyfish tank. Impossibly, it lands on its short edge. The jellyfish tentacles test it once, then twice. It floats over the black device, hovering between it and the surface.

I imagine it has found the device's blind spot.

Are you mine?

[N S F W]
2

Mr. Ray's last official act as manager is to hand out the devices to the staff. Each one in their own special black case; unboxing the future is part of the experience. He's gone with a pompadour with a side part. Early Johnny Cash.

@Jun1p3r's will stay locked up until she returns from her mission. Next to @Babyd011's locker. They are coded to the individual and she will have to be present to activate it.

We are forbidden to contact other Vex offices regarding the new devices, Mr. Ray tells us. He lowers his sunglasses to the tip of his nose, clears his throat to get @Skiny_Leny's attention.

My understanding is cracking the case would make it inoperable, Mr. Ray says. Would destroy it. And no, you can't sell it. These are special models given just to this Vex office. Personalized, if you will, the moment you touch it. Possibly DNA. It's in the fine print.

Mr. Ray says you can leave them out on the desk. But not too close to your monitor. He doesn't explain why and I can see that he is thinking. That he hasn't touched one himself. I note that he was still wearing his winter gloves when he handed me mine.

Congrats on your numbers, he says.

Everyone worked hard, I say. Thanks to you.

I just let you be your best selves, Mr. Ray says. His hair is perfect.

<p>

At the elevator, a ream of typed pages bulges in Mr. Ray's satchel, slung across his chest. In his left hand, a small leather case for his typewriter.

He gives me a hard handshake. I return it.

I left you a parting gift, Mr. Ray says.

Thank you, I nod.

The elevator *dings* and opens.

Mr. Ray steps in, and slips off his wig. The pompadour drops to the elevator floor; his skull is smooth and shiny, a small ridge toward the front. From the typewriter case he pulls out a WWII gas mask and slips it on with practiced ease and looks like a giant black fly.

Any last advice, I ask, because my brain is still processing this exit.

As the elevator doors shut, Mr. Ray says, Don't look back.

<p>

LET THE WORLD IN.
LET THE WORMS IN.

<p>

The black pearls. Is this the bonus? I can't remember who asks, but they ask for all of us. An early release? Incredulous. *THIS* IS THE BONUS?? WE HIT OUR FUCKING NUMBERS!

Everyone has a thought. They verbalize these thoughts:

*f*Ōne?

What about our promotions to full-time jobs?

I thought stock options for the IPO.

WE HIT OUR FUCKING NUMBERS!

I thought cash.

I thought cryptocurrency.

When did you hear that?

I just thought that. It makes sense.

What about insurance? What about our health insurance?

WE HIT OUR FUCKING NUMBERS!

Is this legal?

Christ, what's in the fine print?

Can we unionize?

Oh god, oh god, oh god, are we still temps?

My tinnitus rings with their overlapping voices. Agitation runs through the pod. Heads ramming into the concrete walls.

<p>

Fuck this, @Skiny_Leny says. Imagine what a techie in China would pay for this early release.

The government would just take it, one of the Twins says. Execute the buyer and start to reverse engineer it. The other Twin is dubious.

Already @Skiny_Leny is opening a new cryptocurrency wallet.

<p>

Already @Skiny_Leny is on his burner device, on his secure server and VPNX, and setting up a competing audition for *Wired*, *TekNut*, *Codemonkey*, and *Vice*DE*Vice*. A meetup of his time and choosing for thirty minutes with the *ƒŌ*ne. Bidding starts at $50,000.

<p>

One of the Twins stares at @Skiny_Leny. Just a reminder we have all signed NDAs, he says.

@Skiny_Leny looks incredulous. I'll use part of the money to throw an official office party, he says.

None of us in the office can imagine what that would look like.

There's more than one way to just win, he says.

As office manager, @Skiny_Leny, I am just reminding you of the agreements you have signed. The NDAs.

@Skiny_Leny scratches his scalp where I've removed a patch of his hair. I read in *Codemonkey*, he says, there's no way to take the ƒŌne offline, once it's on. If they all aren't already on.

@OrKa's squeaky desk-bike misses a beat by a sixteenth. She looks over her shoulder, her legs pumping at half speed. She makes a note and picks up the pace.

Rumor is you can't turn them off, he says. We need to find that out. And they're going to pay me to tell. @Skiny_Leny reads fringe websites.

@Sa>ag3, can you find out if this is our reward, a pod-mate says. I already have a device. I need healthcare. Dental. Vision. Prescriptions that aren't forged.

‹p›

My eyes lock onto the floating alien in the black frame. The Gunn legacy. How much the floating alien resembles a jellyfish that evolved to rise into the air rather than stay in the sea. Became the dominant species. An apex predator. Watching me. This is my parting gift.

‹p›

The speed of the present is eternal.

<p>

I expect my staff to put the devices into Faraday lockers and eschew them with disgust. Especially if they think this might be our bonus. Priceless in the moment. Worthless in the long run.

Surely, they won't be distracted by the shiny and new. I expect them to press the issue of benefits, employment. But after the sighs, the cursing, and a free round of Xanax, they all activate their devices. The swirling black pearlescence already gripping them. A pregnant pause.

In the conference room, they all look like they are holding black tombstones. It seems as if we've traded @Babyd011's soul for this, I say. No coworker responds, their heads down.

[N S F W]
3

I think of alien worlds. Alien civilizations. Alien cultures. Did Jesus visit them, too? Did they kill him again or was Gethsemane the first time? What did they call him? What sacrifice did he make? What does the Jesus of Ganymede look like?

Impossibly, time has slowed even more in the Garden. Is this what Adam felt every time Eve went for a long walk?

The ƒŌne at the bottom of the aquarium is communicating to the jellyfish. How to escape. How to evolve. How to outlive me. "Lux Aeterna," a soundscape to my dreamscape. If I am dreaming. If I'm alone in the Garden. If I've macrodosed. And if I've opened myself to evil, it must be purged.

Hardware store. I construct a small Faraday cage, just the size of the object. Triple thick. Even then I do not think it is enough.

<p>

With BBQ tongs and rubber gloves and safety goggles, I remove the device from the tank. I use a sick day to clean the tanks, balance the new salinity. As I sage the apartment, I find four stones at the four edges of our Garden. N.S.E.W. Your work. I burn the old woolen blanket. You would have recommended that. I'm not sure why, but I hear your voice clearly.

The shrimp eggs? I sage them too. No sense throwing out the babies with the brine water.

<p>

I carry the ƒŌne a block away. There is a pothole every ten feet. A mile away, a modern house replacing a historic brownstone dating back to just after the Great Fire. New construction. An illustration on the sign outside the gates shows me what it's like to live in the future. Fully automated. Voice controlled. Radiant heat floors. Full neighborhood surveillance. Smart.

The winter air Is crisp and Invigorating. My head hums.

I slip between the locked gates, and place the Faraday cage into the foundation forms. A crew will pour concrete between the boards and over rebar and the Faraday cage and it will be the cornerstone of this new building.

<p>

I adjust the salinity for the jellyfish, while a kettle heats on the stove.

My feet tingle.

I look down at my blue feet. Numb. I take the kettle from the stove and pull out a casserole dish. My feet soak, working slowly back to pink.

The next morning, with hot chocolate and popcorn I've made on the stove, I watch the workers pour the concrete, work their trade. Then I head into work, pausing briefly at @Babyd011's tree, my bare hand on the cold bark.

Tomorrow will be even better.

[N S F W]
4

Later, when we chat: me at a coffeehouse, you at a coffeehouse in another state. (@Skiny_Leny has installed VPNX on our old laptops.) We video chat, each in a corner, sunken into an oversized chair that looks of espresso and smells of university alleyways.

You tell me you sent a box to me at the office. Keep an eye out for it, you say. I make a mental note to check the drone pad. Only Mr. Ray went up there. I've inherited another responsibility.

I don't ask about your mission, but get frustrated when the feed freezes and audio stutters.

@Skiny_Leny warned it might happen. He suggests using the new *f*Ōne, says it will like being there live. If you don't mind everything you say and do being recorded for offshore analysis.

(I'm tempted to dig up the device. So tempted. People would look at me differently. I'd be held in higher status. Even if just until the *f*Ōne is released wide.)

I want to see your face, hear your voice with crystal clarity.

But it is encased in concrete. A house being built on top of it.

I tell you what I did with it. I repeat myself several times until you can piece together the message.

(What will we do with @Jun1p3r's device when she gets hers? Bury it, I assume. But she doesn't talk about the ƒŌne waiting for her. She's on a mission.)

I hear enough of you to piece together a few questions:

Will the house be possessed? You wonder. Will this be the site of a future slaughter? Will the monkeys use thigh bones to bash in the skulls of their kin? I see cartoon *ZONKS!* And *BAMS!* As you say it.

I tell you I waved to the construction workers. Told them it looks great. Workers that could never afford to live in a house like the one they are building. I offered them warmers for their coffee from my thermos of hot chocolate.

I've doctored the marshmallows with psilocybin. For those that remember the childhood glee of marshmallows and say yes, it will be their best day at work.

As they finish their morning break, the concrete truck rolls up late, its humped back rotating and ready to pour.

I watch the whole process. They're on a timetable and feeling good. No one notices the Faraday cage as it's smothered. For a moment the *f*Ōne resists. A bubble forms with its last breath, then pops, and is swallowed whole.

As an afterthought, I tell you about my promotion. I'm half embarrassed to tell you, but you squeal with glee. You say other things in a rush, but the audio is butchered and I can only smile and nod. You flash and shake your breasts, and I hear Barista Tim behind me snort Frappuccino out of his nose.

My @Jun1p3r.

The workers thank me for the hot chocolate. Already the day is good. I leave the concrete as it cures around the device, and stuff the extra marshmallows in my mouth. My cheeks puffing out like a kid's.

I may or may not have started a snowball fight with kids on the way home. I may or may not have gotten creamed.

[N S F W]
5

Our last night before you left, after the mud-bath cleansing, you had woken me before dawn with another present. You're so good at this.

A straight razor kit. I've been watching videos, you had said, stropping the blade.

You had nicked me just a bit. On the throat.

I'm hard as you lick the wound clean. We both marvel at my erection as it slowly wanes. When it just tips over but is still engorged, you say: What does that remind you of?

The first dick pic you had to flag, I say.

We chuckle momentarily with the nostalgia.

Now my turn to shave you. My hands aren't as steady as I'd hoped. Excited? Tremors? Or the residual images from a double shift?

Regardless, I only nick you once. Eliciting a soft cry of excitement. I lick your wound and do not stop. Until the crying softens and you are a clean little girl.

[N S F W]
6

I can't stop touching my face. The smooth skin. I remember the other shaves, but this one feels different. This feels real.

<p>

PING.

Did you find the box?

I read your message at work. Sitting in Mr. Ray's office, staring at our messenger window, waiting. I've been doing this all morning. I know the pod is grumbling about the loss of manpower. But I can hear the quick tempo of the squeaky desk-bike and I know @OrKa is covering for me.

I'll join them after I hear from you. I'm confused about the box. Finally, I suss out that there are *two* boxes. One coming by GoDronc and another one hidden at home like an Easter egg.

Did you find the box?

<p>

The box is tucked away next to the mushroom bin. It's almost harvest time again. Inside I open it. Another plant. I'm mildly disappointed.

I pull it out. It's a Juniper bonsai tree. With a note: "Take care of me."

I place it opposite the jellyfish. That way there are no blind spots for despair.

The jellyfish hangs just a touch closer to the front glass, closer to the tree, as if remembering a tiny coded impulse to head towards land.

<p>

The drone pad pings a delivery. GoDrone shipments are limited in this weather. Surcharges have been tripled for bad weather delivery. I realize I've never been up there.

On top of the building, a plexi sheet protects the pad from the wind off the lake. The shelter is designed by non-Chicagoans and the wind swirls around it, snapping and whipping my jumpsuit. My cheeks numb instantly. @Jun1p3r's straight razor present having taken away a layer of feral protection.

The drone pad's ubiquitous red beacon pulses. The distant skyline's beacons all pulse out of sync, like an orchestra tuning up. Each sending out their own unique code. I watch, mesmerized. Slowly, the city's beacons sync. All pulsing on the same frequency. I feel my heart sync up to it. A symphony for an audience of one. And, for a short time, there is no more chaos. Even the wind takes a breath.

Syncopation.

The wind exhales. My oversize jumpsuit billows, and fills like a wingsuit. I have the impulse to jump. Take a leap of faith that I will soar and fly. That it will end okay. If nothing else it will end.

I visualize this freedom long enough that the beacons across the city lose their synchronicity and I know I will never leave you.

<p>

I bring the box down from the rooftop. It's from overseas. A Chinese customs form filled out. @Skiny_Leny sweeps it for bugs.

<p>

#Teledildonics

<p>

My three-month-old baby brother stopped breathing when I was five years old. I remember my mother carrying him, running up the street to the hospital. At five in the morning, she left me in the care of the newspaper deliveryman on his route. A man with white hair and black glasses. Looking back, it seemed like the start of a horror movie. My brother died, so maybe it was.

<p>

Aquarists used to inject jellyfish with dye. Make them Day-Glo colors. But that would wear off. Then they went the other way and genetically modified them. Now you can construct an aquatic alien Tokyo. Our store down the street showcases them under a black light.

Because now we have to repackage the perfection of a jellyfish.

<p>

The GoDrone shipment: a tech sex suit. It's complicated or doesn't work properly. I've been off the meds a few days for this. We spend the evening on a conference call with a customer support agent, a woman who does not understand our questions. I don't know if it is a language barrier or a tech barrier. I suspect both. This as I sit at the Grindhouse. In an alien wetsuit, reconnecting wires and resetting the built in Wi-Fi, trying to make contact with you.

<p>

(10:07:56 PM): IN.

(10:08:26 PM): My head goes light. I only sense your lips and a universe exploding...

(10:08:49 PM): I want you to cum inside me... I want to feel you... make you a part of me forever…

(10:08:58 PM): My world...

(10:09:17 PM): my goddess...

(10:09:27 PM): IN.

(10:09:29 PM): Out.

(10:09:32 PM): IN.

(10:09:39 PM): my god

(10:09:39 PM): my god

(10:09:39 PM): my god

(10:09:39 PM): my god

(10:09:39 PM): my god

(10:09:39 PM): my god

(10:09:39 PM): my god

(10:09:39 PM): my god

We are glitching with a spew of copypasta. And then lose the signal, once again falling short of the finish line.

‹p›

Barista Tim comes over to me, hefting a wet mop. I expect him to ask me to leave; instead he tells me he has been promoted to store manager, but will still be making our Cherry Maca Mochas personally and to tell @MØM hello.

I will and thank you, I say.

He apologies for the shabby Wi-Fi and wishes me better luck. Keep grinding. \m/

[N S F W]
7

Excuse me, @Sa>ag3.

It is @OrKa. The first time she has ever addressed me directly.

I have video, she says. For you to see.

I circle to her side of our workstation. My stomach twitches. Then my eyelid. I take a deep breath.

It won't be.

I'd given her metadata to run against all incoming and rerouted videos at Vex. She dropped in a subroutine. She has admin rights from the multiple OS upgrades; Mr. Ray delegating.

A video. For me. She's freeze-framed it. Her legs churn slower. The metronome of her squeaks now more ominous. John Williams, an octave down.

She points at the screen, her finger cautiously inches away. Is that you?

<p>

You look like someone waiting for something important to happen. This with a French accent. I had been sitting at a café in Paris. Posing and wondering if I would be the subject of a tourist's camera. A tourist posing for a tourist.

The espressos had nearly combated the jet lag.

Pardon?

The woman with the comically large scarf repeated herself. Slower. You look like a person waiting for something important to happen.

She had said it offhandedly, and now annoyingly as if having to repeat a joke.

It stopped me mid-sip.

After a moment, I found I could not argue. This, by a stranger. I still think of that exchange every day.

<p>

I'm not looking at myself in the video @OrKa found, though it is me. I am looking at her. The large scarf, the uninhibited dancing. And that smile. And wit. And shotgun laugh.

<p>

I never saw my favorite band, ███████████, perform live in the States. I'd always missed them. This time by two weeks, playing a venue within walking distance. Two weeks. This was before you could track them with your device. Newsletters consumed by your spam folder. They had gotten me through college, a bad breakup. Post-divorce, I had wanted to see them live. Why shouldn't I?

Maybe it would help, the camaraderie, the pure joy.

Another missed opportunity.

But then I found them playing a venue in France. I had a passport and an emergency credit card. *Tickets must be purchased in person only.* I needed church. Salvation.

Also, I rationalized, I've waited in longer lines for things I did not want.

<p>

I flew out days early to line up for tickets. To be present. If I didn't get them, I would stay and explore a city I'd only seen in movies. The City of Light.

New memories to overlay the memories of failure.

<p>

A whirlwind romance. We did not discuss the future. Just the next meal. The next market. The next revival house theatre. Our love of music. Sharing of our soul discoveries. I bought her an expensive scarf from a street vendor.

<p>

I overstayed my visa. The night of the show, we made slow love. We were late—another round of lovemaking, this one primal and a test of wills. I whispered to her that she had the heart of a lion, mind of a criminal, soul of a poet. I thought she would mock me. But she just pondered the words and said in her Romance accent: *tell me more.*

David Scott Hay

<p>

With her smile parting the flock of General Admission early birds, we make our way to the stage.

The squelch of feedback. A guitar being tuned in a historic venue, a cathedral of spiritual gathering. Music our religion.

That euphoric feeling of attention and laughing unselfconsciously with another. The anticipation of your senses being assaulted, of escaping for the near future into a world of music and joy.

Sharing that joy.

A toke from a fellow tourist. The mossy smell of pot lingers in my nose. A bass guitar is tuned. The vibrations reverberate through my chest.

She feels it too and smiles. She puts her hand on my chest. Another note. I feel it through her chest. Her shirt is damp between her breasts. It's going to be a hot one here. Word is that the A/C has already quit. A couple of doors have been propped open with stage weights. We don't care. We'll shower afterwards. Reveling in the night.

The light board op scrolls through a few presets and she glows magenta, yellow, blue and yellow, red and blue, green and yellow, and then red and orange. A muse for every emotion. Every season. Every note. Every word.

And then the lull between final adjustments and the live show.

Blackout.

I pull her in for a kiss. The lights come up and we are looking into each other's eyes.

Ten seconds pass.

<p>

The reason things move in slow motion in a crisis: in a normal situation the brain is not memorizing pedestrian facts or information. Your bedroom walls. Your shoes. Her hair.

In a crisis situation, your brain seems to slow down because it is processing all the details around you, all you might need to survive. It is rewriting your brain and rendering all the new details.

This is why a change of scenery is exciting. All new input.

This is why having an affair stimulates and excites the brain and body. All the new details to render.

<p>

Ten seconds later, the band began to play; the words were on my lips.

Three little words. I said them just as you turned to the stage.

You didn't hear them. But I wanted you to know.

I tapped you on the shoulder and turned you to me. If you couldn't hear me, you'd be able to see my lips. A part of me thought I was going to ruin everything. But I'd vowed when I bought that plane ticket to never to hold back. Never withhold again. Done with emotional calculations. I would not contain them.

I would tell you again the three little words and let fate take its course.

Terrorists and artists have one thing in common: an appreciation of scale.

Our eyes meet wrapped in smiles, ears near-deaf with the opening chords of our favorite song. Now our song.

I lov-

Your lower face disappears with the first three-round burst. The smell of gunpowder chokes the three little words.

Blood pours from my ruptured eardrum. My THX hearing has blown a channel.

Another shot nearly removes your arm at the elbow. Another burst, a through-and-through. Mushrooming inside the other music lovers.

I try to drag you away before going down on the slippery floor. Others go down and never get up. A voice tells me to *play dead.* I do. So much foley to decipher with your face pressed against a dying human.

\<p\>

Stereo: As electronic feedback oscillates against screams, I tried to stifle the blood with your scarf. While staring at your jaw just out of reach. Then the panic of those on the killing floor. Others with their machines waded into slaughter.

Mono: My belly burns. I think I see my guts glisten. There isn't enough scarf to go around.

The spiders had spun their webs.

\<p\>

Vex. The reason I took this job. Inside the ███ the band ██████████. I needed to see the security video. The unreleased video. The sealed video. The leaked video. The purged video. The genesis for the Ludovico 70-second delay. I need to see myself get shot.

I needed to flood my mind with the worst so what I lived through would be normalized. And verified.

What was her name, @OrKa asks.

\<p\>

I ask @OrKa to print out a screenshot for me.

The scar tissue on my abdomen throbs like an alien parasite awakening from stasis.

I needed to see her.

I needed to see her when she was still whole.

I needed to see her when we were still whole.

I needed to see her when hope was still whole.

<p>

A hoax. Actors, they said online. False flag. The misinformation campaign gained traction in the SM platforms, spreading far and wide. Half truths mixed with alt facts confirmed by a web of bots. Tweets to articles to comments verifying a trail of deception. Bots, foreign and domestic. So many lies.

The original video suppressed. People vilified. People exalted. People dead. Broken. The original video purged. Their stories dismissed. Edited for length and clarity. Doxed. Made into a movie with B-listers. My lionhearted companion never making it to the character list, her doppelgänger never on the call sheet. A composite, the producer said. The script mixing and matching parts of the dead. Review bombing from foreign troll farms diluting the truth further. Victims, dead and alive, gaslit to protect what? The status quo. Another distraction from class warfare.

But now I have proof of my story, her story. I have the truth. Finally. My legs wobble and I excuse myself.

The inside of the lactorium is a chapel. I sit with my head in my hands, shaking, sobbing, this private moment. I turn on the white noise. I rub my stomach, the throbbing insect of a scar. A shudder wracks my body. It starts at the base of my neck and travels to my toes, warming them. As it travels back up my spine, my body relaxes. The knot in my chest loosens.

I take easy, natural deep breaths, the inhale and exhale now like opium.

The scar sleeps, and the chill, that chill that never goes away, dissipates.

[N S F W]
8

I wrote a letter to the *f*ace. An exercise my therapist had given me. I did the full exercise. I enveloped it. I stamped it. My therapist is impressed with my participation. I tell him I mailed it with a Forever stamp of an American Flag. It costs me the same to mail it to Hawaii as it does across town.

Did you know that if a woman in Hawaii wears a flower behind her right ear, she is available? my therapist says. If she is taken, it goes behind the left.

I did know that, I say, and then he asks if I put the postage stamp on upside down.

<p>

I used to watch movies. *Vanishing Point. Creature from the Black Lagoon. King Kong. Fight Club. Brazil. Network.* They all end the same: our hero scapegoated. But this is RL

<p>

(10:12:35 PM): I'm breathing you... your liquid turns to blood running through my veins

(10:12:59 PM): we're floating in space

(10:13:57 PM): stars light our way

(10:14:18 PM): I can't let you go

(10:14:33 PM): there's too many stars to share

(10:15:04 PM): I hold you tighter, afraid to let go, afraid to fall away from you

Can half a man live?

At one point, messaging sex isn't enough. But my meds impede the rig. You suggest a new tactic: I'll continue to message you. You program your remote vibrator to buzz every time I type an adjective with more than three syllables. Vocabulary as foreplay. When I type the word "like" my crotch buzzes unpleasantly. You do not like similes.

Thumbing a relationship. Against glass. A prisoner visiting a prisoner. A glass partition. No tactile sensation. I put my hand against the jellyfish glass. My hand no longer trembles.

I imagine a giant hand, maybe God's, outside touching the plastic sheeting.

There's still a crater at the bottom of the aquarium where the *f*ace's monolith stood.

Coffee shop: a coffee clutch. A half-dozen students hunched over their devices. How can I blame them? They don't know of another world. A world without connectivity. They can't fathom how the teens used to get together, plan anything, without texting.

A great mystery.

They don't even have to leave their bedroom to hang out. They've never known anything but horror and terror. At least these here kids have gotten out from under the covers. Two share a set of vintage wired earbuds. Young love.

I grew up on kilohertz (AM) and megahertz (FM). They're growing up on gigahertz (Wi-Fi).

Maybe it's for the best. In the corner of the Grindhouse, I go about unpacking the neoprene sex suit and strip down, my scrotum tight.

<p>

I put on the gloves, the crotch piece, the goggles. The Wi-Fi connection is slow. A tenant nearby must be siphoning their bandwidth for MT bit torrents. I must look like an alien frogman to the students. Nothing works. The UX and UI are garbage. One of the students gives me a thumbs-up. Early adoption is noble, she says. In five years, that's going to be a collector's item. I give her a thumbs-up.

Barista Tim comes over, sweeping up stray packing peanuts from my suit. Looks like you're having a rough one, he says. Apologies for the Wi-Fi—our provider is throttling us. Maybe this will cheer you up. He slips me a packet of Sea-Monkeys.

Thank you, I say.

Tell @M∅M to pop in next weekend, he says.

<p>

My friend says the worst thing he ever did as a parent was give his kids their phones. I just lost them, he says. And when I took them away as punishment, they went feral.

They're offline and missing out and their fear is unmanageable.

Still at the Grindhouse, the pack of Sea-Monkeys at my elbow, I message you this anecdote. Then ask: When are you coming? You send back a wink emoji, flagging the incidental double entendre.

(10:28:08 PM): When are you coming home?

Moments later, you send me a GIF of a suicide bomber in slo-mo HD. A little loop of his body splitting in half, his face still frozen in an anticipation that is looking past the intermediary state of death and towards the great resurrection. The caption: I SHARTED...

I chuckle. The chuckle rumbles into a hitching laugh in my chest, then rolls to my belly and I laugh uncontrollably hard, my body doubling over. I fall out of my chair; I'm laughing violently. The students turn their devices on me. A frogman flopping on dry land. Tiny stars flare in my vision. I can't breathe.

More stars. I laugh and laugh until my vision is filled with light.

[N S F W]
9

The *f*ace is coming to our office. The Vex office. Our Vex office. This in an encrypted email from HQ.

The office spins and I grip Mr. Ray's old desk.

I'm sickened to my stomach. The *f*ace is coming to our office.

A message window pings. @Jun1p3r.

(10:13:57 PM): My magik is useless against the videographer. He's a technopagan.

You explain: To pre-Christian man, digital technology would look like magik. Symbols containing vast information. Runes. The internet, the astral plane. Communication. Transmission. The mouse, the wand. Silicon, their crystals. The screen, their crystal balls.

(10:14:18PM): Isn't that just rebranding, repackaging?

(10:14:33 PM): Yes and no.

(10:14:58 PM): I don't understand.

(10:15:44 PM): He is using blood and sex magik; rituals as well. It seems contradictory. But there are forces at work here.

(10:15:44 PM): I miss you so much.

(10:16:01 PM): Everything evolves. Energy is intention. I'll need a different weapon.

(10:16:33 PM): @Jun1p3r?

(10:17:11 PM): Are you there?

(10:25:59 PM): Hello…?

<p>

COMING SOON

<p>

Let's say you can go back in time and kill a fascist dictator. Or an American president. The line blurs in this metaphor.

This would be a perfect conversation with @Skiny_Leny, but I've opted to talk out loud in the Garden. The jellyfish listens patiently.

Forget the loop logic and marrying your grandmother. Let's talk mission.

Do you blink in right beside them at dinner at their resort or hamlet or villa? Or are you simply where you are now, but back then? You have to get clothes. You have to get a weapon and you have to get access. Let's say you're from the future now. And have to kill, say, the president of the United States. Good luck with that. You'd have to be able to purchase a sniper rifle.

Okay, you can do that during deer season. You need to know his schedule. Maybe. You have to be able to penetrate the world's (arguably) best security force, where you will be outmanned 100-to-1. You have twenty-four hours. Go. What's your plan?

Yeah, I thought so.

What if you go back to when they're a baby? That might be a little easier. Seventy years ago. Not in this day and age. And then say you do, and you're looking at the mother cooing at her baby on a park bench. Can you pull the trigger? You have twenty-four hours. Go.

<p>

@OrKa motions me over to her desk while the others have an impromptu circle jerk in the conference room. Our eyes lock and I notice the slight color difference in her two eyes. A detail only a lover might notice. She allows me to wade into this intimacy long enough to swim out into their depths.

Then shares her own secret, starting with a conspiratorial whisper: *Möchteb Sie etwas bewirken*?

<p>

Because that baby has done nothing wrong. Can you ID the baby? Can you be certain this is the one? Maybe you strike up a conversation with the mother. You have a knife. Can you do it? How immutable does the future seem in the present? At *this* moment?

But you're unwavering. And then what? What's your escape plan? You can't return until the twenty-four hours are up. Do you wait until the last minute, where you wink out of that timeline, blood splattered, in the midst of her screaming. And then what about buying that tech stock, placing that sports bet or whatever? How do you collect?

No. Time travel is not a practical answer.

I'll have to kill the *f*ace in the present.

[N S F W]
10

The act of creating and tending a bonsai involves meditation and mindfulness, the new preacher says.

<p>

I go back to that church later when you are away. I wanted to talk to that preacher, I think. I'm not sure. He at least has a sense of humor and would probably answer questions I had. That is, if I wasn't keeping him from his writers' group.

But a different man stands in his place. A new face. The previous priest having got the call and is now staffed on a new streaming show.

The different man has a bit of a drawl, and dirt in his voice. He talks of westward expansion and the faith to conquer a new land with self-reliance. And its cost. How it could have been done differently and what we imagine our world would be like today without immigrant labor.

Post-service, the new face wearing vestments heads to his office. I catch a glimpse of him pulling out earplugs, this church's choir an acquired taste. Popping them into a clamshell. He sits at his desk and rolls a crisp sheet of paper into a typewriter. It is a curvy, seafoam-green Hermes 3000 with chrome accents.

It's a dandy, I say, and he welcomes me in.

We chat briefly. He's moved around a lot. Bristled a lot of folks.

Why's that? I say.

I can't prove to you there's a God. Or salvation. That's the faith part. There's a lot of bullshit in the world. The one thing I see faith do in this world is help the devoted cope. Not many church boards want to hear that.

Thank you, Father.

That's all faith is, son, he says, a community and a coping mechanism. As I leave, he says me: What's your favorite thing about her?

She has the roundness of an orange, I say, and the grit of a blueberry.

He tips an imaginary hat.

And yours? I say.

He has a sense of occasion, he says.

I tip my hat.

You're still offline. I reread a week-old chat.

(9:40:03 PM): I push your mouth harder into my neck. Pull your hips closer to mine.

(9:40:23 PM): You feel me harden...

(9:41:24 PM): I place your hand on my thigh, under my dress.

(9:41:35 PM): Warm, so warm.

(9:41:59 PM): I buck slightly as you bite harder on my neck.

(9:42:35 PM): I want you to draw blood. To drink me. To swallow my life, to die in your embrace.

My body stays offline.

<p>

Before I go, the cowboy preacher hands me a card. There's a square dance tonight, he says. I play the fiddle and my partner plays the mandolin.

I flick the card, a Mr. Ray mannerism. I can't leave the aquarium twice in one day, I say. I have to tend to the jellyfish.

He smiles. It's always something.

That night, I pick up a small turntable with a built-in speaker. And two-dollar records. I play Hank Williams' *My Bucket's Got a Hole in It*. As I attend to the jellyfish, my feet do a little do-si-do.

[N S F W]
11

I empty the packet of Sea-Monkeys from Barista Tim into the aquarium. On the package they are depicted as friendly cartoons. Mother, father, brother, sister.

"Own a BOWLFUL OF HAPPINESS—*Instant PETS!*"

<p>

The jellyfish tentacles have snared each one by the time I finish the high-school years in the *f*ace's biography. I can see them digesting in each of the monster's stomachs. One per translucent chamber. Dissolving in sight of each other. Until they are extinct.

<p>

Booth. Oswald. Princip. Guiteau. @Sa>ag3.

<p>

I look at the plants surrounding me. Perhaps I can concoct an herbal poison. I put the biography down. WW@Jun1p3rD?

<p>

Your messenger box is dark. @Jun1p3r is *offline.*

<p>

Thoughts connect.

<p>

Anaphylactic shock. Folks living in fear of this carry EpiPens.

<p>

I take a one-day knife-defense class. Judo, I think. They all teach the same thing: run or prepare to get cut.

[N S F W]
12

I'm meeting the ƒace tomorrow at the office. Or rather, he is meeting me.

<p>

Another box arrives. A 20 lb weighted blanket. To simulate the womb. It smells like you, my @Jun1p3r.

<p>

You've missed our nightly chats. So many nights now. Energy is intention. I'm tempted to reach out to your coven, but I don't know how.

<p>

#FREEDOM_IS_SLAVERY

<p>

Rumination is a sign of moderate depression. The thing they don't tell you is how comforting depression is. How normalizing it is. Until it's not.

<p>

David Scott Hay

Where the fuck are the benefits? The novelty of the ƒŌnes slipping to a cracked crown, chronic fatigue, and carpal tunnel.

<p>

I wake up on the sod, fetal. My nose wrinkles. The smell of death in my nostrils. Pungent. Repulsive. I choke on my own breath. The cadaver plant has flowered.

NODE V

"Thus, strangely are our souls constructed, and by slight ligaments are we bound to prosperity or ruin."

—Mary Wollstonecraft Shelley
Frankenstein; or, The Modern Prometheus

[N S F W]
1

Shin Kubota.

My feet on the grass in the living room. I'm naked sitting on the half whiskey barrel. I wonder if it has taken root, this barrel. The potted plants and potted trees surround me, exhaling as I inhale. Inhaling as I exhale. The plastic tarps drip with condensation, a constant reminder of my bubble.

Even the jellyfish tank has fogged over. It and the brine shrimp talk to me through the bubbling filtration systems. My stomach also bubbles. Naked, I go to the hatchery. Tap a shot glass full of salty brine shrimp. I do not strain it.

I down the tiny shrimp in one gulp.

I pour another shot of shrimp and feed the jellyfish. The Sea-Monkey family an *amuse-bouche*.

You're so lucky, I say out loud. The weather forecast calls for more civil unrest. Now let's get to work. I prepare the thermos with saline water.

The clerk at the aquarium store sells me a fishbowl. The assistant manager and a newbie board up the windows. Between the hammering and drilling, the clerk asks where you are, Where's @Jun1p3r? Are we still a thing, she wants to know.

We're all still things, I say.

On impulse, I buy an azure background for the fishbowl. She smiles at the upsale.

<p>

We're pioneers, the *f*ace says. Making the world a better place. He has made it to Vex, despite the gathering mass of protesters. The drone pad must have strained under his private helo.

A world that needs self-editing, I say.

He doesn't perceive it as a slight. AI will handle the bulk soon enough, he says.

Bulk of what?

Everything.

The *f*ace speaks to us as we stand in a circle. Our pod and this outsider. The last time we stood like this was @Babyd011's memorial circle. I don't think the *f*ace realizes he's just told us what will replace us at our jobs. No one protests.

@Skiny_Leny, business plan tucked under his arm, looks for an opportunity to pitch.

The *f*ace asks questions. A mental checklist.

Do you like it here?

Do you like working here?

What would you change?

Do you feel inspired?

Do you get angry or frustrated?

What do you like?

Do you feel you are contributing?

That you are fairly compensated?

Where do you envision yourself in five years?

We give perfunctory answers. We want the dead back, no one says.

You should invest in our cryptocurrency, the *f*ace says, looking at @Skiny_Leny, his eyes clocking the bare patch of scalp dipping below his hat.

We can't afford investments. Vexillum is a subcontractor, I say. Our perks include therapy coupons and coffee drinks. We don't have access to crypto, health insurance. Day care. Job protection.

His eyes blink, not computing.

This is a gig. We're temps, I say. We don't work for you. Directly, that is.

Oh, the *f*ace says. Buffering through a mental maze of legal connections, both public and private. Hmmm. Then: Thank you for your service.

You have met your numbers, he says. It is not an easy number. You have shown us what is possible. I applaud your courage. The ƒace hands us biodegradable envelopes. Our bonus checks.

Mr. Ray was a good manager, I say.

The door to Vex opens and Barista Tim strolls in with a tray of Cherry Maca Mochas. It is Tuesday. Special delivery, he says with a wink to @MØM. She blushes, red creeping up her scoop neckline.

The ƒace's security team hold him at arm's length. Ex-football-player style.

He's one of us, I say.

Barista Tim passes out the drinks. I demur and the head of the security team takes mine. Tasty.

Oh, the ƒace says. Yes. Mr. Ray. Yes. He looks at me. Congrats to you all, he says. He waits for @OrKa to get off her desk-bike. She does not. Awkwardly he slips her envelope next to her. Clears his throat and waits a moment for her to acknowledge him while we peek at the checks. It is more than my parents made in their most productive year combined.

Is it more real as a check, I wonder. Does he curry favor by handing it out instead of direct deposit? US$ instead of crypto. I flick the check. Tangible. I've earned this.

I double glance at the check. It's issued by their own bank, ƒbank.

The *f* is for freedom, the *f*ace says.

@OrKa pedals on. As he turns, she looks at him with a single glance. The glance is loaded with contempt.

Okay, folks. Happy Tuesday, Barista Tim says. Oh, he says to the *f*ace and hands him a legal-sized envelope.

Oh. The *f*ace takes it with curiosity.

You've been served, Barista Tim says to the *f*ace, and then tells us the Grindhouse will start serving an Easter eggnog coffee concoction next month.

The *f*ace scans the paperwork. Oh. Hmmm.

Keep grinding, Barista Tim says. @MØM walks him to the elevator with her dancer's gait.

@Skiny_Leny loses his nerve and hands his business pitch to me. *Please*, his eyes say.

I've never seen anyone be served a subpoena before. Especially one from Congress.

The *f*ace looks up at me as an afterthought. A word in private, he says.

<p>

#BulletinoftheAtomicScientists

<p>

You have five minutes, the *f*ace's security team announces. Things are getting dicey outside. Have I written about this already? Have I told you how the *f*ace

~ 309 ~

had my letter in hand as he walked up to me? Just at the edge of my personal space.

The social engagement continues in my office. A private chat.

I didn't see you on our platform.

I was being stalked.

Didn't you block them?

They're persistent.

Can you handle it?

A vein on his broad forehead throbs. We both stand awkwardly, each with a manila envelope under our arms. His, the subpoena; mine, @Skiny_Leny's unicorn egg.

The *f*ace offers me water. Even though it is my office.

Then a place to sit. As if he's jumbled up the social-pleasantries script in his head. Your letter got me thinking, he says. It was typed, yes, on a typing machine?

I nod.

It got me contemplative. About myths and legends. Eras and epochs. The rise of man. From sea to stars.

I blink.

He blinks. Buffering. Appropriate responses loading. About where we have come from, he says, and where we are heading. What our actual potential is.

For a moment it seems as if he is considering trading his microscope in for a telescope.

There's a loud crash outside, down below in the street. The natives are getting restless. I doubt @Skiny_Leny is making a joke about a moving truck.

He adjusts his body temperature with a tug of his hoodie zipper.

Perhaps you'd like to work for me, the *f*ace says. Full-time.

‹p›

Senator Hurt wants to introduce a bill giving the nation free Wi-Fi. New devices. And mandatory connectivity. Analytics to build a better national defense. Security. A better nation. A better UX.

The new Wi-Fi network is being built in China. Why are we purchasing the spider's web from the spider? The *f*ace tells me this. Something bubbles behind his eyes.

The congressional hearing is to take place in the spring. Once the cold has subsided. After all the spring-break vacations with their families. All the trips to foreign beaches.

He asks more questions: what do you think the users would do if they knew how many lynchings really happen a year? How many plots are foiled? What is really in the drinking water? What man is capable of doing for an audience?

I feel he is reciting discarded copy from his THIN DIGITAL LINE speech. I think of Vex. Our pod. The sex. The drugs. Our Garden. The rituals. They'd cope, I say.

He buffers. But would they continue to use the platform?

The *f*ace stares at the poster of *The Aquarist.* Oh. That stratostation there, he says, the artist's rendering is remarkably accurate to similar projects in our R&D. The tether. The bubble dome. I love these old covers. Did you know the author was executed for heterodoxy? Heresy? Profanity? Sacrilege?

He's glitching on a word. Then moves on.

This book was banned in Russia for many years, the *f*ace says. Tarkovsky wanted to make it his next film project after *Stalker*, but passed away shortly thereafter. Cancer. The results of filming a masterpiece in a nuclear zone. Have you read it—do you know what it's about?

Now, I said.

I place @Skiny_Leny's business-pitch envelope on my desk. Next to the fishbowl.

He pauses thoughtfully. But can't connect the dots. Maybe we will option the film rights, the *f*ace says. We are starting a new production company, the *f*ace says and points to the fishbowl. Is that a *f*Ōne?

@Jun1p3r's *f*Ōne sits at the bottom of the fishbowl. Submerged. The jellyfish hovers over it. With a blue background, it is an invisible monster.

It is, I say.

How long has it been submerged?

A week, I say. Since we got it. He walks near it. We change places, walking past each other as if our movement belongs to actors on a stage.

I stare at the painting, tapping my chin as though I am in an art gallery and being observed. I have no idea if it will still work, I say, indicating the *f*Ōne. My hand trembles against my chin. His movements reflect in the framed glass.

I hear a tiny splash and an *oh oh oh.*

The *f*ace looks at his hand with a tilted head. The *f*Ōne leans against the inside of the fishbowl, askew. Droplets of water blossom on the desk. The jellyfish hangs on his hand, dangling by its tentacles. A distorted mirror image of his hand.

Oh. Oh.

He looks up at me.

Oh. Oh.

I stare at him.

Oh. Oh.

He flicks his hand. The jellyfish slides off his hand and plops back into the fishbowl. A few tentacles still dangle from his fingertips. He flicks them and they wrap around the back of his hand. More venom is released.

Oh o—

Color drains from his broad face. He blinks. He holds his hand out, staring at the red welts as they pulse. His other hand goes to his heart. Then to his hoodie pocket.

His EpiPen.

The *f*ace is allergic to shellfish. You can learn so much from an unauthorized biography.

Let me help, I say and take the EpiPen from him, @Skiny_Leny's business plan forgotten. No judo moves necessary. Are you in distress, I say. Answer me. His throat bulges and no air comes out. Are you in distress, I say to the pale face.

Do you need me to administer this shot, I say. His hand on my arm. Do I stick you with this end, I say and drop the EpiPen. Oh no, I say, I fumbled it. I remove his hand from my arm, scratching it. A white harvest of his skin under my nail.

The *f*ace stares at his hand. The red lashes of prehistoric death. Another epoch. Face to face. Our eyes lock. His mouth forms an O, puckering like a fish.

The leg or the arm, I say? I've never used one. I stumble-kick the EpiPen under the desk. I'm useless in a crisis, I mutter. Please tell me. I say it softy to the *f*ace. The jellyfish knows the script. The same lines rehearsed countless times in the Garden.

Then he keels over. With a loud thump.

@Skiny_Leny looks at his bonus check and rethinks his business plan. One of the Twins talks about Vegas. The other about starting a no-kill animal shelter. We've talked about a tiny house by the lake. Maybe a river. @H₁pp3 would have built an Earthship or started a scholarship fund. Those can be tricky, everyone agrees.

But @MØM looks at her bonus and worries everyone is going to quit their job. And then where will she go?

His security team barges into the office.

He dropped his EpiPen, I say. I can't find it. A tear even manages to slide down my cheek. It does because I know I have failed.

They tear off his hoodie. Strange rune and symbol tattoos cover his arms, a calculus of protection. They stab him with another EpiPen, even as his heart stops. They begin CPR. I do not volunteer the location of the office AED. But they are certified EMTs and he will live.

Booth. Oswald. Princip. Guiteau. @Sa>ag3.

History will not remember my name. I will not join the list of infamous assassins.

David Scott Hay

@MØM needn't worry. We will all arrive early on Wednesday. Hump Day. The *f*ace's near-death by jellyfish will not make anyone's feed.

[N S F W]
2

The door buzzer rings in the Garden. A loud old-school alarm that rattles the hatchery and the jellyfish tank.

I become momentarily disoriented as I cannot find the door in all the dripping plastic. I use the aquarium, the bonsai, and the sunlamp to triangulate my position in the Garden. I find the doorknob poking against the plastic. But I cannot find an access slit.

The door rattles again and again. I take a box cutter and cut a slit. I'll fashion a patch later. I open the door.

You look like a person waiting for something important to happen, you say.

<p>

I had offered you a key once. You declined. I would never presume the assumption of my company, you had said.

<p>

You drop your bags and you jump into my arms. Your cold clothing a shock against my naked body.

I rip open your outer skin, like the first time. Buttons fly, zippers jam as you join the fray. We do not make love on the grass. We are not quiet or gentle or civilized.

The downstairs neighbor is home. But does not disturb us. Certain things have to run their course.

<p>

As we catch our breath, you wrap yourself around my leg, breathing in my ear. My fist in your hair. Your thighs clench and unclench with aftershocks. You tremble and are still, drifting away into slumber.

My fist won't open.

Afterwards you say, You're not on your meds, are you?

<p>

In the glow of the jellyfish, you say, That man, that videographer who did those things. He'll never do it again.

You have succeeded in your mission. I have failed at mine. I stroke your hair. New silver strands glint pinkish in the light. The hatchery hums. I soothe you.

I fear what I did to you, you say. The Rule of Three. I haven't spoken to the coven and I could justify it. But the backlash could be horrific.

I don't want you to leave our Garden. We're just getting started, I say.

I can leave you and you'll find peace, you say.

I pull you closer. But I already have, I say.

We're not blood bound, you say.

I wish we were, I say. I want to commit to something in this ever-shifting world.

You dig up the piercing kit from the closet. The mushrooms have escaped the bin and now line the closet walls. Several things thrive in darkness.

<p>

I pluck the cadaver flower and tuck it behind your left ear. I missed this face, you say, knife in hand. I hold up my hand, palm out. An offering. You take it, speaking in ancient tongues. My head goes light. And by the pricking of our thumbs, we are bound.

<p>

Now what do we do?

[N S F W]
3

We do a double feature at the revival theatre. *The Blob* and the remake. We take the jellyfish. We do this so it will not feel left out. Both times we side with the blob, booing a young Bullitt and a Drugstore Cowboy's little brother, and cheering its oozy kills.

In the original 1958 version the blob comes from space, an extraterrestrial. In the 1988 remake, it's a government experiment gone amok.

We leave before the end of the first movie. The remake seemingly hitting too close to home.

I cradle the clear thermos. The jellyfish almost invisible. Small buds are already forming, regenerating the tentacles torn on the *f*ace's hand. How does it feel, this revisionist tale, I ask, turning you from one of God's children into a scientist's experiment? It bobs and coos in my ear.

You laugh.

<p>

Creature to monster.

Outside the theatre, I see that white cargo van from our first date. I stop. Your lip trembles. You tell me it's okay. Your hand finds my shoulder. But your hand's shaking.

It's okay, I say and remove your hand. I hand you the thermos. I can feel my head tilt like a curious dog's as I walk slowly towards it. I touch it. I lean and listen. I move to the front and peer into the window. Blinds separate the front from the cargo area. The blinds are a tartan color. I recognize the pattern. It dawns on me.

I think this is @Skiny_Leny's van.

LSD death run. The van is sluggish and threatens to roll, drifting towards the guardrails on the right-hand curves. I'm pressing the van to her limits. One hand on the wheel, the other on a thigh.

A country assassinates the leader of another. That country does a small, ineffective counterpunch. The country, fearing reprisal from their meager retribution, gets on edge. Shoots down a civilian jetliner that wiggled its wings. 200+ souls. Who fired the first shot? The original aggressive country's government gives contradictory explanations for their initial killing on a foreign land.

What if Lovecraft was right?

\<p\>

In the van, @Skiny_Leny and @Jun1p3r and the baby and me. Parked at the harbor.

Star lights glimmer around the van. All three of us lay out on the foam bed.

We are the only life—*period*—in the universe, @Skiny_Leny says. But not with his normal confrontational edge. Carl Sagan says it's a lot of wasted space, if so. But think about it: of the entire universe after the Big Bang, *this* planet, this is the only one that grew into the Beatles. Into language, into sentient beings. The *only* one.

The rest of the cosmos, every universe, and there are millions, every solar system, every planet, we are *it*. That's how many rolls of the dice, that's how many chances it takes to get just *one* with life. To get us. It's like how much coal and time and pressure it takes to get an uncut diamond.

Just one, he says.

I think of the Chicxulub asteroid. The final ingredient.

Just us, he says. That's how special we all are. And when we fuck it all up, that's it. There is no Plan B. That's how special life is. He takes another toke. What's your jellyfish's name?

I kiss him.

@Skiny_Leny lives in his van. Got arrested for passing counterfeit twenties. I wear a LoJax, he says. It's an implant. Can only leave for work. But since I live in my van, they can't do much.

Why don't you just head for a warmer climate?

He shrugs. I like my job. I like the people I work with.

Black ice is clear and forms on roadways, rendering it nearly invisible.

We've made love, us three. I lay spread-eagle on the van's bed. Marveling at the LED star lights hanging down. The universe in miniature. @Skiny_Leny slips on a pair of sweats with embroidered monarch butterflies. And catwalks up to the passenger seat and starts chatting with you as you roll a nightcap.

He cracks a window and a blade of chill air off the lake cuts through the van. The glowing lights strung along the ceiling are tiny and provide no illumination, just sparks of firefly light. The chill air is the vacuum of space; I am traveling in a starship. Survivors of a society that has eaten itself. I am traveling through space. We have provisions, each other, and the will to live. We will find another planet and do it right this time. We'll send a postcard to @H₁pp3. To @Babyd011. She'll think it amazing.

The cold shifts and lake-effect snow blows across LSD. I think of @Babyd011 alone in the park, slumped against an oak. Maybe it was a maple. A tree as old as the city itself. What she saw. Still clutching her Cherry Maca Mocha. I think of her walking out to get fresh air. I didn't say anything. She would be back. We all came back.

Until we didn't.

It broke her spirit. It broke her and she recognized it and she said to herself: *this is where I get off.* And she found a quiet peaceful place. A park. And she listened to the wind in the trees. The distant-city-sounds background. She found her peace.

And in the dead of winter, she headed for the Summerland.

[N S F W]
4

Everything in its right place.

For a few miles.

A hundred-thousand-dollar vehicle driven by Van Lifers distracted by their devices clips ours as LSD bends away from the city. Black ice ensures reflexes are useless. Until impact, you are behind the wheel.

<p>

The Jaws of Life appear as a surprise guest star for the Van Lifers' final livestream. For every Good Samaritan there are a dozen devices blinking red. Media outlets pay extra for bodies.

<p>

@Skiny_Leny gets a souvenir head plate and an erratic line of staples. Half his head shaved. Per his wishes, the hair is donated to an organization that makes wigs from human hair for cancer patients. After the blood is washed from it.

You and I are treated and released at the scene. Bumps, bruises. Dharma, karma. Our jellyfish intact under the driver's seat. Shaken, but not stirred. The van limps back to the Garden, a shudder in the front axle; you refuse to yield the wheel.

<p>

#Turritopsis_dohrnii

<p>

When he is released, we bring @Skiny_Leny back to Vex, back to the pod. He doesn't remember the accident.

In the office, the smell of disinfectant stings our noses. It's chemical, man-made and foreign to my sense of smell after a weekend convalescing in the Garden. Everything is clean. The dust bunnies under the lip of my recycling can are gone. The abandoned Post-it notes @Skiny_Leny put under everyone's desk chairs. I find one wedged up under @Babyd011's chair, which sits now in the corner with her jacket draped on the back. Tall candles and carnations surround it. Our own memorial.

It's as if everything has been replaced with an exact duplicate. Are the walls a different shade? you say.

In this early winter light, it's hard to tell. The walls are not tacky to my touch. And there is only the faintest odor of new paint. As if the office spaces next door have been painted and carpeted for new tenants.

I flip on the office light to Mr. Ray's office. I still consider it his even though I know I'm in command. I still feel like any moment an authority figure will come relieve me from duty; always the second, always the backup, always the adviser, the Hand of the King. @Sa>ag3 can figure it out. I wonder how long I've felt like I was walking in the shadow of a thing larger than myself. Is that how Mr. Ray felt growing up in the shadow of *The Aquarist of Ganymede*?

#MoonArkProject

The lights flicker and buzz atmospherically. I blink my eyes, adjusting to the artifice. The A/C kicks on. I wonder what additions to the ventilation system have been made. Are there new circuit boards and routers and servers? Are there new arteries and veins pumping alien information into a new head? A new heart?

Through stinging eyes, I scan the room. Right in front of that oak desk, I attempted murder. Murder by jellyfish. The grain of the office carpet lies to the north instead of west. It too has been replaced. Where I can imagine the chalk outline of the *f*ace, the water stain is still there, but the shape of Idaho has become Arizona. Or Oklahoma. What does it matter? All the forensics have changed.

Paranoia will destroy ya.

A yelp and clapping draw me out of the office. @MØM sings a light cabaret tune and sways her hips with a Welcome Back sheet cake held out like the cigarette girl's tray on the back of my grandpa's playing cards. @MØM catches my look of concern. I paid for it out of petty cash, she says. As if my look was concerned with cake and not reality.

A loose ball cap hides all but the tail of the stapled wound that zags down @Skiny's scalp. Just a headache and haircut, he tells @MØM, adjusting his crutches as she croons.

One of the Twins offers his condolences to @Skiny_Leny regarding his half-shorn hair.

Business on the left, party on the right, @Skiny_Leny says.

Later, a sexual favor for go pills is exchanged in a bathroom stall as I stand solo at a urinal.

Before @Skiny_Leny can acknowledge the Twin, your arms drape around @Skiny's neck and you whisper for absolution even as your tears drop down his neck. His eyes meet mine. Longing and forgiveness.

@MØM's mouth curls with an edge of jealousy. An intern I don't recognize starts to sing "Happy Birthday."

‹p›

A news GoDrone buzzes the building. Slows. Moves on.

[N S F W]
5

My aunt won't let my uncle watch R-rated movies. He'll never see *Cinema Paradiso*. *The Butterfly and the Diving Bell*. My poor uncle who has his open carry permit. A .45 strapped to diabetic hip. Grocery store. IHOP. PG-13 movies. My uncle carrying a firearm and relegated to watching cartoonish depictions of violence. My aunt the true law west of the Pecos.

At my usual urinal, I tell the shaggy Twin this, as if I'm talking to Mr. Ray. It's odd not having him piss on my right anymore. This as @Skiny_Leny thumbs down the front of his yoga pants at the urinal to my left.

You know we slaughtered the Chinese once they helped us build the railroads, @Skiny_Leny says. Mass graves out in New Mexico. He's trying to pick a fight, but his heart isn't in it.

That's why they're slowly buying us, the Twin says. They want to reclaim their dead.

The Twin and @Skiny_Leny politely debate whether or not crypto or the return to the gold standard constitutes a better personal firewall against China's hostile takeover. The Twin's bet is on food and ammo. Then the Twin asks @Skiny_Leny about go pills.

<p>

@MØM snorts Cherry Maca Mocha out of her nose. We go to her video. A little boy is pushing his baby brother in a stroller. It hits a rock and the stroller dumps the baby headfirst onto the sidewalk.

The pod laughs. A bit strained, bracing. My stomach cringes as @MØM laughs again.

Oh, he's okay, you can see there are no obvious cracks in the glabella or coronal suture or frontal bone. And now, watch this. The boy picks up his brother. A little girl runs up in a red wagon and they put the baby in it and rush off, the boy making a foreign siren sound.

Isn't that the most adorable thing?

I FLAG it and walk away.

<p>

Science advances quicker if it enhances bread and circus. If it takes sacrifice, progress is slower.

Except for the Manhattan Project, you say.

Or the moonshot.

Yes, we compressed a decade of R&D into a few years. Twenty-four-hour shifts, food and lodging for the best and the brightest to end the Great War. Just a decade to leave the planet. Then it became normalized. Can you name the last person to walk on the moon?

We could do the same for cancer and homelessness.

But neither is in the interest of national security.

And cancer is a 200-billion-dollar industry.

Companies are racing to create a cure for hair loss. In subscription-pill form. That's the golden goose, @Skiny_Leny says, testing his new hairline of staples with a pawn from his mini magnetic chess set. His statements lack conviction these days. As if he's a touring band performing their one hit for a drunken middle-age crowd. He tries to see the pawn stuck to the staple with a compact mirror, but it slips through his hands and cracks on the edge of his chair. I start to make a joke about him neglecting to use a screen protector. But I see he is genuinely upset. It was @Babyd011's compact. A gift.

Already my memories of her are fading. Did she have a mole on her left breast or right? I clear the rumination with a practiced deep breath. Jews cover the mirrors in mourning for seven days, I say. They say it's because ghosts can carry away souls into the reflection never to find peace. Or that the deceased can enter the physical world through the mirror and seek retribution.

But I believe it's for protection from accidental breakage, I say. No one wants to remember Uncle Saul's funeral as the start of a bad streak.

@Skiny_Leny laughs. Appreciates the levity.

<p>

His cock pushes past my hesitant lips.

<p>

It started with the Greeks and Romans, @Skiny_Leny says. In Europe it's a common superstition. Even the Irish Catholics still do it. Heard of an Irish wake?

I just thought that meant folks got shit-faced at a bar and told stories about the deceased, I say.

That too, he says. But they still cover their mirrors.

<p>

He fills my mouth with his pulse. I milk him, swallowing per your direction. You watch with stolen glances in the van's rearview mirror. Harbor lights blending with buoy lights. Star lights blending with streetlights.

<p>

Speaking of Romans, @Skiny_Leny says, and starts talking about their belief in a seven-year soul cycle. I start to wonder if we have talked about my seven-year cell replacement issue, but I'm distracted by a video of two teenagers stabbing each other. I flag it for copyright violation. It's a scene from a movie. One of the actors is Shakespearean-trained and will have a hit movie where he gets into a farting contest with an imaginary dog.

<p>

The soft pop as I enter him. Making a fist in his hair, pulling like the reins of a horse, riding him. The van fills with our moans. You, one hand on the wheel, the other digging into your damp panties. As the road hums under the van's tires. City lights blending with headlights.

Then oncoming headlights.

Make 'em laugh, make 'em laugh, make 'em laugh.

I look over at you, my @Jun1p3r. Headphones on, swaying to an unknown beat, while watching gay Muslims in wheelchairs being pushed off roofs by other gay Muslims proving their masculinity.

My heart swells.

Meanwhile, @Skiny says, my biggest thrill? Working here.

I nod. Now you're looking at acid face victims.

I love you.

@MØM comes and reminds us that it's time for the *Mt. Rushmore* conclusion.

I throw it up on Mother/Screen. @OrKa apologizes for her squeaky desk-bike, but it doesn't even register. The desk-bike, not @OrKa. Out of the corner of my eye, she looks like @Babyd011.

On Mother/Screen, the reluctant brown-faced terrorist brother pisses on what he thinks is his brown-faced brother's Koran, but is quickly revealed to be his own *Martha Stewart's Dinner at Home: 52 Quick Meals to Cook for Family and Friends.* He becomes apoplectic. There is a knock at their apartment door. Then the feed cuts to black:

C O M I N G NOW

[N S F W]
6

All the workstation monitors go black. Yours reboots first, another upgrade from @Orka.

Possible school shooting, you call out. Live feed confirmation is glitching.

I've been walking around like a teacher supervising test-taking students. Hands clasped behind my back. The fob dangling around my neck. I've ironed my jumpsuit by pressing it between thrift-store encyclopedias. I stroll over to your desk. The shooting is first-person POV. Looks like a video game, I say.

One of the Twins, the one keeping it highand tight, leans over.

Is this game footage? I say.

Negative, he says. Frame rate is wrong. But that's an AR-15 with high-capacity magazines. Nice grouping. He can tell this by the holes in a campus security guard.

Where is this happening? It becomes a guessing game.

The first school shooting took place in 1764, @Skiny_Leny says. A group of Native Americans shot and scalped a teacher. Killed almost a dozen students.

Is this archival footage? I ask. Columbine? Virginia Tech? Parkland? Sandy Hook? Parkland? Santa Fe? Santa Clarita? Buffalo? Uvalde? Izhevsk? It could be footage from a hundred shootings.

I roll the fob between my fingers like a poker player with his last chip.

Clothes are too current for any of those, @MØM says, peeking over my shoulder. That's from the Johnny Simonetta fall collection. @MØM has learned a lot from @Babyd011. It's not an inner-city school. Probably not even public. Most likely private, @MØM says.

Do we have a location? I ask you. Give me a metadata read.

It's blank, you say. No metadata.

Movie? I ask @Skiny_Leny.

None that I recognize, @Skiny_Leny says. He picks nervously at a staple in his head. Newest vehicles are this year's model, he says. Domestic, with the steering wheel on the left side. It is not archival.

Your voice is strong, even without software verification: *This is a live feed.*

Do it, I say.

Sixteen million watched news coverage of 9/11.

Three quarters of all TV viewers. This before streaming. Before the social media explosion. Before smart devices.

<p>

You mash the red panic button on your desk. The pod snaps to attention. All business.

The feed kicks up to Mother/Screen. Workstation monitors come back online and minimize sophomorically bad choices captured from YouTube and replace them with predictive metadata and animated infographics powered by algorithm equalizers.

This video is the only one that matters. Chairs swivel, eyes glancing between Mother/Screen, desk displays, and me.

It's my decision alone.

Do I kill the feed? The fob feels light in my fingers, heavy around my neck.

I take a deep breath. Let's figure it out, I say.

<p>

@Skiny_Leny hands out Adderall. @OrKa's wheel squeaks quicken.

<p>

On Mother/Screen, a clock tower flashes in the foreground. But I know it's not the University of Texas. I know it's not 1966. It's a religious university or prep school. Selling the business acumen of the Pharisees wrapped in an American Jesus costume. The clock tower is an hour ahead of us. That gives us a time zone. Per the training, one of the Twins confirms our 70-second delay synced to the NIST's clock.

IRL.

IRT.

In 70 seconds, the world will be privy to this horrific livestream. We are the thin digital line.

Give me a ten-second-interval countdown to Live Feed Event propagation, I say.

<p>

Live feed from San Antonio.

Everyone's head turns to the German accent. It's @OrKa. She's running her own software on a third laptop. She bypasses the audio input from her earbuds for a moment. A group of tourists scream from her laptop. It sounds fake, but littered with real screams.

I can tell the difference now. My adrenals are pumping, but a part of me believes this is a hoax, even as they fall off the River Walk and splash into the shallow water that winds through downtown. Beer-ritas create inky clouds like frightened squid.

Designate shooter one: *Adam*, I say. Shooter two: *Bravo*. I wish @Skiny had handed out alprazolam.

The Twin calls out: *T-60 seconds to Live Feed Event propagation.*

Another window blossoms on her laptop. Louisville, Kentucky, @OrKa says.

A third shooter.

Kick it up, I say, and now Mother/Screen displays three shootings in three cities at three different settings: A college campus. A tourist strip. An arts district.

Designate third shooter as *Charlie*, I say.

@Skiny_Leny, who has interned at a local news station in the sports department, says, this looks like a live production. A 2nd unit follow-the-ball style.

Adam: the POV of the gunman races across the campus on foot. He reloads as he does. Covering fire crackles in the background. Automatic weapons. Muted like real life. Not sweetened for THX.

Multiple students go from run to crawl to still.

A trio of would-be Christian student athlete heroes armed with devices charge *Adam*. One, two, three, they go down as *Adam* reloads. *Adam* is not a lone wolf. He has backup. Multiple shooters. Any movement by the wounded is arrested by another three-shot burst.

T-50 seconds.

They must all be background extras, I say. Stunt performers.

We have blood, you say.

Do I kill the feed?

Nothing on this scale, the cleanup and reset, @Skiny_Leny says. This is a one-take only.

My fingers tighten and release on the fob, but not the kill button. Could be squibs, I muse.

More windows blossom on @OrKa's feed.

She's calling out locations, a new one every few seconds, pinning them on Mother/Screen. Los Angeles... Seattle... Laramie... Oklahoma City... Tulsa... All mass shootings. It's like a string of firecrackers across the Lower 48. A long-burning fuse, expertly rigged.

Eleven UHD video feeds become a stress test. Mother/Screen glitches momentarily.

T-40 seconds.

One of the Twins begins to quote live-feed specs from a dusty manual. A server overheating. We need more power, more bandwidth, more this and that.

I sequence the monitors to feed from West Coast to East Coast. Designate: *Echo, Foxtrot, Golf, Hotel, India, Juliet, Kilo, Lima, Mike, November.*

An explosion. A community center collapses into rubble. A dust cloud choking vision and breath. Clouds of sickly green and yellow begin to roll down the main street of the president's hometown. An ethereal blob absorbing citizens. Melodramatic screams become the echoes of PTSD.

They glance to me.

It's a hoax, I say. It has to be.

Like ORMAC training for the mass casualty incidences. Like Quantum Grammar. Like maritime law. The moon landing. The flat earth. Chemtrails.

@OrKa's wheel squeaks merge into an ominous tone, a flatline.

Do people need to see history in order to believe? Should I sweep this under the electronic rug? My finger trembles over the fob's switch.

It's bigger, this event. It is history happening now.

I think of *The Mercury Theatre on the Air*. Their little radio play in 1938. The panic. The legend of the panic. The legends of panics. 1975, 1981, 1989, 2001, 2008, 2021, 2026.

Now.

T-30 seconds Live Feed Event propagation.

Finger hovering, grasping the fob like a crucifix and hearing my dad's voice talking about pearl-clutching.

You at my arm. You've left your workstation post.

Is this real? Has it gone live?

The clock is ticking.

My brain slows everything down. Rendering everything in a visual clarity that my intellect cannot yet grasp.

I've got visual on HD cameras, @Skiny_Leny says. Red Ones. Dragons. All digital. Dolly tracks.

Does not compute.

Adam's POV camera catches another shooter running beside him. His weapon mounted on his back, an exoskeleton, with a large weapon on an arm extending in front of him.

But it's not a weapon.

That's a Steadicam, @Skiny_Leny says. They're streaming everything.

T-20 seconds.

They have multiple cameras. In multiple cities. A person is directing this like a live-action sports event. Close-ups, crowd reaction, wide shot. GoDrone shots. Car rigs. It's terrorism with a budget and cinematography.

There must be mics planted everywhere. @Skiny_Leny explains it's probably a mix of hypercardioid shotgun mics and parabolic mics tuned to various predetermined sweet spots. Wireless transmitters. Sound pack, and a location field mixer. Maybe even a few ambisonics.

The sound is not flawless, field mixing its own art, but there are terrifying moments of crystal clarity. We've all heard the sounds before. The flow of the images defies Eisenstein's theory of montage. A shot is held long enough to get orientated before cutting to a new shot, but they all flow together. Cause and effect.

T-15 seconds.

This can't be right. My brain fighting what can be real and what can be fake. It's one or the other. None of the extras get back up. None of the people on fire are extinguished. A school bus is hosed with lead. No more pencils. No more books. No more teacher's dirty looks.

No one calls CUT. Just more ACTION.

It can't be real. This has to be a mistake. A movie. A hoax. Anything other than real. Everyone looks to me and the fob.

Instant messages coming in from other Vex offices, a Twin says. They all say the same: They are requesting assistance. None of their kill switches are working.

You glance at a power graph. Our kill fob is charged and synched, you report. System signal strong.

A news helicopter loses a tail rotor, goes down in a crowd of gawkers. Metal shreds, bodies pulp. A yawn any other day, but now spectacular. The pod gasps.

Pull up the Big Three and the Big Two, I say. Plus, PBS.

Mother/Screen goes black.

Pull it up, I bark.

That's it, sir, a Twin says. None of the national three broadcasting stations are on air. The two big cable news channels, ideologically opposed, show the same placeholder: ONE MOMENT PLEASE. They are dark.

Freedom of information.

Freedom from information.

OKC.

9/11.

1/6.

The Hack.

War of the Worlds.

Restore the feed to Mother/Screen, I say. We watch the horror in 4K.

The fob feels like a grenade in my hand. Sweat stings my eyes.

What thing of beauty is formed from regret?

Will all this footage come back to us down the road? Will my pod spend the rest of their careers flagging this footage over and over, being overwhelmed a thousandfold? Not only this footage, but those that livestream their dying words to loved ones.

What would Mr. Ray do?

@Skiny_Leny under his breath, *it's beautiful.* Finally, cinema and scale converging. @OrKa's wheel squeaks faster, higher peaking in a solid tone. My tinnitus activates its old scream.

And now I understand. I take the fob from my neck, dangle it from my hand.

The by-the-book Twin protests. Your fob, sir.

T-5 seconds.

Five seconds and the genie is out of the bottle. On Mother/Screen, a yellow cloud blooms. It is not tear gas. Would-be livestreamers lose their bowels and weep blood. Birds fall from trees. I can't keep track of the cities. Let alone the dead.

You and I hold hands. The thin digital line.

T-2 seconds.

Noted, I say curtly.

He defers to my authority per his training.

I think of Paris. I think of her.

I stomp the fob into a dozen MADE IN CHINA plastic pieces. Let the world in, I say.

The Twin says, *Window for termination of the Live Feed Event has closed.*

[N S F W]
7

Among the chaos on Mother/Screen, a metallic rattle pings my ear, beckoning me. I wander to the Vex employee lockers as the crew settles back to witness. I can hear a faint transmission, as if a whistle in the upper frequency is being blown. My tinnitus flares.

<p>

@MØM's *f*Ōne starts to buzz. A news alert. She starts to cry. It should be in her Faraday locker. The other lockers begin to vibrate.

<p>

I open your locker. Your *f*Ōne rattles. It shouldn't have a signal. Not here in the locker.

I touch the *f*Ōne. My hand feels a tingle. Haptic feedback, as it starts to charge off my own bioelectricity. It is showing a video.

It mirrors the feed on Mother/Screen.

Oh no.

On all the *f*Ōnes, the biggest-selling tech item of the decade. Every new device will play it automatically.

The top news story. Autoload. There is no opt-out. The end of the live feed is just the beginning.

Oh god.

‹p›

The live feed transitions from city to city. Cloud to cloud. Event to event. Body to body. Fire to fire. Explosion to explosion. Even security-camera footage from CCTV, which should be impossible. That's what we've been told. This group, they know their audience, giving us what we really want. A juicy bone to fight over.

We have lost the war on savagery.

‹p›

Wall Street stalls. Banks close. ATMs locked. Our life-changing bonus checks locked away in the purgatory of DEPOSIT PENDING. Riots. Grocery-store lines a kilometer long. News sites can't find a font big enough for the headlines. Pundits shout. Bunkers are dug. Devices are never set down. Conspiracy theories abound. Images bombard the country to the point of desensitization. Of being triggered.

Half the country yawns.

Half the country panics.

The pod gathers behind me. Reeking of shit, cum, alcohol, weed, cherry chocolate. We haven't stopped watching replays of the Live Feed Event (LFE). We are merely spectators now. We live on glass slides. The satellites, the microscopes.

A news reporter reading off a scrolling teleprompter says the unimaginable has happened. This is false. Someone imagined it and made it a reality.

@MØM grabs her stomach. Swollen with bile and anxiety. Not this world, she chants, not this world. *Oh, Tim.*

One of the Twins drops to the floor and starts doing clap push-ups in time with @OrKa's desk-bike. The other Twin makes notes in a small journal. His military wristwatch chimes with an alarm I've never heard. You light a bundle of sage.

<p>

Can half a country live?

<p>

Sa>ag3@vexillum.com:> AUTOREPLY - OUT OF OFFICE

<p>

GoDrones fly through clouds hunting and gathering footage of citizens clawing at their throats, their eyes. Just drifting over us on the wind. News streams report the clouds of nerve agents are still rolling over the heartland, over amber waves of grain. The Event's chemical encore.

<p>

The president takes a page from his congressional colleagues: Now is not the time to overreact with a legislative response. The same speech given on the Senate floor after every school shooting dramatic enough to make the front page. Keep calm and lobby on.

The *f*ace finishes strong-arming the purchase of ancestral land on a big island untouched by the Event. His Fortress of Solitude built on the bones of a people whose name he can't pronounce. There is to be ceremonial purging of spirits.

This is buried deep in a feed.

Because of the bleeding edge of savagery and production values of the LFE, right-wing radio claims it is a fake. Hollywood liberals finally getting their master plan out of turnaround and jacking up fear to boost ticket sales for theatre chains. Streaming subscriptions. Escapism. Creating new storylines to twist and distort in their writers' room, their imagination bankrupt. Ripped from today's feed.

#Content

Whether it was fake or not, they only had one shot. No retakes. No resets. No fixing it in post.

It was real.

They showed it.

<p>

The men in suits want to ask me questions. I don't have time to chew a Xanax. If we had any.

They interview me at Vex. I am the Office Manager and electronically we are the epicenter of the LFE. I ask if they prefer the "family room." Sensing, incorrectly, that it is the least likely place to have surveillance at a tech firm, they agree. They want me to be comfortable. I believe this is a standard technique.

(the tremors again)

These men have taken Specialty Security Training. They talk about the training videos they have watched. They talk in front of me to each other. I don't recognize this interrogation technique. They say they had watched videos used by the LAPD. Their top five favorite videos are Columbine, Virginia Tech, Binghamton (NY), Beslan (Russia), and Mumbai (India), with Newtown an honorable mention. They wonder which cities from the Event will become training videos for the future.

(what do you see? here?
here? here? and here?)

They ask questions about Vex. About the people that work here. They ask about relationships within Vex. They have their questions, their If-Then statements memorized as if we are just having a conversation, while their brains try to draw red yarn strings from connection to connection.

*(someone has to be
blamed)*

I don't tell them about the flogging breaks. Or Mr. Ray's philosophy. I don't tell them about @MØM's maternal habits. I don't tell them about @Skiny_Leny's pharma desk. I don't tell them in detail about our daily tasks of sorting through the bombardment of human cruelty. They ask about you. I tell them basic-cable things about you, our relationship. I don't tell them about the cutting. Or the jellyfish. Or the jungle aquarium we've built. Our own personal Eden. The mushrooms.

(americans need closure)

They don't understand how I don't know your real name, where you are from, how old you are. Because we connected in the present, I tell them. That is where we live. We made no plans for the future. We were busy coping with the now.

(they will scapegoat me)

This kind of talk makes them yawn.

#Cord_Cutting

The first Special Agent asks if I happen to know how *Mt. Rushmore* ends.

I shake my head.

He asks his partner if he would have hit the kill switch. His partner shrugs. That's above my pay grade. But not his, he says, indicating me.

The other Special Agent in an off-the-record kinda way asks, why didn't you stop the Live Feed Event?

His partner: Yeah, why did you let it spread?

<p>

#Mise_en_scène

<p>

At the break, @MØM sneaks in a red-white-and-blue sheet cake. She's so proud of the Twins.

Their service records. True patriots. Their guard unit is being prepped for deployment. Her smile is forced. Putting on a good face for her children. The cake is gluten-free. Her therapist says baking is a good hobby for anxiety.

@MØM announces that the red is made without Red Dye 40. It causes aggression and violence and hyperactivity in children. My babies love cake, she says. From the way she winces when she cuts the cake, I can tell her nipples are sore. Both Twins craving mother's milk.

The agents tell me they'll be in touch.

I take a slice of white.

The agents both take a slice of red and a finger of blue icing.

<p>

The subpoena Barista Tim delivered to the *face* comes from Congress. The spring hearing has been moved up. So many watched on his devices, and Congress have to act like they are being proactive. He's to be the face of their biggest hearing.

For a few days, we all live and sleep at Vex. GoDrones dropping off food, go bags, cots, and sleeping bags. Only a quarter of the shipments make it. @MØM watching through the big window as unmarked GoDrones perform aerial attacks like hawks.

@Orka never gets off her desk-bike, refusing to activate her after-hours auto mode. @Skiny scrounges for more go pills.

<p>

Who do you fear most: a scientist, a terrorist, or a politician?

[N S F W]
8

Mother/Screen.

<p>

He's before Congress, the *f*ace. Talking. Glancing at his notes. Not blinking until he sees the prompt in his notes. He cocks his head; his trained physical gesture for *oh, I've just had an idea.* He reaches into his jacket pocket.

I can still see the blemishes of my assassination attempt wrapped around his hand like a red henna tattoo.

He unfolds a piece of paper. Even in a wide shot I recognize the ink-stained fingerprints. Mine. He has my letter. He faces all the elected officials. He reads a quote I typed with Mr. Ray's machine.

> **"I was benevolent and good; misery made me a fiend. Make me happy, and I shall again be virtuous."**

A weathered senator asks the *f*ace to clarify his quote and a young well-read Ivy-League-educated senator asks if he is suggesting that the people/government/American culture created the *f*ace.

The *f*ace smiles. It's genuine.

<p>

As soon as they put a hood over your head, you no longer exist as a human. Before you drop from the gallows. Before the firing squad. You're dead before they execute you.

This is why they put a face to products. To the news. To the company.

<p>

The president has ties to the big smiling *f*ace. He was one of the first 300 users. Was one of his first donors. The inner group. In return, that faith was rewarded with a superweapon. The *f*ace's algorithm. 302 electoral votes can't be wrong.

<p>

No one remembers victory gardens. Any sacrifice made for country is now an assault on personal liberties.

<p>

An in-depth article on Cinephiliabeyond.com draws comparisons between the Live Feed Event in terms of sound, cinematography, and choreography to the cult film *Midnight Shelter* and the best foreign-film war movie, the dreamlike French film *Asleep Apart*. All the key crew profiles from both movies have been removed from IMDb. The Cinephiliabeyond.com website is supported by donations. Shortly thereafter, it shutters.

No one wants to pay for anything. Even before the LFE.

<p>

Now I understand why my father went back into the jungle. He figured it out.

<p>

Your husband is arrested; facial recognition software picking him out of the first sequence of action, where he gunned down the would-be heroes charging *Adam,* thinking *this is my big break* and *don't screw up the shot.* The evening news showed his actor's headshot. No longer twenty feet from stardom.

That's an old headshot, you say. I took it with a Nikon.

Your husband also took a lot of headshots with an AR-15.

<p>

The men in suits are back. They take you into the lactorium for questioning. More than a witness, but less than a person of interest.

<p>

After your interview, they pull me into the lactorium for a follow-up questioning. I'm an alibi for your time leading up to the Live Feed Event.

I'm clean. No media accounts. No smartphone. The agent gives me a quarter taped to his business card as a joke. His partner laughs. I pretend I don't get it.

Between both our extensive interviews and brief chats with the pod, the authorities exonerate you, my innocent @Jun1p3r.

The first special agent asks if there is any more cake.

The other special agent wrinkles his nose. What is this room used for again?

<p>

A federal task force the size of Delaware parses the video of the Event, watching for bad actors. A civilian task force the size North America does the same and for free.

<p>

It was all a hoax. The radioman with a microphone and spoon-hungry audience repeats it *ad infinitum*. Hoax. Followers. Actors. Meant to what? he says so that he can tell you the answer: Shock us into submission.

Call in and tell us what you think: 1-888-253-3139.

<p>

Your husband uses his one call to his talent agent. I know what really happened, he says. I was there. Book me on the talk-show circuit. I know the truth. His agent drops him.

His career ends at the end of the bedsheet tied with a knot beyond his skill set.

<p>

#Syphilis

#Sisyphus

<p>

Before the congressional hearings happen, the Live Feed Event is dissected by cinephiles. Trying to match the style with classic directors. Too restrained for a film student. I research to see if the disgruntled masters of cinema were in the country at the time. Sometimes you never leave the jungle.

Two weren't.

<p>

Already the term *Parser* trends. As in a person who spends his time parsing the Live Feed Event into smaller and smaller bits looking for clues. Also, trending is the term *Placer*: a person who spends his time piecing together footage of a particular individual until said individual leaves the picture or is killed. Placers who post cobbled footage of a citizen that ends in death are given higher status. No one wants to be left hanging.

<p>

The citizens of China and North Korea are blissfully ignorant of the Live Feed Event, their governments each having a handle on their own brand of terror.

<p>

The cinephiles create an open-source project of the LFE. Videos of the first three cities are posted on a split screen: running side by side are comparison shots stolen/homaged from classic movies. Text underneath names the movie, year, and director. The rack focus, the swish pan. The handheld. The aerial. Under the Live Feed, when the audio is enhanced, a subtle ominous tone from a Korg synthesizer is laid in the soundtrack, adding an additional sense of unease. Occasionally it drops out, a sudden sublime shock, letting the body know: here comes the money shot. *Citizen Kane* is referenced more than once, as is *Hard Boiled*.

Forum fights break out on reddit, arguing the sources. The internet being scoured for proof from obscure underground films. The Parsers feel co-opted, culturally appropriated. The Placers leave the chat room.

What do you think, @Sa>ag3? the special agent says.

We don't really watch movies anymore.

What do you watch? the other special agent says.

Nature. We have a jellyfish.

One special agent turns to another and says, I can't keep up with today's slang.

<p>

Every sporting event is canceled. The nation finding it hard to get back up on this horse. Everyone knows someone that knows someone. Two degrees of terrorism. There will be no rousing sporting pregame speech. No T-shirts. No motto. No campaign slogan. No tattoos.

<p>

> Los Angeles, CA.
> Seattle, WA.
> Salt Lake City, UT.
> Sioux City, IA.
> Laramie, WY.
> Oklahoma City, OK (finally in the big leagues).
> Tulsa, OK.
> Philadelphia, PA.
> San Antonio, TX.
> Shreveport, LA.
> Memphis, TN.
> Atlanta, GA.
> Pittsburgh, PA.
> Louisville, KY.
> Toronto (yet again a production proxy for NY).
> Pensacola, FL.

A scattering of small towns hit not with bullets but with gas. Their entire populations wiped out, now modern ghost towns. Goodbye, Cupertino. Goodbye, Dry Hollow. Goodbye, Independence. Goodbye, Jackson Hole. Goodbye, Sun Valley.

<p>

The Live Feed Event designed and choreographed like the opening ceremony of the Olympics.

<p>

They were actors! All of them. The shooters, the *victims*. Look here: there they are in other movies. The talking dog. The depressed chicken. The corporate odd couple. Here are their IMDb credits.

Here. Here. And here.

The 21st-century fog of war.

<p>

Several in the crowds are, in fact, background actors. Extras hired for a peas-and-carrots street scene. Several promoted to Featured Extras. The pay is the same as the bullets are real.

A number of the terrorists are actors. Americans. Canadians. Getting their big break in a production with a budget. All will be gunned down by police or friendly fire before they realize they are not shooting blanks. But no one stops. No one wants to ruin the shot. No one wants to be "difficult to work with." There's too much at stake. The conspiracy built into the production of slaughter.

<p>

You had to be there, I say to the special agents. It was real. They showed it.

[N S F W]
9

Post-Event.

<p>

A scientist, a terrorist, and a politician walk into a bar. The bartender calls the cops and says he feels threatened.

"The scientist fills my head with facts and figures to make me feel stupid. Because I am stupid, the terrorist wants to blow me up."

"And the politician?"

"Oh, I gave him a hand job in the bathroom."

There's a pause. "Did you wash your hands?"

"No, I called 9-1-1."

The cop shoots the bartender because he did not comply with "all employees must wash their hands." It's the law. And we are nothing if not a country of law and order. The terrorist hires the scientist. It's a free and fair market. And we are nothing if not a country of fair and free markets.

<p>

#American_Carnage

\<p>

We have our pick of train cars. Armed SWAT officers stationed at either end. You notice the young parolee curled up in a dirty coat on the seat bolted over the car's heater. I pass you a handful of protein bars from the office. You slip them into his coat pocket. Kiss the top of his head. We both know what it's like to be alone and lost.

\<p>

Still in our jumpsuits, we pass through the airlock into the Garden. The plastic has been slashed. There is no sound save a *drip drip*. And the smell of bleach.

An invader has taken a bat to the kitchen. Clorox to the sod floor. A hatchet to the Garden.

Salt water drips onto the floor. The last of the brine shrimp zipping around in tiny tide pools. I swallow hard, as I recognize the severed limbs of the bonsai tree.

The jellyfish tank a thousand shards on the dead grass, sparkling like dew. Like precious blood diamonds. My heart breaks. I pick through the slivers looking. Looking. Looking.

I find our jellyfish. Shrunken and colorless. Nicked and tattered like the plastic over the door. Humless.

The whiskey barrel slats broken, swollen with the last puddle that might have given our baby a chance to live.

It looks like a Shrinky Dink, I say.

You put it in a baggie. The only safe space we can find.

<p>

You eye the kettle. Want a cup of tisane? you say, gathering up a handful of strewn leaves.

There's probably glass powder on them, I say.

We've consumed worse, you say. Your voice cracks.

I agree.

<p>

@Skiny_Leny asks if anyone cares for a bag of popcorn. We all raise a hand, our jumpsuits unzipped, the sleeves tied around our waists showing off our concert Ts for Casual Friday: T.S.O.L. and Violent Femmes.

Mother/Screen hums to life. We observe, but do not report. The Twins are gone. I list them as MIA.

At the hearing, the senator asks the *f*ace how the sales of the new phones have been. An aide hands him a scrap of paper. Excuse me, *devices*. Then another aide hands him a second scrap of paper. Excuse me, *fŌnes*. How are sales?

Sold out.

How many units is that?

All of them.

The senator takes a sip of water. Batteryless, I hear, he says. How does that work?

The *f*ace makes the perfunctory gesture of consulting with his lawyer and cites trade secrets. The senator waves a paper copy of the patent and trademark. It is vague and useless. This would be of great application to national security, the senator says.

I look forward to seeing what our government comes up with, the *f*ace says. In our free market.

I get political emails. The machine can't decide if their opponents are fascist or socialist.

However, when citizens die politicians solicit thoughts and prayers. When they run for reelection, they solicit cash.

Another senator says that the Live Feed was watched on 99.99 percent of the new devices, the *f*Ōnes. The senator mispronounces the name of the device.

The *f*ace's face ticks a fraction. Whether from the accusation, disappointment in the percentage, or branding misfire, I can only guess.

Then the senator asks: Did you have the resources to orchestrate this Live Feed Event?

#DEWEYDEFEATSTRUMAN

Is it true an employee of yours waived this Live Feed through your firewall?

That's not how firewalls work.

Is it true an employee of yours was married to one of the featured terrorists?

An employee? No.

Is it true that you have to give personal information for a discount on your new device? Including your social security number?

No sir. We already have that information.

How?

<p>

#Apocalypse_Now

<p>

The *f*ace sits at the hearing, before men born in an analog age. Impassive. His little-boy haircut. Claiming it's only a tool. Claiming the First Amendment. Freedom of choice. Freedom from choice. Capitalism. The American Dream.

Then they push him.

They threaten to break up his techopoly. Rewrite legislature that protects him from content delivered on his platform. A senator with a BA in theater pounds his desk, red and puffy faced, refusing to yield the floor to the lady from Illinois.

Blood flushes up the *f*ace's neck and face. I know an imminent explosion when I see one. I credit my OJT. He reads from my letter once again.

"When falsehood can look so like the truth, who can assure themselves of certain happiness?"

His finger dances on the surface of his own device.

Cell phones and devices supposedly not allowed in the chamber suddenly vibrate. The whole room vibrates. It is a plague of locusts. Aides breach protocol and rush to their charges. The hearing is abandoned. Decorum forgotten. The gentleman from South Carolina is the first to clear the exit.

<p>

The direct-line number the president has had for the *f*ace since they first shared their secret ambitions in the Ivy League now goes directly to voicemail. The voicemail box is full. The president is being ghosted by the *f*ace.

<p>

Live on air at the congressional hearing, the *f*ace names names. Speaking not with his mouth but with his thumb. Electronic press kits are spammed to all the major and minor news outlets. Liberal, conservative. Neo-Nazi to far-left fascist. A push of a button. He doxes them all. What they watch. What they buy. Taxes. Foreign banks. Slush funds. Offshore accounts. Who they fuck. Ages. Kilos. Clips. Videos. Texts. Embezzlement. Misappropriation. Tax evasion. All this information locked with blockchain technology. You cannot alter it. It is a permanent record. All organized and searchable in a nifty EPK.

All the skeletons. All the bodies. All the money. Everything. Everyone who opposed him. Thinking their secrets were safe in a digital vault when they awarded the *f*ace a robust government contract under one of his shell companies. Owned solely by the *f*ace. The only legal entity without an NDA.

Read the fine print. They all agreed to terms. Clicking the box.

\<p\>

Enthusiastic White House interns write pages and pages of speeches and type them into teleprompters for an audience that no longer listens.

\<p\>

Two freshmen congressmen come out unscathed. Standing side by side, they call for unity and vow to rebuild America's government from the sky down. Rebranding as the Grand New Party and the Blue Star Collective. A week later, they attack each other's platforms.

\<p\>

News media: one outlet calls it the Purge (until a movie studio sends out a volley of C&D letters). This when Congress hanged themselves that spring morning. Took their pills. Took their own lives. Had their lives taken. Righteous indignation no defense for crimes against humanity. Those without shame fled to South America, following in the *Gröfaz*'s footsteps.

Six months later, they are culled by an isolated viral outbreak. The last of them dying with desperate black-market vaccines filled with bleach. A spokesperson asks that the families be given privacy.

If I could, I would email their families my ruminations and meditations. Thoughts and prayers now passé.

<p>

This is the fall of the American empire.

[TERMINATION]
10

Druids consider Fate *where you allow the currents to carry you.* Destiny is *where you swim towards.*

\<p\>

I wonder, was I targeted? Did my profile point to me as a bad actor? A revolutionary? Did I loathe my fellow man so much that I let him see the world? Did I love him so much I wanted him to witness the truth?

Or was I merely another algorithm? A culmination of decades of data points?

\<p\>

#Transdifferentiation

\<p\>

Why did the *f*ace give me a choice? Did he know what I've experienced? Since my own experience with a terrorist slaughter in Paris. Was my decision not to press the kill button preordained? Why are any of us given a choice? Was I being tested? Was I simply another variable in a grand experiment?

In the end it served the needs of only one person. One country. Not me. Not us.

The term "drone" was first officially used in 1936, by US Navy Lt. Cmdr. Delmer S. Fahrney.

After the congressional cleansing, the *f*ace introduces a news feed. The first big story is an exclusive interview with the *f*ace. He talks about his new venture into Big Pharma. He talks about a cure. He introduces us to his pet jellyfish, Adam. This little creature is the key to so many ills plaguing mankind, he says. It is the new face of pharmaceutical science. Expect an announcement on our platform very soon.

Meanwhile, I'd like to introduce to you a new security initiative that will make the world a—

I mute Mother/Screen and follow his eyes as they twitch in his skull, reading from a teleprompter.

The term "keyboard activist" is an insult. But at the keyboard is where the war is growing. Power grids. National defense. Banking. Infrastructure. Elections. But many folks believe if it isn't happening on their block, it doesn't exist.

Eventually, the bread turns moldy and the circus leaves town.

The *f*ace is deleted. On an island driving to a ground-breaking ceremony on holy land. There was an explosion. No one knows if it was an IED, a car bomb, or natural gas. There is no footage. It's a no-fly zone. Hobbyists and renegade news outlets watch their mini GoDrones fall from the sky.

Veterans of recent wars agree it was an unmanned combat aerial vehicle (UCAV), but disagree if it was the Reaper or Predator version. I wish the Twins were here so I could ask their opinion.

The newscasters do not report this theory as they've exhausted their superlatives with the LFE and the Congressional Massacre.

<p>

The druids know nothing of riptides.

<p>

Of course, the video of the *f*ace's assassination ends up in our office. We all watch it. A sense of dread fills our pod. Our nuclear family.

<p>

Video gamers routinely score better than trained aviators when it comes to drone training. Raised with no real consequences, emotional or otherwise, to their actions, they have honed the ability to be a top gun.

The high and tight Twin had told this to @MØM in the lactorium before shipping out to Nevada.

<p>

#KillDieRepeat

Within hours, a new *f*ace is introduced. A doppelgänger for the woman in the doctor's office with her rolling back bag. This woman has a more expensive backstory. This one has more expressive eyes. All the better to showcase her glycerin tears. The work will continue, she says. His legacy not forgotten. They will forge ahead. Making the world a better place. Saying this as smoke and ashes rise in the distance and gunfire crackles on the street.

#Project_Bluebird
#MKULTRA
#Operation_Midnight_Climax
#Milgram_Experiment
#Operation_Sea_Spray
#Stanford_Prison_Experiment
#San_Antonio_Contraceptive_Study
#Tuskegee_Syphilis_Experiment
#Operation_Big_Itch
#Operation_Big_Buzz
#Operation_May_Day
#Operation_Drop_Kick
#Project_Shipboard_Hazard_and_Defense

#A_Study_of_the_Vulnerability_of_Subway_Passe
ngers_in_New_York_City_to_Covert_
Attack_with_Biological_Agents

David Scott Hay

#Operation_Riptide
#Project_SnowFall

<p>

Just win, baby.

[TERMINATION]
9

Up on Mother/Screen, *Singin' in the Rain* is our night's entertainment; our pod does a sing-along, our drunken voices drowning out the casual squeak of @OrKa's desk-bike. Her finish line still on the horizon.

We don't make it to the finale. Our pod receives a GoDrone shipment with a box addressed to Mr. Ray. The return address: *Ganymede.* Otherwise, it is an unmarked box. Inside, an old-fashioned thumb drive. It takes us thirty minutes to find a dusty adapter to jack it into the vid system.

<p>

You kick it up to Mother/Screen. The last video we will watch as a pod comes in.

We should not watch it.

We should have it removed from the global archive.

We should never speak of it again.

We should pack our bags.

We should drop our devices into wet concrete.

We should run.

It is behind-the-scenes footage of the Live Feed Event. Not just a ten-minute PR puff piece for the infotainment shows. This is a master class in coordinating the logistics of moviemaking with terrorism never seen on this scale. The grizzled director about to tell the Academy what they can do with their Honorary Award. @Skiny_Leny says, Laurence Olivier, Charlie Chaplin, Lillian Gish, Alec Guinness, Mary Pickford, Groucho Marx, and Orson Welles were all recipients. No one comments, the time for trivial pursuits gone.

The video is comprehensive. The supply chain. The choreography. The technical details. The funding. The documents. The experiment with whole-city-block facades constructed by nonunion labor in Siberia. Fine-tuned with another set of city blocks on a private ranch in South Dakota under the watchful eyes of Mt. Rushmore.

The production of the LFE was funded by Russian oligarchs. State-sponsored. Their citizens unaware, their war with the States forever cold.

The great bear finally sinking its claws into the eagle.

<p>

#Deep_Fake

<p>

The metadata stamps on the behind-the-scenes videos are clear.

@Skiny_Leny runs a calendar app of current events against national, regional, and local happenings. "This day in history"-type thing. It's on a public-school-system history website updated thanklessly by a history professor turned librarian.

@Skiny_Leny beckons me over. Points to the date. The time stamp on the treasure-trove compilation of data is within ninety minutes of the poisoning (and subsequent death) of Professor Snowden. Moscow Institute of Physics and Technology.

The rehearsal videos geotagged from fifteen different locations in Siberia. The information making it to Snowden. Who then got the incriminating flash drive out of Russia using his own person as a diversion. This before he was executed with poison.

Snowden once again a lone figure rising up against a rogue nation, collecting and disseminating data to protect US citizens who would have had him hanged for treason. The ultimate global whistleblower failing to realize America hates a snitch. Ignorance is truly bliss.

This time he paid the ultimate price. No statues will be built in his honor.

And now our pod has witnessed the truth of the LFE, the truth of it all. Yoked like beasts of burden.

<p>

A GoDrone buzzes the outside window of Vex. I toggle the windows to opaque.

@Skiny_Leny yelps.

What?

Oh no, @Skiny_Leny says. Points to a block of code, now visible, within the flash drive.

It's a GPS, you say. Active. The color drains from your face.

They're coming for us.

<p>

#The_Tyranny_of_the_Should

<p>

The fight-or-flight reflex is primitive and primal. If the fight reflex wins, the sphincter tightens. If the flight reflex wins, it loosens. A pod-mate apologizes and rushes to the bathroom.

@Skiny_Leny shaves the rest of his hair over a trash can. Lights it with the latest draft of his Big Idea. The air stinks of human waste and char. By the time we've ditched the jumpsuits, he's wearing combat fatigues and a leather jacket. Combined with the head scar from the van wreck, he looks like an apocalyptic chieftain.

I'll miss you, @Skiny_Leny says. He hands me a paperback-sized box. The one Mr. Ray left for me. I'm sorry, he says. I got jealous and took it. He kisses the corner of my mouth. Tastes like cherry.

<p>

#butterflykisses

@Sa>ag3!

The volume of her voice startles me.

@OrKa motions me over to her screen. She's tapped into the CCTV for our building. All from her keyboard.

The camera on the drone pad shows electronic snow.

But at ground level we see @Skiny_Leny limp out of the building lobby, key fob in hand. The lights in his van flash as it unlocks, like the final blip of a heart monitor. He drops his key fob. Before he can retrieve it, an identical unmarked white van pulls up next him. Men in urban fatigues pop out like spiders and drag the ant into the van and speed off.

Another white van pulls up. More spiders pour out and into our building.

#LooseEnds

@OrKa takes a 5.56 mm NATO copper-plated hollow-point round to the head. Violence as a first resort. @OrKa pedals still, the momentum from her legs still cranking.

Look at the thighs on this one, one of the armed men says. They are not professionals. Just paid like ones. Start grabbing hard drives, one says

Slowly, @OrKa's legs stop. The wheel is no longer squeaky. When the wheel stops, a five-second If-Then statement requiring input from the desk-bike is tripped on @OrKa's computer, detonating a worm within the Vex IT system. The worm replicates laterally, breaching the Kubernetes containers, deleting each root directory, including all files and subdirectories. All our personal information is eradicated. The entire history of Vexillum electronically vaporized. Tracks covered.

<p>

Orcinus orca. "Killer Whale."

<p>

In addition, Trojan Horses are activated in the *f*ace's system. @OrKa and Mr. Ray had believed they had cracked the *f*ace's firewall with help from their ally in Moscow. An ally who helped create the nation's backup system for the CIA. They just needed the *f*ace's DNA.

It's easy to take a DNA sample when your subject is prone on the floor in anaphylactic shock. One scratch gathering tissue under my fingernail. If I couldn't kill him at least I could do that. My own Plan B. My one contribution to Mr. Ray and @OrKa's underground resistance. I didn't ask questions. I just wanted to win for once in my life.

<p>

Mr. Ray understood what happens when men with guns come knocking at the door. Sacrifice or submission.

<p>

We hear the spiders seize @MØM outside the bathrooms. She's screaming, *I'm pregnant, I'm pregnant. Tim! Tim!* Muffled thumps like a heavyweight champ hitting a heavy bag. Then retching. Her shredded voice fades as she's dragged away. I think this is what I hear. White noise masks our hearts, our breathing. I hold you as close as possible. Your heavy breathing muffled by my chest even as it warms it.

Boots outside the door. A hand brushes the lactorium handle. Pauses.

I feel you tense. We are a ball of steel. Vibrating with adrenaline of impending death.

Then the boots are gone.

This from inside the lactorium. A place that gives insecure men pause.

[TERMINATION]
8

I'm behind the wheel of @Skiny's van. The pink mace key ring had been easy to find in the dirty snow.

We're heading north. In the back of the van where we counted constellations on each other's bodies are boxes of protein bars, the industrial first aid kit, and whatever else we could scavenge quickly from the Vex office. The frame of *The Aquarist of Ganymede* was smashed, the poster missing.

Nobody took a sledgehammer to Mother/Screen.

‹p›

I imagine that Snowden reached out to Mr. Ray, offering the warning of the impending LFE. Who better than the son of a Soviet sci-fi writer whose father was a political prisoner? But then the package never arrived. No treasure trove of intelligence. Mr. Ray believed Snowden had been found out. The counterplot foiled.

At least his pod got their bonuses.

I imagine this, because I did not ask @OrKa questions when she asked me if I wanted to make a difference. I did and I did not want to read the fine print.

#ITEOTWAWKIAIFF

I imagine for @OrKa it had been easier to become an employee at Vex than a manager. Especially with the constant turnover. So, she arrived before Mr. Ray. Her German grandparents forced to make propaganda films for the Reich Ministry of Public Enlightenment and Propaganda, @OrKa understood more than most the power of film.

Maybe the office's *Maschinenmensch*, and her dead man's switch, could have negotiated additional leverage. Maybe she had a plan that had yet to be activated. Maybe she thought she could bargain with them. Spare our lives. Maybe the descendant of silent movie stars had final words to proclaim for posterity.

But they didn't ask her anything.

You can't bluff a player who isn't paying attention.

@OrKa's slag code erased Vex. It is supposed to worm its way into the *f*ace's system, doing the same, sniffing out hidden server warehouses around the globe.

Snowden's BTS package is sent out into the world, to the exact same media outlets on the *f*ace's media congressional hit list. All too late.

The truth is an antiquated idea now, another resource to be weaponized.

David Scott Hay

You scramble to find an AM news radio station.
They are beheading journalists in Times Square.

[TERMINATION]
7

At the sporting goods store, the small-town clerk is heavily armed. The windows are boarded up. They're having an end-of-the-world sale, which means the prices have tripled. But you can't put a price on self-sufficiency, she says. Clearly, she believes the Event to be a hoax. She winks and talks of theater. A warning. An opportunity. A false flag.

Cash or trade only.

All the ATMs have been offline since the Event. The banks are closed in a vain attempt to prevent further economic collapse. Our bonus checks sitting untouched in untouchable bank accounts.

To save time, I show her our list. Rifles and ammo. Field dressing kits. Camo. Netting. Propane. Waterproof matches. Saws. Tarps. Water purification straws. Tablets.

Yeah... she sighs. She's seen this list a hundred times today; it's a PDF checklist from theamericanprepper.net. Looks like you folks have a busy weekend, she says, trying gallows humor. Whatcha hunting?

Freedom, you say, in your anthem voice.

God bless America, she says and shakes your hand, unsure of your tone. Then eager to stay in your good graces, that voice, those eyes, she says, You heard about the *f*ace, right?

I make a noncommittal noise.

Was a drone strike, she says. By the government.

Which one, you ask.

But you and I know. We've seen the footage.

The clerk takes another look at the list. Shakes her head. Tells us how many reward points we'd have earned if we'd signed up on their mailing list. How she could have reserved supplies for us. But, she says, and turns and looks at shelves that I see now are stocked mostly with ripped and torn and empty boxes.

What do you have? I say.

She pulls out a survival knife from under the counter. From her own private stash. It has a sawback and a blood groove. That knife don't need batteries, she says. When the EMP hits it'll still get a signal, if you know what I mean.

I'm the battery, I say.

That's right, she says. An American battery. With elbow grease, bushcraft, and that knife, you can build a shelter, build a fire, kill and dress prey for dinner and clothing. And carve yourself some art.

Kinda like the Native Americans did before the Puritans showed up, you say, more out of habit than conviction.

You mean before the western expansion, she says. Manifest Destiny. They had a chance to drive us back into the sea for 200 years. Anyone telling you different is just trying to sell you an alternate history, she says.

We trade mushrooms and petty cash for the knife, a saw, and camo netting. She throws in a cheap compass. I offer my hand to seal the trade.

She sniffles and her eyes water. She's prepared for this her whole life. The Kraken. Adjustment Day. The Rapture. And now that it's here, there is no one left to convert. Her smile falters, but she finishes the handshake. Thanks for buying American, she says.

I think of the Twins' jumpsuits. Their drone-footage acumen. They weren't pretend pilots, you say. I wonder which piloted the faceless drone (UCAV) machine that fired a single Hellfire missile from the wild blue yonder. The word LIKE and a cartoon thumbs-up scrawled in chalk just beneath its warhead. The last message the *f*ace would receive as his compound turned to crater.

The Wiccans own undeveloped land. A stopgap against the failing crypto standard. This is where we are heading. I start to open the package from Mr. Ray, but instead I am lulled to sleep by the hum of the tires and the AM radio. Sounds like 1963.

The radio waves will reach Jupiter in 43 minutes. By then we'll be 43 miles down the road. A signal chasing noise.

That's how this all ends: a signal chasing noise.

<p>

We drive @Skiny_Leny's van to a looted big-box-store parking lot. The RVers and Van Lifers have circled their vehicles. We offer Xanax and antiseptic in trade for a place in the circle. The Vex industrial first aid kit becomes our life savings.

The community gathers around their screens, watching the news. Hot takes. Politics. Tech war. Foreign policy. The lost, upcoming baseball season. Class war. Domestic terrorists. Foreign intervention. Too many slants and angles. Nothing you can distill to a bumper sticker or a T-shirt. We feign silent interest.

A prepper with everything trades one of his several old offline GPSs, preloaded with the maps of thirty-seven states, for the unauthorized biography of the *f*ace.

<p>

In the biography, the *f*ace jokes about being a mad scientist. And that he is truly the happiest when he is jacked in, coding, experimenting, and that his dream would be to have a place where he could do his work uninterrupted. Unfettered.

The casual reader would assume this to be our island-state of Hawaii.

But that is not what Russia offered him.

According to Snowden, they had offered the *f*ace his pick, save Ukraine, of traitorous republics of the former Soviet Union to experiment on. Unfettered. Unregulated. Just like the US had done so many times to its own citizens. If you can't win in a tech war, you acquire your enemy. Palo Alto Warfare 101.

All the *f*ace had to do was enable the new devices to broadcast the true end of the Cold War. To everyone. So much data to mine. It would take decades to parse. Or place.

They offered the *f*ace citizenship, freedom from persecution, impunity for his experiments. As long as they had access to the data.

The PR nightmare of Hawaii was just a distraction. The *f*ace was never going to live there after the ground-breaking ceremony. He timed it so he and his family would not be on the mainland when the curtain raised on the stage-managed and coproduced apocalypse. And now his bones are mingled with the bones of others in Lua-o-Milu, the land of the dead.

<p>

I have every former Vex employee's email and social media accounts. I have the message prepped. I only need to hit SEND. Let them know where we are going, let them know there is a safe space. It's a short message. An invitation, no RSVP required. Come as you are. A string of coordinates to a green star.

<p>

In the morning we find a deserted library. From one of the dusty library computers, I click SEND.

We "check out" as many books as we can. Off-grid living. Maps. Water sanitation. Gardening. Waste disposal. Rope skills. Bushcraft. Compass orientation. Classics. Erotica.

I refresh the computer before we leave. All the emails have bounced back. Receiver unknown. @OrKa's scorched-earth plan having burned all bridges. We are an island, entire of ourselves.

<p>

Before we leave, I make a copy of a map on a dusty fax machine. I mark a spot with a green pen. I star it. If we ever get separated, we will meet here. I make you show me how to use the compass over and over.

What happens if we get separated? I quiz, repeatedly.

Get to the green star.

[TERMINATION]
6

One needs a 4x4 vehicle to reach the Wiccan camp. @Skiny_Leny's van bottoms out early. We park in a small clearing and drape the camo net over the van. We hike miles. It feels good, the burn in the legs. The land here free from pollutants, pesticides, and nerve gas.

<p>

The witches welcome us with open arms. I count nine, including yourself. The others may have fallen victim to the LFE. They show us around. Where the paths are. Which ones have roots to avoid tripping over. It's a new moon rising, chasing stars so thick they look like liquid poured across the sky.

I tear up. At the beauty of it all, and then start to laugh.

What, you say.

Land a plus.

<p>

The fire warms our outsides. The tisane, our insides The huddling of our bodies, my soul. We are given a tent and privacy. I look forward to sleeping in woods not lined with plastic. Tomorrow we will be assigned chores best suited to our skills. And teach others the same. I will set up a library for the coven. Tonight, the musk of our sex is camouflaged by the hardwood smoke. The smell remains in my jacket, like a disinfectant.

My sleep is dreamless, but restful. When the moon is full and overhead, you wake me gently with a kiss, then a touch. We make love slowly. It's the first time we do so where we are not fending off foreign invaders, or anger, or frustration, or using each other to purge mental images. I trace the tattooed Bride on your arm. Even she seems at ease next to the Wolfman, bathed in this moonlight. We do not deflect the moment with humor. We see only each other. Feel only each other. Feel relief. It is church.

Everything in its right place.

<p>

Why did I ever need more than this?

<p>

We rise at dawn. Join the community. I feel a sense of relief. My brain does not idle in high. My alpha and theta waves calm, allowing me to be fully present. I can breathe deeply, as if my rib cage will allow my lungs to fully inhale this alien atmosphere. My body starts to shudder, my vision blurs, and my chest hitches with fresh oxygen. It's not quite a sob, but a release. The body can only hold together for so long under stress. We have crossed a finish line of sorts. In the clear. You steady me with a warm hand on my back. You make some joke, but the punch line catches in your throat.

We're home, you say.

We are assigned chores and do them happily. We eat as a family. A community. Tonight is a big night, they say. We will celebrate Imbolc to welcome in the Spring and this year's new life. And purification, another adds. Yes, purification.

Hand in hand we take a walk at dusk, circling the camp. They remind us again which paths to take and which are a bit trickier on the ankles. We cinch our laces and head out. Our visible breath, proof we've made it.

Winter is harsh and Imbolc is a calendar observation. Spring still feels far off, but the pioneers did it. And we are the new pioneers. It will be a simple life. A satisfying one. We reflect on our journey as we walk, before we officially join the coven.

Does that make me a warlock? I say.

You slap my arm. You have to eat your firstborn before you can call yourself that.

Oh, Jun1p3r.

Why did we ever need more than this?

<p>

I pull out the compass and test your acumen. You're a natural. As we admire one another, a half-buried root takes us both down. We laugh and help each other up.

You stop laughing. Looking over my shoulder. I turn.

A blackened timber stake rises from the ground. Chains dangle near the top. Kindling at its base. The coven's chant drifts into the woods.

Oh no.

Oh no.

The Rule of Three.

Purification.

The chant grows louder. Wolves and owls respond.

That's for me, you whisper. We shouldn't have come here. They are going to burn me alive for using blood magik. For what I did to that pornographer of children.

I'm sorry.

Is this real life?

I'm so sorry, @Sa>ag3.

<p>

We run, stumbling through the woods, over roots, dead branches. Until we reach the van. We've left behind our packs, our Vex sleeping bags, and sundries. And our library. But the van is still a luxury and it starts on the second crank.

<p>

Miles and miles down the road, our stomachs grumble as you pull out protein bars. We pass a diner, miraculously still open at the end of it all. We debate pulling in. Have we put enough miles between us and the coven? We decide to move on. Then you retch. The protein bars are made with powdered crickets. Protein-rich and chitinous. Sustainable. Our stomachs agree with our skepticism and we decide to conserve the protein bars.

<p>

The smell of corned beef hash fills the harshly lit diner. We've seen plenty of burned and twisted bodies. Withering and shrinking. Not all were a result of self-immolation. At Vex, we were not subject to the smells. But here it is what I imagined it would be like. And still, my mouth waters.

We sit across from each other as to watch each other's back. There's a jukebox on one side and an old-fashioned cigarette machine on the other. The kind with the pull knob.

The short-order cook, prison tatts. FUCK and COOK on opposing knuckles. We can see the puckered flesh from a grease fire on his chest peeking out from the top of his stained apron.

I'm not going to be burned at the stake, you say. This as though it were a daily affirmation.

The brittle-haired waitress makes a burned-steak joke, mishearing us in her attempt at folksy charm. We are her only table. Each table a quartet of mustard, ketchup, salt, pepper. The chosen few have a half-empty bottle of hot sauce. Including ours. You slip the bottle into your pocket.

We start with coffee and pie as the waitress slips the cook the order for our last civilized meal. I peel the quarter from the business card the man in the suit gave me. I pass the pay phone and stop at the jukebox. Drop the quarter in. It clanks but does not fall all the way, getting stuck. I give the jukebox a small whack and the waitress' look stops me from a second attempt.

<p>

Back at our booth, I fiddle with Mr. Ray's gift box. Should I open it? I say, my mouth filled with apple and cinnamon.

Let's open it when we get settled, you say, your mouth filled with flaky crust. Your eyes dart between the employees and the parking lot. Your eyes say we did not put enough miles between them and us.

A black semitruck pulls into the parking lot. The trucker's been here before, knowing exactly where to park without blocking anyone in. As he enters, the waitress cuts him off before he can even say hi and he chuckles. She hides a smile by talking trash to the cook about his gravy. His order is started. He bellies up to the counter. A hot cup of coffee is poured expertly and a handful of cream cups is stacked pyramid-style in front of him with a wink.

They talk of the LFE. A hoax. City slickers. A return to Christian values. God's retribution, the waitress says. All clichés, the trucker says as he shrugs her off. He lifts reading glasses from a granny chain around his neck. Perches them precariously on his boxer's nose. He begins to read from a dog-eared paperback. The cook stops to listen.

"Even broken in spirit as he is, no one can feel more deeply than he does the beauties of nature. The starry sky, the sea, and every sight afforded by these wonderful regions, seems still to have the power of elevating his soul from earth."

I swallow hard, my throat corked with embarrassment.

"Such a man has a double existence: he may suffer misery, and be overwhelmed by disappointments; yet, when he has retired into himself, he will be like a celestial spirit that has a halo around him, within whose circle no grief or folly ventures."

Our hands find each other's, respectful of the moment, this intimate performance.

[TERMINATION]
5

A tear runs down the cook's face. He abandons his post and takes the hand of the trucker and they climb into the back of his sleeper cab.

The waitress finds no cigarettes in the trucker's crushed pack. Eyes red with rejection, she takes a meat tenderizer to the cigarette machine. Glass shatters and she treats herself to a stale pack. She inhales her rejection and exhales her disappointment.

<p>

#ThíchQuảngĐức

<p>

You take a moment to sit with the waitress at the counter. Sisterhood. Heads bowed. Hands clasped. Energy is intention.

I sweep up the broken glass, happy for once the mess I'm cleaning isn't mine.

As I pass you on my way to the restroom to wash my hands, you reach out to me. Introduce me to the waitress as your soulmate. Then you stand and embrace me. Long and warm. I'm surprised, but return it.

I start to whisper in your ear my real name. You hush me. I know all I need to know, you say. You caress my cheek. I see my reflection in your pools of amber. *This face*, you say.

In the stained restroom mirror, I see a hint of emotion I have not seen in many moons. Joy. Last Halloween, I dressed as myself; a fictional character I did not recognize.

When I return, you are gone. As is the waitress. Our meal ticket hangs in the window carousel. The parking lot is empty save for our van.

I scream your name. Echoes of it, the only answer, ring in my ears.

I can't breathe. All the air has been sucked out of the diner. Out of my lungs. Wave after wave of anxiety rocks me on my heels. The fluorescent lights buzz like trapped insects. I frantically open every door, cabinet, and storage area, hoping to find it's all just a joke, a misguided game of hide-and-seek. There is nothing.

I am alone.

I throw a chair against the far wall. The lodged quarter falls in the jukebox with a *clink* and a dusty 45 record drops. A crackling Conway Twitty sings, "You've Never Been This Far Before."

[TERMINATION]
4

You did not come back.

I drive as far as I can to our emergency rendezvous place, that delicate little green star on our photocopied maps. I drive until the fuel gauge pings its warning. I drive past E. I coast until gravity eases the van to a stop. I find a duffel bag crammed into one of the small compartments. I pack what I can. And start walking, following the green star.

<p>

Lewis and Clark wrote they could hear the ocean thirty miles before they reached the coast. Can you imagine living in a world so quiet of human endeavor?

<p>

The green star. Set my pack down. It will be a good place to camp. Close to the river. A natural white-noise machine. A clearing not far away and trees I can harvest for our cabin. Freeze-dried supplies. If we're not followed.

<p>

Each morning I'll get fresh water for the day. I'll take my binoculars and stand on the high point and watch. I hope to see you before I see black rafts. Before I see a chopper following the river upstream—however they'll come for me.

Until then, I'll wait for you.

[TERMINATION]
3

In that twilight between wake and dream, I hear you laugh, feel the warmth of your flesh, the cut of your wit, the smell of sweat tainted with our mingled musk. The smell of the greenery. The earthiness of our tea on your lips, your tongue. The sting of your hand. The trust in your eyes. The armor of your mind. Its chink. Surviving the tidal shifts of our orbit.

We grew mushrooms, read books out loud, and traced constellations—stars and freckles—with our fingers. We ate when we were hungry. Slept when we were tired. Explored the land. Our minds. Bathed each other's bodies. Chopped wood. Fetched water. Watched the jellyfish.

This was the dream.

I wake up in the woods, naked and surrounded by witches. The waitress from the diner. The hunting-store clerk. Others I cannot place. Brilliant disguises all. They must have followed your green star. A witch with a blood-red streak in her hair appears silently from the woods. I recognize her: the receptionist from my doctor's office. Sage masks a sweet sickly smell I cannot place. I brandish the survival knife, its sawback blade. The blood groove. She does not run nor prepare to be cut. She speaks for them.

"Juniper did not know your true name," the witch says.

(her real name was Juniper)

"And thus, Sa>ag3, we have no power over you."

(except you do)

She hands me a small sack. A large Mason jar. Inside, a rolled piece of parchment. Energy is intention, she says. The Rule of Three. The knife falls to the damp earth.

"You are no longer bound to her."

(except I am)

"You are free."

(even as the chain grows heavier)

The witches evaporate into the woods, back to their gingerbread houses, sated on childhood dreams.

<p>

The sack contains gray ashes, fine as silt, and pieces of bones I cannot name. I remove the thick parchment from the jar. A tiny object clinks at the bottom. But my focus is on the parchment. It's like thin leather, charred at the edges. I unfurl it, this message in a bottle.

The tattooed Bride stares at me; lightning-streaked hair highlights her scream frozen on your excised skin.

[TERMINATION]
2

And then I was alone.

<p>

I scatter your ashes into the river. You will continue into the future without me. Perhaps to the Summerland. Back to the ocean. The home of our familiar. And just maybe the stars, your destination.

<p>

Another loop.

[TERMINATION]
1

Birth. Life. Death.

‹p›

A pearl is formed from an irritant. What thing of beauty is formed from grief?

‹p›

A muted glint catches my eye. Something out of place at the bottom of the Mason jar. A shriveled, hard contact lens.

A spark in the darkness.

‹p›

On the edge of a cliff, over the river, I stand. Behind me, stars blanket the night sky, vast and watchful. The gift from Mr. Ray at my feet, the box stained with hot sauce from the diner. Inside is a paperback of his father's banned novel.

‹p›

I sterilize the Mason jar. Mix the saline just right.

‹p›

I drop the dehydrated tissue into the small aquarium fashioned from the jar. It flutters to the bottom. I wait.

My thumb throbs; the old scar from our blood ritual. Still receiving a signal. The scar on my abdomen inert, now ancient history.

The lens softens.

I hear choppers, low and over the river. Heading upstream towards me.

The Mason jar in my hands, held up; through it, a distorted Milky Way. Inside it, hard edges expand. Reshaping.

Echoing up the river, the *thump thump* of machines, no different than war drums.

The lens twitches, expanding like a miniature balloon. Tentacles unfurl slowly. The jellyfish floats to the middle, whole again. It hums a welcome greeting. I hear it clearly.

Life. Death. Rebirth.

[TERMINATION]
0

Because this is a love story.
the end
</p>

ACKNOWLEDGMENTS

All quotes from the node breaks and the *f*ace's letter are from various editions of Mary Wollstonecraft Shelley's *Frankenstein; or, The Modern Prometheus.*

The poem Mr. Ray recites is "You Will Hear Thunder" by the great Russian poet Anna Akhmatova. Special thanks to Elena Koposova for tracking down the rights holder and Dmitry Tsvetkov at FTM Agency, Ltd. for granting permission.

Special thanks to the estate of Raymond Gunn, Sr. for permission to reprint Chapter 1 from the novel *The Aquarist of Ganymede* copyright 1953, translation by V. V. Glinski.

Tyler Miles Lockett for the fantastic cover.

Grit for the interior design and layout.

Teresa Hartman for the sharp edits.

Scott Storm for the amazing trailer.

Anthony Miller for the webs.

Jess Hollen for the SM panache.

Darren Callahan for the introduction.

Brian Alan Hill for the audio book performance.

Miette who said yes before reaching the end.

Allison for calling this one my mistress.

The first draft of this book was written on a phone. Insert joke here.

DSH is an award-winning playwright and screenwriter. As a novelist, he is a 2x Kirkus Prize nominee.

He currently lives with his wife and son and dog and chickens and a dozen typewriters in a valley between the ocean, the mountains, and the desert.

© Mycki Manning

[NSFW] is his second novel.

Davidscotthay.com for more whatnot.

WHISKEY TIT attempts to restore degradation and degeneracy to the literary arts. We are unwilling to sacrifice intellectual rigour, unrelenting playfulness, and visual beauty, often leading to texts that would otherwise be abandoned in a homogenised literary landscape.

In a world gone mad, our refusal to make this sacrifice is an act of civil service and civil disobedience alike, and our work reflects this. We welcome like-minded readers and writers.

Soviet Sci-Fi Classic

THE AQUARIST OF GANYMEDE
by Raymond Gunn

Arson Books

35 c

First English Translation

~ 412 ~

The Aquarist of Ganymede

By Raymond Gunn

(Translation © 1969 Vladislav Vladislavovich-Glinski)

Chapter 1

Upon waking, Adaam's feet ached with the usual cold. He stepped out of his sleep pod and took a deep breath. His lungs filled at 69%. That would be enough.

He thought of her and made another gesture, one only she would have recognized. Their last three months, they had developed such a shorthand; they often had to repeat themselves when communicating with the other stations. When the other stations started communicating in like language, they would change it and use it only in private.

Despite his feet, he performed his morning ritual of stretches and asanas. Holding each for a time only felt and not counted. They used to do this together. Side by side, occasionally face to face; a dark-skinned mirror image of each. Then they added kata. And made it a dance. This was logged only as Morning Calisthenics. Each morning a move added, until their waking moments were spent in motion, the exertion fighting off the malaise of a limited living space.

Adaam changed out his bodysuit's capture-filter so that the sweat could be recycled. He slipped in a dry filter. His feet still ached. He dialed up the temperature of his suit in the lower third by a few degrees. His chronometer beeped an early alert. Feeding time. Almost. In another Ganymedean hour, it would be time to churn the protein tanks. Occasionally, Adaam forgot whether he was getting older or younger with time here. Not that he knew his date of origin.

He took the hydro-lift down to the protein tanks. The temperature in the lift and all sections between the bubble and nursery were frigid. Only essential areas of the MSA Station *Tsikavats* maintained any heat.

As he descended the lift, the alternating design of window and solar panels created a calliope effect, one like the vid-package on early cinema. The hydro-lift slowed as it neared the protein tanks. He felt a slight vibration through his feet. Curious, he stopped the lift, aligning with a sol-window. Nothing seemed amiss.

Close to the horizon, he could see a dark dirigible shape. It was little more than a smooth silhouette. A sheen of light reflected off its westernmost side. Even from here he could see it slowly rotating as its float sacs expanded with the distant sun. Adaam checked his chronometer and made a note in his personal log. The floaters were coming sooner and sooner.

The vibration again. Maybe it was just the sun warming the outer skin of the station. The station's temperature tolerance had fallen in narrow parameters since the storm ravaged the pod of eight stations. A shadow crossed the sol-window. Startled, Adaam looked up as a giant hidden floater emerged from a large hydrogen cloud abreast of the station. A flattened half sphere, like a mushroom cap, tilted on its axis. The floater rotated toward the sun and cast Adaam in an eerie shadow as it filtered sunlight through its bluish translucent body. Did it do this to gather light? Possibly. Four enormous sacs pulsed as they shrank and expanded, minutely tilting its body and keeping it stable. An organic gyroscope.

Adaam caught himself raising his hand as if he was able to touch it through the G-glass. They had never come this close. Being this close was a gift, but not without danger. If it floated too close to any of the intake filters, it could jeopardize the already crippled life-support system.

He felt the mystery vibration again. A secondary sac inflated and the floater drifted from the window, up and up. Its body bumped and yielded to the structure. No proximity alarm had sounded.

At least he knew what was causing the vibrations.

Another floater appeared on the horizon. He glanced at his chronometer. They were definitely coming earlier. Noted dryly that the floaters did not wear chronometers. He reset the hydro-lift and continued down to the protein tanks.

———

Rotten. His nose told him the room was wrong. The new crops were diseased with fungi. The artificial light can't fend off the decay, he thought. Not even worthy of fertilizer. Perhaps they should embrace the fungi. He churned the protein tanks. They needed more and more crops to get a minimal yield. They were losing effectiveness even before they had begun to ration. He adjusted the centrifuge filter in the churner and shortened the separation cycle. In a few minutes, the protein was packed into honeycomb cells for removal and the waste was jettisoned into the atmosphere. An unintended effect was this brought the floaters from the dark side of Ganymede.

Adaam always released the floater food on the opposite side of their approach. This gave him enough time to take the hydro-lift back up into the observation bubble before they had consumed all of it. His stomach gurgled and churned. The foodicator was long dead. He scooped up root veggies and fungi cultivated from their final harvest. He released a flush handle and pulled out a small honeycomb cell packed with a small yield of protein. He headed up to the observation bubble.

Adaam chopped up the fungi and mixed it with the protein he scraped from the honeycomb cell with a tined spoon. She had preferred to keep her portions separated. They had long-ago run out of salt, but they had soon found that the bland food became richer. A pleasant surprise given their rudimentary taste buds.

He took a bite. The fungi were earthy, more so than the root veggies. The protein rich, but slightly bitter. They had experimented with drawing salt from their sweat, but that experiment was quickly forgotten when they first caught a glimpse of the floaters eating the waste from the protein churners. It was a majestic sight and they watched in silence, before they started whispering questions to one another, as if they might spook the floaters. Where did they come from? What did they normally eat? The protein waste couldn't possibly be their only food source. Perhaps there was more on the dark side of Ganymede, mysterious and wonderful among the electrical storms.

A floater expanded its sacs and lifted quickly and drifted over a swirl of protein waste, then it deflated and dropped over the swirl. It dropped too quickly and the compressed atmosphere pushed them out from under its umbrella. Another floater inflated two of its primary sacs and tilted, opening its underside. The swirl of food disappeared under its flotation sacs, thanks to its rival. Or were they working together?

She had said they weren't scientists anymore, but space farmers. They ate naked in the observation bubble. They toasted the other lost stations with a brew made from leaves, spices, and a powdered supplement. They had started with eight. Enough to generate the requisite data points for the Ministry of Space Activities to determine if the project was viable. The best and brightest Ministry minds could not have foreseen the hemisphere-wide, once-in-a-century storm. It had rained, proof that the surface had jarred its treasure loose: moisture from beneath the surface. As the jet streams came, and the lightning storms coalesced, the sister stations of Project Alkonost could do nothing but ride out the storm and collect data. It was a dazzling reminder that they were not here by invitation.

MSA Station *Veles* exploded inexplicably on the horizon. A single light flash of warning among the storm clouds. *Mokosh* and *Zorya* lost their primary sky tethers, the storm exceeding theoretical stress points. The two-person crews abandoned ship, and on advice from her and Adaam used the weather-sac in hopes of drifting to the *Svarog* as their stations fell to the cracked and frozen surface.

Miraculously, three of the four mission crew made it to the *Svarog*. By the end of the storm the *Svarog* slowly lost its O_2, the crew crunching numbers up until their margin of error stayed past another theoretical point. With its last gasp, the *Svarog* sent out a razor cast of data collected. Then went dark. *Jarilo* just drifted away, its surface anchors mysteriously moving with the ebb and flow of an unseen force. An EPIRB sounded and then faded, lost in the electrical storms and the rise in the magnetic fields at the poles.

And then the two scientists of MSA Station *Tsikavats* were alone.

Adaam and his companion knew that the Ministry for Space Activities had created them in a lab for these specific tasks. The compatibility bred; the genes engineered. Even then, only the top 3% made mission crews. It was an honor. Adaam and his companion ranged just in the 3%. Still an honor. Veneration if, perhaps, not as much of the mem-bytes devoted to the top 1% in the Ministry's History of the People.

The MSA couldn't have known that putting the two of them together would create a pairing less predictable, if not stronger. She was gone now. But he was not the same. She had infected him.

His appetite was gone, but Adaam finished the modest meal mechanically, calculating caloric intake for the tasks ahead.

———

He brewed himself a cup of tea. Thought of her. Inhaled the steam, let it flush his senses. Summoned her face. Still, calm, peaceful. Not the screaming visage that haunted his sleep.

Adaam lost his partner in an EVA to repair their razor-comm caster. Without it they could not communicate with the Ministry. Transmit their research data. The station vid feed captured the fall from 15,240 meters to the iron surface below, where temps hit -200° Kelvin.

Falling, falling, her face one of disbelief, sorrow, and perhaps relief. That last look haunted him the most. Disappearing through the clouds as though a soft landing awaited her just below the station. That had been her gift. Impregnating him with a sense of calm and peace, when the experience should have flooded him with terror and trauma. If only it worked within his dreams. She did not deploy the weather-sac, the only chance of buoyancy. But she was successful in the repair.

Soon after, he began to bring plants from the nursery up to the observation bubble. Moved his sleep pod in there as well, though that took complex engineering. It wasn't the isolation that made time crawl, though he felt that as well. But the sameness of his surroundings. Clean, sterile interiors. Polyplex, that left no fingerprints or dust motes. The scrubbers took care of that. Soon, the plants were flourishing. Breaking up the engineered angles and colors. He did not run artificial audio of birdsong or other creatures. The subtle language of the station was enough, and the plants' song filled his dreams.

If only the observation bubble had been big enough for the churners and rest of the garden. Eventually, Adaam rerouted several routines, electrical and menial, to the observation bubble. It required less heat; the plants provided more oxygen and provided an amazing view. Why had they not done this sooner? Once, before the EVA, the fall, they were blessed with the glimpse of Mother Jupiter's red eye. Wordlessly, their fingers found each other's hands. For several seconds, they were as reverent as scientists could be.

An electronic sound buzzed. Then pinged.

He blinked himself back to the present. It sounded again, a low rattle and buzz like the vids of insects. Adaam pushed himself to his feet, staggered a step, and regained his balance. It wasn't vertigo or a loss of blood circulation. The observation window visible through the rows of greenery. Condensation coated it now, blurring the stratosphere outside, but Adaam could still make out the distorted horizon. It was out of level by three degrees. The station was listing.

The electronic buzz sounded again.

He flipped three switches with practiced case and the main power of the station including life support dropped to minimal levels as he manually engaged a gyroscope. The calcium carbonate crystals in his ear shifted ever so slightly. The station was level. He could tell without verifying it with instrumentation. He opened the flood of energy back to the station and felt the temperature rise slightly. He took a deep breath. 56%.

The buzz again. He looked at the Spectrogram. A spike on the higher frequencies. It did not match any of the Ganymede sounds they had catalogued. He plugged in his Tel-met and lowered the eye filters. Dialed up the audio tuners. Through the lens and Tel-met, the frequencies merged to create an image in the soundstage in his head. And then, with a low rattle, disappeared. He tried to strengthen the signal, but dared not reroute power.

Hmm.

Adaam logged the ghost-ping occurrence in his personal recordings. Not the Ministry recordings. Maybe it was an EPIRB from the *Jarilo*, though unlikely and not supported by any data. That storm had transformed the moon into one for which they were now ill-suited. He would form a few theories first and explore them before any formal presentation.

Unofficially, the MSA would not bother with unknowns without two working hypotheses. That is what she would have said and done.

He finished his tea. It had cooled, the taste pungent now, but lost in thought he did not notice.

———

Unable to sleep, Adaam stepped out of his sleep pod. His feet ached, but he did not adjust his suit. Before he stepped into his grip-boots, he slid on an extra pair of socks. Hers. He powered up a single processing center and brought up the station status at the time he had received the ghost ping. The computer had resolved it, saying it was the echo of the station's own EPIRB. But that made no sense. He prepared cross-reference solutions using the orientation of the sun, wind speed, station temperature interior and exterior. The visualizer inside the Tel-met synced with the station and he muttered through a number of variables before authorizing calculations. The only data he could confirm was that it was not a ghost echo.

That meant endless possibilities. Adaam felt himself get excited. A new off-the-books project was always engaging. The *Tsikavats* asked if he wanted a mild sedative. He declined, but the excitement, however, was short-lived.

———

MSA STATION
TSIKAVATS
PROJECT ALKONOS

TERMINATED.
PREPARE ALL
CURRENT DATA FOR
RAZOR-CAST...
AT NEXT COMM
WINDOW
EVACUATION TBD

———

Adaam's hand hovered over the TRANSMIT button. Dutifully, per his breeding, he had organized all the data, analyzed it, and written a draft of the conclusion: Ganymede was not viable for colonization, commercial industry mining, or as a communications relay.

He doubted the Ministry would read anything more than his conclusion. He checked his chronometer. The comm window was arriving shortly.

A local alarm sounded.

At first it was a distant wail from within the station. Then it hit the speaker comm in the protein tank chamber. Adaam checked the gauges. It was mid-churn and he didn't want to shut it down or it would spoil this precious batch. He checked his chronometer. It was too early in the process; the yield would be minimal. Adaam watched the gauges rise and timed it with his chronometer. It would burn out if he let it run. He'd have to clean it ASAP to prevent it from clogging. The MSA station was not built for the churner; it was a manufacture of Adaam's own device. The storm had shorted the foodicator along with most of the kitchen module. Project Alkonost considered multiple stations redundancy enough, so Adaam repurposed what he could for the churners. They worked.

And, as an unforeseen result, brought the floaters. Naturally, scientific curiosity took over.

They refrained from naming the floaters, and often weren't sure if there were different ones or a pod of the same that arrived every few days, as if they were a feeding-ground stop on their G-weekly migration. They kept their findings on a separate mem-card. His personal journal on the same. Various other experiments were set in motion long ago, with Adaam merely recording the data and giving perfunctory summaries that were razor cast out into the great beyond to the Ministry.

He doubted few scientists with the resources at hand and with the time would have done any differently. It also gave him purpose beyond duty. Beyond grief.

By the time the Klaxon sounded station-wide, Adaam was already on his way down in the hydro-lift. The muted strobing of real and artificial light played in his face. In the chamber, Adaam pulled a full stop on the protein tanks and hurried to the central IntraFace. The small subset of monitors in the protein tank did not contain an input source. He speed-walked to the central hub; his grip-boots slipped as he broke into a full run and he accidentally launched himself in the low G. The sensors worked and emergency handholds emerged from the stations. He grabbed on to one and forced his feet down, where they stuck. He resumed a powerwalk, pulling himself along the handrails, and made it to the hydro-lift and punched in to the main floor. The windows barely strobed as he moved up the hydro-lift. Visibility was poor, the *Tsikavats* enveloped in a cloud of hydrogen. He slowed the lift briefly to verify he could see nothing. A shadow perhaps. Elongated. And dark. But unidentifiable. Then it hit him: a floater tentacle. It must have gotten caught in the filters. The *Tsikavats* shuddered, almost imperceptibly, but after seven years Adaam could read the vibrations. This one was not benign. The HUD on the hydro-lift pinged as life support shifted from green to yellow.

The central hub confirmed a clog in the westernmost air filter. He engaged the auto-scrub, following protocol. Then the manual. It was resisting. Life support shifted from yellow to orange. Red, and disaster, would be next.

He typed in:

ALT ACTION?

The *Tsikavats* spelled a reply back.

EVA.

A shock ran from his belly to chest.

EVA.

Watching her float slowly but inevitably to the surface 15.24 kilometers below. His heart palpitated. The *Tsikavats* asked if he wanted a mild sedative to take off the edge.

His fingers trembled, as he typed:

NO.

He closed his eyes and forced himself to take a deep breath. He typed:

COMPUTE   OUTCOME
IF NO EVA.

The screen blanked, the normal pause, then the ship had to draw extra power for the more complicated calculations.

STATION TSIKAVATS
INERT IN 12 GM
HOURS...

———

His breath echoed in his head. The Tel-met refused to click into place. He double-checked the seal. Perhaps it was his body refusing to enclose itself in such a claustrophobic device, but he had been through training and passed a psych evaluation. She had sensed his hesitation and volunteered to fix the razor-comm cast, taking his place in the EVA. He had uncoupled the Tel-met umbilical and plugged the helmet into his suit's power pack.

Visually, Adaam double-checked all connections and harnesses in the mirrored ready room. Normally his partner would have done the check, this reflective open booth built as a backup should one of them become unavailable or incapacitated or... lost. The *Tsikavats* verified and recommended a mild anti-anxiety. Which he declined. With patient wrangling, the Tel-met finally clicked into place.

All systems green. He proceeded through the airlock; his heartbeat now competing with his lungs for the cacophony in his Tel-met. He'd already shut down the power feed for the clogged duct.

———

The airlock pressurized. The suit overrode his verbal protest and injected him automatically with a mild sedative. Adaam's heart rate stabilized. He took long deep breaths, oxygenating his lungs, in case of panic-induced hyperventilation. He visualized the exterior filter. The safety harness. The walk, the removal of the floater. At 50K feet, he would not look down, lest vertigo overtake him. He dialed his Tel-met visor iris to minimum to block his peripheral vision. He could still sense objects and changes in the light but not a clear picture. He would look straight ahead and do the task and return, like a workhorse with blinders. He tried not to think of her.

———

Adaam stepped out into the Ganymedean oblivion and missed the first handhold. His boot caught and he leaned out over the white abyss bending by the ankle. His heart rate pinged a warning and he muted the alert until it sounded like a faint distant drum.

The shimmer in the dead floater had dimmed. A thin membrane covered it now. A death caul of sorts? Past the membrane was a light spongy mass. Gelatinous at its inner layer and thicker than he had hypothesized. Probably to survive the windstorms that had been creeping up. Movement flickered to this left, and a luminosity grew, lighting his work area. Adaam focused on the task at hand, assuming it was a lone floater, perhaps wanting to see what had become of its companion.

Adaam pushed away the anthropomorphic thoughts he had assigned the floater. The task was imperative, and he could not afford to be curious. Time was of the essence and essence meant oxygen. He took his scrub rig, a hastily repurposed tool, and began to spatula the jelly-like mass off the station. It jammed more than he liked, but less than he feared. It hummed, and soon he found a peace in the work; a rhythm that was efficient and less taxing. The outer hull was cleared the easiest, but Adaam found portions that had been pulled deep into the filtration system. This would mean going into the narrow duct.

He removed the grill and tethered it. The duct disappeared into shadow. He widened his iris and pulled himself in. With the scrub rig, it was a tight but not impossible fit. Steady, easy breathing. The walls of the duct were irregular and he squirmed to keep moving. His suit snagged here and there, but he managed to keep moving until he was in position. He powered on the scrub rig and got to work.

———

He had cleared 59% of it when his Oxy alert sounded. Too soon for his level of exertion. He was bleeding O_2. His lower leg had snagged a non-flush rivet head and torn it. With both arms working the scrubber, he could not reach down and seal it. He could reach the pocket-sleeve SlaPatches on his forearm, but not his leg. The Oxy alarm sounded again. He needed to clear more of the filtration system. The thought of another EVA terrified him, even through the sedative. A creeping feeling of claustrophobia started to tighten his chest. The rig slipped between his chest and a wall. For an instant his whole suit vibrated and his teeth rattled. Without thinking, he released the deadman's trigger on the rig and thrust himself out of the filtration duct, and fell.

The safety harness jolted him. Another alarm sounded. He palmed open the forearm sleeve and watched in horror as the winds of Ganymede whipped the SlaPatches into the air like a deck of cards. His hand shot out with animal instinct and he caught one between the thick fingers of his gloves. He took a deep breath and focused. Slapped the patch, the edging melding and sealing the leg gash.

The Oxy-burn meter slowed, but did not stop ticking down. Another leak. He headed for the airlock, numbers and timers buzzing in his Tel-met like an awakened hornets' nest. He worked his way back up the tether to the filtration pods and then up the main cable tether to the station airlock. He did not conserve energy or air. His breath echoed in the Tel-met, mixing with the insistent alarm tones and buzzes. Darkness crept in at the edges of his vision like an old vignette photo. His suit hummed and jolted him with a tiny electrical shock, his vision sharpened. Warmth flooded his veins.

He made the airlock and completed re-pressurization. He stripped off his suit, letting it fall in a heap, like a molted skin. He activated the life support that ran through that duct. He felt rather than heard a small hum. Then a clunk and clanging sound echoed throughout the *Tsikavats*. He thought of the loose rivet. But the *Tsikavats* settled down and the duct was functional.

At the IntraFace he requested a recalculation for the central hub regarding the westernmost filter.

STATION TSIKAVATS
INERT IN 92 GM
HOURS...

If only he'd been able to clear out the rest of the filter. It did buy him significant time. He dialed up extra sleep time and ran a rudimentary scan to make sure no more emergencies loomed on the horizon or otherwise. His eyelids drooped and he felt his body begin to crash, post adrenaline and stim. The scan revealed another ghost ping. He dialed in another scan and scratched his chin. Felt the grit of new growth. He programmed another rudimentary sweep to be followed by a secondary scan—any other time and he would have given this his full attention. The *Tsikavats* had a bit of energy to spare for it now. But he did not. He stumbled to his sleep pod and fell in. He was in REM before the pod finished its seal.

—

Adaam heard a ping. His eyes opened. He started to hyperventilate and realized he was in his sleep pod. He couldn't wait to tell her his dream and then remembered that she was no longer there. It was still the middle of the Ganymedean night. He'd slept for two days. His feet ached, but he ignored them. Did he hear a ping?

AUTO TRANSMIT FAIL.
RETRANSMIT.
AUTO TRANSMIT FAIL.

Apologies, I was sleeping, he thought.

Adaam stroked his cheeks and neck. The beard was coming in. He hadn't picked up a razor in some time. At least since he came back in from the outside. Ominous clouds gathered in patches across the Eastern horizon. The tilt of the station kept the western view hidden in the observation bubble. He kept life support on here and in the protein tanks chamber. The life support generated enough oxygen to refill one station path to the chamber and back. He set up a small lab and analysis corner here in the bubble. Rerouting the electrics and inputs. All this to extend the *Tsikavats'* life, and her memory. And to avoid another EVA.

—

At his portable InterFace, Adaam began another sweep for the ghost ping. Replayed the recording from when he slept. Found a small spike. He worked through several calculations, letting the *Tsikavats* reroute as much power for the calculations as needed. He tightened a scan frequency and oscillated it, sweeping in a tightening radius around the *Tsikavats*. Soon, his breath became visible and crystals formed on the observation bubble. He dialed back and let the temp rise again. When the sun rose the plants would be fine, but killing off his supplemental oxygen supply with an artificial frost would not help him survive until the Ministry extraction. He hesitated and let the *Tsikavats* run a last calculation. If something was out there, it was just beyond the terminator, the line between Ganymede's dark and light side. Where the floaters came from.

He brewed a small batch of tea. Added an extra stim pack.

The floaters...

He replaced the vid and viewed the images from the EVA suit-cam. The handgrips had been coated in the floater skin. That's what made it slippery. The shadow had been a floater. Its tentacles extended out teasingly. He had only seen that done as a feeding behavior. He wondered if it was trying to reach out to its companion or if was testing for protein in the EVA suit. He gathered up his discarded EVA suit and examined it carefully. There it was. A bit of the floater tissue.

He ran the analysis again. And again. He turned off the razor-cast cache constant stream of data from the

Tsikavats to the Ministry. His mind raced. The floater contained traces of "unobtanium." He ran more tests. Founds more experiments to run. Found more positive results. The floater's skin and regenerative properties seemed promising. Unexpected. His mind raced with all the possible applications. They would write of him gloriously in the People's History.

———

The comm window for the Ministry arrived.

> STATION TSIKAVATS
> TRANSMIT ALL DATA
> RELATED TO
> PROJECT ALKONOST
> FOR RAZOR-CAST...
> IMMEDIATELY.
> PRIORITY ONE.

Adaam scratched his chin. Typed in a reply:

> *STORMS.*
> *TRANSMISSION*
> *DELAYED TIL NEXT*
> *WINDOW.*
> *ETA EVACUATION?*

The comm window neared its close. Then a reply articulated across his screen.

> EVACUATION TBD

To be determined, Adaam thought. And then it dawned on him: he was the sole survivor of Project

Alkonost. They would not come for him. He would receive that news, if at all, after his final razor-cast.

Moisture dropped on his face and startled him. At first he thought it was sweat, but then realized it was from the vines overhead. The *Tsikavats'* observation bubble tilted toward the sun and condensation began to form along its clear Vue-Glass.

If Adaam did not razor-cast again, they would send a Scientary Explorer Unit to determine what had happened and to retrieve their data. They would not be pleased with him.

If he tried to alter the data, they would send a SEU and they would not be polite when interrogating him and his motives regarding the Ministry of Space Activities' Mission Statement. He would still not leave the *Tsikavats* alive.

If he razor-cast all his findings, they would see commercial value in the floaters. The Ministry would deploy an Industrial Unit. They would set up more stations. Harvesters. Processors. He might leave the *Tsikavats*. He might receive a medal. He might make the primary text of the Ministry's History of the People, not just a footnote.

He ran through his options again. As she would have done.

If they got the *Tsikavats* data, they would come.

If they got his personal data, the mission would change.

They would come for the floaters. Turn them into bioweapons. Spice or med supplies. The only known cure for Phalanx. But the only people suffering from Phalanx lived in the luxury dome on Oceanus Procellarum or the House of T and all its bloodline. They took their chances ruling from a seat of power they dared not give up, disease or no.

If it took farming a species to extinction to retain their status and trade power, they wouldn't hesitate to throw Ministry resources at it. They would reward Adaam. A medal. A role of status and rank. A People's Hero. Or they would prefer to keep the mission covert and he would simply be cast out the airlock as Lucifer. Or perhaps, they would throw his body into the churners, where he'd become floater food. He chuckled. Another posthumously celebrated comrade.

The only way to keep the MSA from responding would be if there was a catastrophic event on the *Tsikavats*. There was no possible way for the Ministry to retrieve the data once the station hit the surface. They would write off the project and move on. And he would die.

Another ping. The comm window opened:

> AUTO TRANSMIT FAIL.
> RETRY.
> AUTO TRANSMIT FAIL.

A few kilometers away, a floater appeared outside the observation bubble. Maybe it could sense the *Tsikavats'* slowly failing systems. Or maybe it was coming back to mourn the floater that got caught in the exfiltration system. Or maybe it was only here to eat.

Tea slopped on the keyboard. His hand trembled. This is how it ends. The future never arrives as advertised; he'd read that in a banned novel from his youth. He thought of what he might do. He sipped slowly. Sparkles appeared at his periphery. A warmth blossomed in his stomach. Contentment.

And then he knew.

He thought of her and started the final protein churn.

———

By the time the protein tanks jammed and started to burn, Adaam had taken a last look at the observation deck and all the greenery. His memorial to her. He stood in the airlock, hand on the emergency handle. The odds of making it to anything were astronomical or infinitesimal depending on one's predilection for scale. And yet here he was. The *Tsikavats* listed and he fell and banged his Tel-met. A small crack spider-webbed above his forehead, but no suit alarm sounded. A shuddering vibration rocked the station. As the horizon tilted, the metallic shriek of metal became thunderous. Without a second thought, Adaam twisted and tugged the red handle and blew the airlock door out into a cloudy oblivion. He stepped into the white void.

As soon as he cleared the *Tsikavats*, he pulled the cord on the weather sac. His last act of defiance.

It inflated instantly and lifted him up. He felt weightless. All the mass and density and dark left his body. He teetered and wobbled against the pale nothingness. Like a foal on earth. An Oxy alarm pinged. Another leak in his EVA suit; a small tear. Maybe from a thorn. A few of the plants had grown needle-like thorns on their main branches. Or maybe it had worn thin. He wasn't sure when he'd last taken it off.

He lost his bearings and then steadied himself. Finding and riding equilibrium between suit and sac. He dialed the iris on his helmet. It opened to maximum and Adaam could see the expanse and glint of the *Tsikavats*.

Already he could see it venting. It began to list like a ship in the Caspian Sea. And then began to sink. Adam watched as the *Tsikavats* dropped slowly into the 'sphere. For a moment it gave the illusion that Adaam was soaring upward, but enough clouds broke to adjust the perspective. He was floating now above the *Tsikavats'* death (and with it the new knowledge). He looked down on the off chance he might see the bottom. See the surface, see her.

He felt the shock as the observation bubble exploded. Bits of now-frozen greenery fluttered in the air. His memorial to her gone in a shower of ragged confetti. His heart and stomach sank, not from emotion, but from free fall. He jerked back, looking up. His weather sac wrinkled and wilted with rapid decompression, now just a useless flutter of fabric. He pulled the harness free and let the fabric flutter on its own journey, like a war-torn flag of surrender. As he fell, he closed his eyes and tried to summon her face. If he could, it would be enough.

Instead, his whole body jerked with impact. A soft impact.

For they had come and bumped him. Like children with a balloon. Long slow parabolas, and when the sinking feeling in his gut came on and he resigned himself to the fall, he would be bumped from underneath or the side, usually a blind spot. At the apex of each bounce, he would see the creatures. Finally, he bounced face-first on a spongy mass, saw up close the floater's skin, their mass, their grace. Lightning and static storms flashed to his right and left near the poles. Through the floater's bodies, the flashes distorted and looked like a Victorian experiment.

The Ganymedean clouds broke and Adaam gasped. The swirling clouds of Mother Jupiter rose above, its red eye greeting him. It filled the entire sky, a colossal presence. He drank it in. The majesty, the mystery, a view no other had seen before. He was the first. His body flushed with heat. His toes stopped aching. He looked for her face in its clouds. A gentle bump and Jupiter moved from his field of vision. He dropped back lower into the clouds, a final glimpse above of the red eye as he moved away.

Slowly, the children of Ganymede pushed Adaam to the terminator, that line between shadow and the sun's reach, closer to the darkness and the unknown. Sparks flickered randomly just inside the darkness, like giant matches flaring and extinguishing with the breath of the cosmos.

As they bounded him one last time into darkness, he hoped he was not alone. Behind him the dying *Tsikavats* appeared so small, so infinitesimal. Had he bothered to look back. But the Aquarist did not.

For his journey had just begun.